AIRSHIP 27 PRODUCTIONS

Jezebel Johnston: Devil's Handmaid
© 2015 Nancy Hansen

Published by Airship 27 Productions
www.airship27.com
www.airship27hangar.com

Interior illustrations © 2015 Rob Davis
Cover illustration © 2015 Terry Pavlet

Editor: Ron Fortier
Associate Editor: Peg Livingston
Marketing and Promotions Manager: Michael Vance
Production and design by Rob Davis

ISBN-13: 978-0692524039 (Airship 27)
ISBN-10: 0692524037

Printed in the United States of America

10 9 8 7 6 5 4 3 2 1

by Nancy Hansen

PROLOGUE

Long Tall Tom, they called him, and for good reason. Thomas Johnston topped six feet, and he was lanky even for an Englishman. He was the tallest man Monifa had ever met, and of the mahogany skinned former slave's lovers, her absolute favorite. The blond haired, hazel eyed privateer only showed up in Tortuga once or twice a year, but he would often stay a week or two before restlessness swept him back out to sea. Even her impending pregnancy the year before had not silenced the siren call of the waves. Now he was back again, but only for the day. After hours of lovemaking, their sun bronzed and rich brown limbs intertwined and sweating bodies pressed close; they had finally both fallen asleep.

The sun was rising over the bay a scant few precious hours later when he quietly disengaged himself and rolled out of bed. In the gloom, he dressed, pulled on his boots, and fastened the belt that normally held his cutlass. He already had his hat in hand and was reaching for his jacket and pistol when she awoke.

"You leave me again," she stated in her soft spoken patois of French and English, her voice low toned and sultry as always. She had her back to him as she slipped into loose clothing. She already knew the answer to that.

"We sail on the morning tide," he answered by way of explanation. "I have to report."

There was no use arguing; he'd go anyway. Captain and company always came first, and the sea was his one true lover. A proud woman did not beg.

Babbling came from across the room, splitting the silence between them. "Come then," she said, lacing up her bodice under full breasts and tugging it tight so that they crowned in the loose peasant top she wore with the long skirt. "Meet your daughter before you go." She led him to the other corner of the hovel and lifted the netting over a rough crib.

A dark haired, coppery-skinned infant of barely eight months old stirred and looked up when he whistled in appreciation. She was big for a girl child!

Monifa lifted the baby and handed her up. The infant never cried, just gave a yawn and then stared at Tom with interest in her very dark eyes.

"She's a Johnston all right," he said, chucking her under the chin. "She's

5

got the family's stubborn jawline." He smiled down at the baby until she grabbed at his curling beard, and then winced. "Strong little bit, too!" He had to pry her fingers free before he handed her back down to her mother. "What did you name her?"

"I picked a name from your king's Good Book, as you desired. I call her Jez-e-bel." She pronounced each syllable slowly and carefully, and smiled up at him. She was surprised when he sighed unhappily and shook his head.

"You don't like her name?"

"I taught you to read wench, but I can see I neglected to teach you to *think*. Queen Jezebel was far from a proper Christian. She kept her own Pagan gods, and corrupted King Ahab and all those around her with idolatry and murder. You could have chosen better..."

"No, I chose carefully," she said in a low tone. "She is named for a queen who fought for the rights of her own people in a land that did not love them. She stood up to everyone. My daughter...your daughter as well," she added, holding the baby up so he could look deep into her eyes, "she will not be ruled by the powerful. She will not wind up a whore on the docks. She will not work in some master's kitchen or cane fields until she drops of exhaustion. She will be a free woman who makes her own way in this world; a woman who comes and goes as she pleases. Just like her Papa."

He gave her a lopsided smile. It really didn't matter what she thought. Monifa was only a freed slave turned serving wench, and the babe just one more colored bastard. He had a wife and two sons back in Liverpool. No one in Tortuga cared what your name was, and even if the girl survived infancy, she'd not be leaving the island.

"I'll bring you both something when next we dock here," he said, kissing her cheek and then the baby's before he left.

Long Tall Tom was as good as his word, for every time he was in port, he brought Monifa and Jezebel some bit of his take from the last voyage. Often he was there only on a turnaround, other times he might have several weeks to spare while the ship was cleaned and repaired, and another crew signed. He would speak of his adventures at sea with great reverence, and his stories always captivated mother and daughter. He left out the ugly and dangerous truths, and those bits that were patently illegal. As Jezebel went from baby, to toddler, to a long legged young girl running after her mother or chasing the other children in the streets, she learned to look forward to those visits of the man she called Papa Tom. He was a hero to her.

One year, he did not come at all. Nor did he come the next year, or any year after that. Monifa always had other lovers to turn to, and Jezebel now had two younger brothers. With careful management of the capital from selling the trade goods Tom brought her, the former slave had squirreled away a healthy nest egg. She purchased the failing tavern she had worked in for many years, which was doing well again, with all the pirates in town. Now she was opening a brothel down the rutted street, and life was good for them in Tortuga, except that Papa Tom never came back to visit any more. Only Jezebel seemed to mourn his absence.

"Men…bah, they are best enjoyed from a distance anyway," Monifa told her daughter on a daily basis, once Jezebel was old enough to understand. "A wise woman can manage her own affairs. You see how well I have done? It is because I am in-de-pen-dent. That is what Papa Tom wanted when he bought my freedom, and in truth, he gave me a new start; but I am the one who made the most of it. It is what I want for you too, Jezebel. You were named after a proud queen who would die before she would give in to anyone, even her king. Do not think on marriage and settling down too soon. Tortuga is a good place for a woman of color to make her own way. You must become someone important that the others look up to, just like your Mama. Learn all you can, and make no man your better."

It was a life lesson that the impetuous young girl with the copper skin and the long, dark curling hair took to heart.

CHAPTER ONE

The island of Tortuga in those days had been claimed by several countries in rapid succession. Its big port town was perpetually busy, as well as dirty and unkempt. The docks were rotting, the buildings surrounding it weather-beaten and leaning. A motley assortment of sights, sounds, and smells filled the air around the waterfront. The heady salt breeze mixed with the steaminess of the thick jungle on the slopes above, punctuated by the rank stench of sewage and rotting vegetation, acrid pipe smoke, and the tar and rust odors of the multitude of vessels docked or anchored in the bay. None of the respectable folk lingered long there. Day and night, the streets were full of colorfully clad swaggering pirates, garrulous fishwives, longtime sailors with rolling strides, various outlaws, escaped slaves, scurrilous rogues, and local scoundrels. Strutting, skimpily clad whores flaunted their wares openly on the rough board sidewalks or called out from sagging balconies. Grubby, half-starved children screamed as they were chased by wary-eyed and cantankerous shopkeepers with brooms. Pitiful looking adult beggars thrust their bowls and baskets in your face; trying to catch your eye while they were picking your pockets. Roaming animals, piss and vomit, crushed produce, and unmentionable filth were perpetually underfoot. Squawking sea fowl, squealing pigs, barking dogs, and vendors hawking their wares competed with loud voices raised in laughter or anger, raucous music accompanying off-key bawdy singing, and the occasional gunshot. A multicultural crowd of men and women of all ages, races, and hues jostled and reeled in the roughly cobbled or mucky streets, many of them drunk and barely able to stagger along. Cut-purses and murderous louts lurked in the shadowed narrow alleys and byways, where baking sun or the sparse evening lamplight never reached. Panhandlers haunted every corner or sheltered doorway.

Tortuga was a haven for the lawless, the restless, and the dispossessed; a true pirate port. But to Jezebel Johnston, Tortuga was home.

Now, she was going to leave it all behind.

The tall fourteen year old with the cinnamon skin and unreadable dark

8

eyes, was dressed like a sailor youth as she hurried down to the docks. Small busted and on the thin side, with the broad shoulders as well as the high cheekbones and an outthrust square jaw she inherited from her English father, she easily passed for a boy. A stained and threadbare linen shirt, old and baggy; faded brown breeches, and tall boots that were a size too big, had all been purloined from men either staying at the popular tavern her mother owned, or got left behind in her brothel down the street. The girl had roughly chopped off half her long and curling brown black hair, and the rest was corralled by a wind of colorful red bandana. A small but sharp kitchen knife was thrust into a makeshift sheath in her right boot, and what little she was taking with her was bundled into a ratty blanket tied shut with strands of discarded dock line.

She was working her way down the row of ships, looking for an 80 foot brigantine *Devil's Handmaid,* captained by Dandy Dan Abrams. She had fallen for a handsome pirate she had been serving ale and turtle stew to the past week…a man who had known and respected her long lost Papa. She could not get this dashing, blue eyed, dark haired pirate out of her mind, and feared losing him too, so Jezebel Johnston had decided to join him on the high seas, where she would seek her fortune and live happily ever after beside her one true love.

At least that was her plan…

When she had asked him about the ship's name, Walter had laughingly mentioned the figurehead was a red painted, naked hellion with horns. They'd be leaving on the evening tide, and when she protested, he had asked for a kiss for good luck to send him off. When her mother intervened, he pushed the young girl away; but before he left, whispered he'd come back next year when she was older.

Always rebellious, Jezebel had dressed as a boy and slipped out at mid morning. She intended on joining the crew, so that she and the object of her infatuation would never have to be apart. Surely a young man who spoke English, French, and some of the native language would be welcomed aboard!

The quartermaster was standing on the pier, overseeing the loading of barrels of salt pork and dried meat, clean water and local fruit. She stepped up smartly, and waiting until he stopped shouting orders, cleared her throat. The stooped and balding man removed his cap, and wiping his brow, turned to stare at what appeared to be a tall boy. What was left of the older man's white hair was tied back in a tail, and he had a bristly fringe of white beard. His clothes were common cloth, once well cut but now stained, frayed, and faded. His ruddy face was lined and weathered, with squint marks around the eyes, and while unsmiling, it was not an unkindly expression. He threw up his callused hands with their ragged, chipped, and blackened nails, in a gesture of annoyance.

"Well go on now lad, speak up! I've plenty to do here without waiting for ye to find yer tongue." He had a slight brogue that put his origins back somewhere in the British Isles, perhaps green Eire.

"I... I've come to sign aboard Sir," she said hesitantly. Her voice was naturally low toned enough to pass for a male youth. "Master Armitage said you might have use of me." She was fishing for information, trying to be sure that Walter Armitage was actually part of the *Devil's Handmaid* crew and hadn't just been using a ruse to encourage her often professed devotion into a tryst.

He studied her a moment and then smirked. "Did he now? And does your mother know that yer down here at the docks?"

"No," she said truthfully, shuffling her feet. "Does that matter?"

"Not to me," he said, turning back to direct someone rolling a barrel up the plank. "That un goes to Cap'n's quarters." He turned back to Jezebel, taking in the smooth copper skin, thin body, and beardless face. Probably a runaway house slave. "We're not taking on crew presently, but ye don't look like ye eat much. We can always use deck hands and such. I warn ye; 'tis a hard life, 'specially for a boy who's never been a'sea. Ye'll be expected to sign Articles, and pull yer own weight."

"I'll do all that and more Sir," she said eagerly, following him up the main plank. "I speak some of the trade languages, and I can read and write a bit too."

"Fine, fine, lad. See the captain up yon?" he pointed to the main deck. There was no missing Dan Abrams, because the blustering little man in the foppish clothing was the focal point of a heated discussion. "When he's done he'll read ya them Articles, and ye can make yer mark. I'll see ye get yer kit, quarter, and rations, and enter ye in the account once ye've scrawled yer X. Tell him Gully sent ya. Now go on, get aboard and let a man do his work!"

He stumped off and Jezebel Johnston tentatively set foot on a pirate ship for the first time. She took a deep breath, and after glancing around at the sweating, grunting, rough spoken men who were stowing rolls of sailcloth, barrels, chests, and coils of rope, strode quickly toward a colorfully dressed one in a brocade frock coat of gold and burgundy over black velvet breeches and buckle shoes.

Standing politely by, she waited until the captain was done shouting and gesticulating. The men with him nodded and went off to their various duties. Atop his shoulder length brown curls, he carefully seated a black tricorn hat with gold braid and a long black plume, turned abruptly, and almost bumped into her.

"Get out of my way, you stupid lump!" he said, shoving her aside with a be-ringed hand surrounded by frothy lace cuffs before pushing past. As long-legged as she was, Jezebel had to walk very fast to catch up with him, as even encumbered with a basket hilt sword that wanted to drag, he moved like quicksilver.

"Captain Abrams, I've come to join your crew," she said breathlessly as she drew abreast. He stopped immediately and regarded her with eyes so pale blue they appeared gray. There were crow's feet around them, and his features were craggy, but there wasn't a gray hair in his mustache or neatly trimmed chin whiskers.

"How nice of you, dear boy," he said in a precise tone dripping with sarcasm. "And you feel compelled to stop me on the busiest day of the year and tell me this because...?"

Jezebel was taken aback. "Um... Gully sent me about the *Articles*?" Her voice went up nervously at the end. Though he was half a hand span shorter, the way he was glaring at her made her knees wobbly. If her gender were discovered, she'd be put off the ship.

"Ah yes, the Articles," he said with indifference and pointed to a yellowed sheet tacked to a cabin door. "Go find someone to read them to you and then make your mark."

"I can read, Sir," she told him proudly, knuckling her forehead respectfully, as some of the other men had.

"Splendid. We shall take your oath when I've more time. Now get you gone, and leave me to my command!" He stalked away.

Plenty of eyes were on Jez as she walked slowly over and stood by the door. Squinting up at the parchment, she read very carefully through the entire document. It was extensive and very specific list. Some of the words were long and hard to understand.

I. After Engagement, with Funds for Provisions and Repairs duly set aside, the Captain shall have Two Full Shares. The Quarter Master is to have One Share and a Half more. The Surgeon, Carpenter, Master Mates, Gunner, & Boatswain; One Share and a Quarter. Remaining Company will have One Share each.

II. Good Quarters and Proper Victuals with Adequate Strong Liquor will be given to any Man Grown who Signs his Mark. All Unblooded Boys below the age of Ten and Six who Sign a Mark shall share Dry Quarters as Out of Weather as possible, with Proper Victuals and Watered Liquor as deemed Rightful by Age & Constitution.

III. Any man decreed guilty of Cowardice at the time of Engagement shall suffer what Punishment his Captain and Company deem fit.

IV. Any Man found guilty of Drunkenness to the Dereliction of Duty at the time of Engagement shall suffer what Punishment the Captain and Majority of the Company deems fit.

V. He that shall Threaten or otherwise discharge and use Weapons Aboard when not Engaged or In Training; or Wills to Strike and Abuse his Brethren in the Company; shall suffer Punishments to be decided by the Captain and the Company by Majority Vote.

VI. He that is found Guilty of Scheming to Defraud another to the Value of his Share, shall forfeit half his own Share as Recompense, as well as receive any Punishment the Captain and the Company Majority deem fit.

VII. If any Undeclared Prize of Silver, Gold, Jewels, Coin, Sundries Else be found on the Person or within Affects of one of the Company; who did not deliver it to the Quarter Master within the space of Four and Twenty hours; that Breach of Solemn Oath to Community Property shall be Punishable as Captain and the Majority of the Company deem fit.

VIII. No Women are allowed aboard While In Port without the Express Permission of The Captain. Under No Circumstances are Women to be taken Out to Sea. Offenders of the First Part will be Dismissed and their Shares Divided amongst The Company. Offenders of the Second Part shall receive Extreme Punishment as Captain & Company deem fit.

IX. He who has the Misfortune to lose a Limb at time of Engagement, shall have the Compensation Sum of Four Hundred Pieces of Eight. He who loses One or Both Eyes during Engagement shall have Compensation to no more than Two Hundred Pieces of Eight per Loss. Those deemed still Useful after such Loss & Healing may remain aboard as long as they shall think fit. Those no longer able to Serve shall be Set Ashore in a Lively Town with Compensation of additional Three Hundred Pieces of Eight.

X. He who first spots a Sail that leads to a Profitable Engagement, shall have In Addition to his Share, a choice of any Blade, Pistol, or Small Arm aboard her.

XI. No Man Aboard may Refuse to Work, Sup, or Repose near to another Simply for the Cut of his Cloth, Hue of his Skin, nor the GOD he keeps or eschews. All such Personal Disagreements resulting in Ongoing Enmity shall be handled by Duel declared at the Will of Captain and Company.

XII. No Ransom Prisoner, be it Man, Woman, or Child; nor any Guest Aboard; shall be subjected to Torment, Ridicule, Harassment, or Otherwise Disrespected. Any man found Torturing or Forcibly Fornicating with a Ransom Prisoner will be subject to Gelding and Flogging.

XIII. To Speak Of or Conspire To Incite Mutiny and Rebellion will result in being Put Ashore in some Forsaken Place, with a single Skin of Water and a Pistol. Any & All Grievances against the Captain shall be decided by The Company.

XIV. No man shall Kick, Poison, Shoot, Knife, Scald, Drown, or Consume the Captain's Cat. Any Man found guilty of Harming the aforementioned Master Puss shall be Executed without delay.

Below and around it were the signatures, Xs, and sometimes thumbprints with initials of the men who had signed on. She read it several more times before setting down her bundle at her feet and drawing her knife. Pricking a forefinger, she smeared the first three letters of her name with her blood on an open spot.

JEZ

Jez is who she became from that moment onward. She tucked away the knife and picked up her things, before walking over by the starboard stern rail. Standing out of the way, she looked out over the bay, past the moored ships, to the boundless ocean. What adventures would this journey bring? Yet also; what dangers? Many of the men working around her had scars or missing fingers and toes…even entire limbs. At least two she saw had lost eyes. It was a hard life they lived, no denying that.

Other than the one visible scar, Walter Armitage had appeared whole in body and faculties, and very eager to get himself back aboard. There had to be something positive to this life. He had spoken so wistfully of his time at sea, Jez could almost picture every scene. Anything had to be better than rotting in Tortuga as the sullen keeper of a waterfront tavern. Leave that life to Mama then; she'd be far happier tethered to the shore.

"Hey ya lazybones, move yer scrawny shanks over here and lend a hand," called out a squint-eyed man with a long beak of a nose and sandy hair straggling out from a dirty yellow rag tied around his forehead. He was attempting to heave along a crate of something too bulky for a single person to hoist, and a twisted slat kept hanging up on the deck. Jez stowed her bundle in the long boat lashed to the deck and hustled over to help. She was fairly strong for her age, but didn't have the muscle bulk of a man who hefted heavy loads and hauled rigging for a living, so she couldn't lift her end more than a couple inches.

"Ah, ye'll be useless for naught but fish bait," the deck hand said with disgust as he set it down. He spit towards her feet. "Fine boots and lady's hands, another blasted runaway brat. Go home and play wit' yer toys. Come back when yer worth yer salt."

"I got this, Sol," said a booming voice behind Jez. An ebony mountain of a man, all sweat and huge muscles over a loincloth and some seashell bead strings, pushed past her and lifted the other end of the crate. "The boy has yet to come into his manhood. Give him six months at sea, a blade in his hand, blood beneath his feet, and a few women to warm his nights, and then you'll call him brother."

Sol snorted and gave Jez a wry glance. "Yeah well, I ain't no stinkin' nursemaid. A shipmate pulls his weight, or he goes off ta bother someone else."

They moved away from Jez, lifting the crate together as if it were a feather. She angrily snatched up her bundle, and stalked off to see if there was something more useful she could do to redeem herself.

She wound up spending the next couple hours helping the cook set up the galley. The small, wizened old salt with the peg leg and filthy apron was called Rat Stew Andy Boone by most of the men aboard. He gave Jez a toothless smile and a clap on the back.

"Yer a right fine 'elp lad. Ye come down 'ere anytime, and I'll make good use of ye, and teach ya all I knows. It's nigh on thirty five years I been at sea, or so they say; and 'twasn't always as cookie. I was a right good fightin' man, I was, and a damn fine sailor. But I lost me leg, lost all me teeth, and three fingers on me shootin' 'and. So now I'm king of the scullions."

Jez smiled as they moved barrels and swung big kettles into place. With Andy, she felt like she had somewhere to fit in.

"Does ya know any music boy? I sure do love a good song now 'n' den..."

"I sing sometimes, but not right now." Her singing voice was higher pitched and she needed to learn some of the shanties and bawdy tunes the sailors seemed to enjoy.

"Aye that's bully news, I loves me some singin'." Andy Boone loved to talk too, but most of all, he loved his pipe and rum. He was quite knowledgeable though, and kept Jez both busy and entertained until they were called topside.

The loading done and the evening tide coming in, Gully whistled loud and long, and all hands came running to assemble on the main deck. The Oath was basically a rereading of the Articles before the company with further explanation to those who had recently signed on. There were plenty of jeers and ribald commentary. It was a last chance for port recruits to have their names scratched out and leave before they cast off, or for the regular crew to reject someone they didn't like or trust.

There were seven new company members that day; four men and three boys, including Jez in disguise. She kept her face downcast and her voice just loud enough to be heard, but as she squatted on the lightly rolling deck of the still tethered ship, she was surreptitiously searching for Walter Armitage. With the rough estimate being 111 men and 3 boys aboard, it was a large company to ogle.

She finally located him, standing behind the gunners with his arms crossed on his chest, looking very different from the dashing adventurer she recalled from the tavern. The faded breeches, worn boots, and a sweat stained, loose linen shirt made him blend in, though he carried himself far more proudly than most of his brethren. His waving black hair was still freshly shorn to the nape of his neck, though it was now covered with a faded blue calico scarf; his cavalier hat with the jaunty feather having been set aside for more practical wear aboard. The scruffy beard and mustache was growing in again to cover the thin scar from ear to corner of the mouth, but above that his eyes were still a blue that you could see across a room. Next to her bold Papa, he was the most handsome man she had ever met, and Jez had to resist the urge to smile and wave. Feeling the flush running up her neck into her face, she fought to steady her breathing.

Master Gully indicated it was her turn by holding out before her a worn Bible in Latin script with the back cover and half the New Testament missing. It was just a prop, for pirates were not known for piety. Hardly any of them could read anyway, and certainly not Latin. Gully laid a ceremonial sword that belonged to the Captain atop the battered book. Jez raised the sword in her right hand as the others had, and placed her left palm and fingers on the tattered book.

"Do ya swear ye be one of the Company; that ye'll abide by the Articles and do as yer told, work like a dog, fight like the devil incarnate, mind yer betters, and vote with yer heart?" Gully asked her. Jez could feel all their eyes upon her.

"I swear all," she said like everyone else had, albeit in a shaky voice. They dipped her a mug of bumbo…the sweetened and spiced rum favored by pirates…and handed it over. Jez gulped it down as she had seen the men do, almost choking on the unaccustomed burn. She'd never had more than watered wine, beer, or ale. The boy next to her that everyone called Pah-*kay* was a full blood Panamanian Indian slave who had run away from a sugar plantation. He signed aboard with no more than his ragged breeches and a crude bow with a sinew string and small set of arrows that he bragged he had made to kill his cruel overseer before he escaped. Pakke managed his bumbo just fine, but the tow-headed skinny fellow on the other side, named Neville Felton, coughed, sputtered, retched, and gagged. Someone had to bang him on the back before he could get his wind.

The men laughed and pointed, slapping their knees and beating hard callused feet on the deck. The captain, shaking his head in disgust over the weak and wastrel youth of these latter days, walked away. Master Gully stumped over to break things up.

"Tides up, wind's seaward; all hands make ready to sail," he hollered and every man scrambled back to his feet, including Jez and Pakke. Neville was far slower, and accepted the Master's hand up, which was more of a yank that would have dislocated a shoulder had the boy not been so reedy thin.

"Got yer wind back yet laddie?" Gully asked with a chuckle.

"That savage drank from it before me," Neville said bitterly once he got his breath back. "Their spit is poison."

"Bah, none o' yer nonsense now!" Gully retorted, boxing his ears until Neville ducked and howled. "Yer not some bloomin' Earl's son; jist another freebooter, as good or bad as any aboard be. C'mon ya three useless brats, and I'll learn ye yer place afore I turn ye over to our gunny, James Reuben.

That's *Master* Reuben to the likes of ye, so show 'im some respect. He'll assign ye to powder monkey or swab dipper as he sees fit." Men were already climbing into the rigging to trim sail as needed once they had cleared the docks and pilings.

As it turned out, Master Gunner James Reuben was none too happy to have three green lubber lads to deal with. While the shouting and singing commenced upon the main deck as lines were cast; sails raised, bent, and snapped, and the creaking timbers around them began to groan, the trio were led between decks. It was down to the gun deck first. There they were introduced to the life of a 'powder monkey'…those lads who brought the charges and shot to the gun crews. James Reuben quickly explained that this was their main duty while engaged, and stressed the dangers involved. The small man stood with hands balled on hips, his well-callused bare feet beneath wide legged slops spread far apart to take the roll of the big ship as the *Devil's Handmaid* came to life and back tacked cautiously out of her berth.

"Now mind, we won't need you every day, and so I'll not be wanting you laying around awaiting your turn to make yourself useful," the squinting man with the braided pigtail and tricorn hat said in his clipped and cultured tone with a bit of noble breeding showing in his precise diction. "You'll pitch in as necessary on trimming ballast, holding watches, mending sail and lines, and just generally learn to do your share elsewhere; whether that is bilge pumping, hunting rats, or fetching sacks and casks for Rat Stew Andy. And do look lively lads, or you'll be tossed off at the next port. I've no room for shirkers nor crybabies. You want to eat; you work."

That first day was full of adjustments. Since none of them had a sea chest, they were each given an empty nail keg to stow their things along with a marlinspike for picking knots and splicing, and bone needles for mending sail. There was no room for any more hammocks where the main crew slept, as men got first choice, so they were told to bed down in the orlop deck, where the spare lines were stored. "Nothing like a cozy nest of hemp when you be new to the sea," Reuben said sarcastically before he left them in the hands of the men stowing cables in tidy coils.

"Ye'd best put way them foin shoes and boots first off," one of the old timers said when saw Neville and Jez's footwear. "Get yer tender feet toughened up right off. Ye'll want te keep the leather good fer when ye're in port. Gotta be impressing the fine ladies, iffen ye want te get 'neath their skirts," he added with a ribald chuckle before turning back to his work.

They stowed their things, and Neville and Pakke wound up helping some men move and lash down spare yard arms. After all the bumbo, Jez was desperately in need of relieving her bladder, but unlike her male counterparts, could not just drop her fly front and aim off the side. She finally made her way down to the bilge, and found herself a quiet spot to partially disrobe, reasoning that she couldn't make it smell any worse down there than it already did. The bilge had the worst reek aboard, but the entire ship stank of far too many seasons of salt and tar, sweat, blood, fish, and dysentery outbreaks. Jez was a little disheartened about her choice to sign aboard as she worked her way back up to the galley, to see if Andy needed any help.

"Why, ain't ye a fine and considerate lad, te come back and 'elp an old man," he said in greeting, his smile filled with rotted teeth and big gaps. "Now that we be 'eading out, I was just settin' up te get me stove goin'. The fellas will be 'ungry no doubt, after 'auling and cartin' all day, and I've too much te do as tis."

As the ship left the harbor and gained the open water, Jez lent a hand in preparing food for the Captain's dinner. There was more of a pitch and roll to the movement of the craft and it took getting used to, but she voluntarily carried the tray up to his quarters without slopping too much of it. That was where her experience waiting tables in her mother's tavern came in handy, though it was a tough climb while encumbered with the heavy pewter trencher loaded with food that wanted to slide off at the slightest tilt.

The door to the great cabin was shut, but there was a buzz of men's voices within. Jez shifted the tray to one hand and knocked lightly with the other.

"It's bloody open!" came Dandy Dan's imperious answer as the voices hushed. "Get in here, it's about time we were fed! These men have work to do once we're at sea, and they've not got all night to wait on a meal."

Stinging from the second rebuke from her Captain in a single day, Jez pulled the handle, and grabbing the tray with both hands against the ceaseless rolling of the ship, used her rump to keep the heavy wooden paneled door open while skillfully swinging her tray inside without a mishap.

The captain's table was arranged below the stern gallery windows to take advantage of daylight whenever possible. He also had a desk and large upholstered chair, a bunk, a couple of chests, and various oddments that had to be dodged while avoiding stepping on a monstrously fat and rather rough looking cat sprawled in the only open space. She had to negotiate her way along carefully; the unaccustomed rocking motion making every movement more difficult in the cramped space filled with long legged men seated on hastily drawn up benches. She didn't dare take her eyes off the path her bare feet were treading.

Finally reaching the table without a mishap, she heaved a sigh of relief. There were pewter tankards and a couple of flagons on it, so while men leaned out of her way, Jez gently nudged things aside to set the tray down. There was a clatter from the far end as a tankard slipped from a careless hand and some of the contents spilled, and men swore and brushed themselves off.

"Wally me bucko, I'm sure a hopin' to hell yer gun hand be less shaky than yer drinking one!" someone said as Jez was getting things set out. The rest of them laughed as the careless man scowled and said little.

Her delivery of the meal was all done so skillfully, she got a grunt of satisfaction from the Captain. Before she could turn away, he grabbed her wrist, bringing her roughly around.

"You have some experience serving, don't you lad?"

"Yessir... I've some," Jez answered quietly, uneasy at having to meet his eyes.

"Well done then, considering you've not been aboard before. Tell Andy I said you can bring me my meals daily, and if Master Gulliver approves, I'd like to see you assigned to assist in the galley."

Gully nodded, and thumped his tankard down, indicating it was empty. Jez bustled over to refill it from one of the two flagons on the table. He eyed her and said, "Aye Cap'n, that old tar is struggling as it is, so I've no issue with using a boy where I don't have to assign a man." He pointed at Jez though, frowning. "Now mind lad, that doesn't excuse you from main deck duty. Ye'll serve watches and the gun deck as you be needed."

"I will Sir," she said politely, and the rest of them laughed.

"Boy thinks he's in the bloody Royal Navy," the chief Gunner, James Reuben, said with a lift of his own tankard. The slight man took a long quaff and set it down gently. "He's bloomin' polite for a gutter rat."

"Ah, leave 'im alone boys," Gully said dismissively. "He's likely had the manners beat inta 'im by some plantation owner that fancies 'imself a great lord."

Jez was uncomfortable with the scrutiny as well as their all too easy familiarity. "I... I should get back to the galley, so if this is all you need for now..."

"Leave us," Captain Adams said dismissively and waved her off before he reached out for a hard-boiled egg and then whacked off a wedge of

"You have some experience serving, don't you lad?"

cheese with his knife. "Set to lads, we'll not have a meal this good for a while."

Jez edged away as soon as the captain gave her leave to go. From over by the door, she dared a quick glance around the room. The one person sitting there who had not said much was Walter Armitage. He met her gaze with a calculating one of his own. There was no warmth in the blue ice of his glare. She knew then and there he had recognized her for who she was, and that only the company's presence had kept him from questioning what the devil she was doing on his ship.

The Master of Arms caught up with her later, as he made his rounds to introduce himself to all the new men aboard, and remind them that he'd be teaching them weapons basics. The galley was his last stop. "I'd like a private word with your helpmate, Andy," he said, after greeting the old man and inquiring as to his health, which gained him an entire litany of ailments.

"Go on lad, I'll manage." Andy Boone waved them off.

They went off silently together, single file down past the main hold, where the cargo would be stowed. Walter Armitage's carriage was stiff and his manner brusque. Once they had passed the last knot of men working to more safely stack hogsheads of rum and found themselves out of sight and hearing behind a great stack of sailcloth, he rounded on her. His face was a mask of barely controlled fury, his eyes almost shooting sparks as he snapped in a low but obviously enraged tone.

"Jezebel Johnston...what the bloody hell are you doing on this ship?"

Well there it was, the moment she had been dreading since she first saw his face. How easy it had seemed to slip aboard; how incredibly right the urge to be with that handsome devil who had stolen her heart. How lame that all seemed now, with him towering over her, every pore oozing anger and exasperation.

"I knew you wouldn't stay ashore if I asked," she said, her dark eyes downcast, "And I couldn't let you go on without me, Walter. So I did the only thing I could think of..."

"You did the stupidest, most unconscionable thing I've ever heard of!" He wanted to shout at the top of his lungs, yet just barely managed to control the vocal intensity of his response. "You read the Articles! You made your mark, and gave your word; and that's all a lie! This could get us both booted off...or worse! You have to confess before we're too far from Tortuga, so they'll send a boat out and get you safely back to the docks. See Gully about it immediately."

"NO!" she insisted, a bit too loud before he shushed her. Her fists were balled at her sides, her stubborn chin up, while her dark eyes snapped. She was only a head shorter than he was at twenty and nine. "I don't want to leave. I want to be here with you, raiding the seven seas, seeing all those wondrous sights you told me about, sleeping in your arms of a night..." her voice broke, and his eyes softened.

"Jez," he said with a frustrated sigh, giving in to emotion for just an instant, "I know you're Tall Tom's daughter, and I adored the man when I served with him. But you're only still a *child*. You don't understand the predicament you've put me in. I can't hide you in my cabin...I share it with James Reuben."

"If my father asked, you would have done it," she hissed in an accusing tone.

"No I would not," he said flatly, "Because at least he understood the code better than you do, and he honored it. Your father would have told you this is a hard life even for a man, and always dangerous. A ship is no place for a woman anyway. It's a bad omen to these freebooters to have one of the fair sex aboard while we're underway, and they're a fierce lot that don't scare easy. If they get wind of me consorting with a female stowaway I'll be marooned at best, and you'll get dumped in the nearest port."

"I won't let that happen! I can pull my own weight here, and they'll never know who I am."

He shook his head. "They'll find you out eventually, especially if you keep going down to the bilge to piss!"

"How did you know about that?" she asked in a shocked tone, but managed to keep her voice low.

He glared at her. "You're not as sneaky as you think you are, because Master Reuben brought it to my attention, though he assumed you were just shy of exposing yourself in front of the others. At least take a bucket with you next time!"

"I will," she promised. "But see? Things can be worked out."

He shook his head. "No they can't, not forever. You have to go back before you get us both into a greater mess. I'm not losing my berth aboard for you. Abrams is a good captain; well respected and fairer than most. I can't afford to have word get around that I defied him."

Oh, so it was all about what he wanted. That put her temper up, and she lifted angry, glittering eyes to glare at him in the gloom.

"Fine then; I'm on my own, and to hell with you! Look after your own arse Walter Armitage; because I can bloody well take care of myself," she retorted hotly, and dodged away before he could say another word. She sniffed back the tears that threatened to overspill her eyes and stomped off to see what else needed doing. Jez wanted to lift and haul, toss things around, and make her young muscles strong as a man's. That would show him…that would show them all!

She strode off filled with angry, injured pride. Jezebel Johnston was going to be as good a pirate as any man aboard.

CHAPTER TWO

Many days had passed with fair winds, and the *Devil's Handmaid* was traveling at a good clip. Most of the new men, the two boys, and occasionally Jez had been sick to the stomach with the rolling and heaving of the deck. She and Pakke seemed to adjust fairly quickly, but Neville was seriously 'green about the gills' as Master Reuben called it, all hours of the day and night. They'd had to force him to sleep up on deck to keep the stench down. He got chided a little, but the others mostly left him alone, for it was obvious the boy was miserable.

Jez spent most of her time eagerly learning about what the deckhands did, which sails were which, how to tie knots, and safe ways to climb rigging. Out in the sunshine and fresh salt air, she felt far less queasy. Once the smell of food didn't send her stomach lurching, she went back to being part time galley help.

"Well jist lookit ya," Andy Boone complimented Jez when she came striding in to fetch the Captain's dinner after a gun deck drill, "Ye seem to 'ave got yer sea legs right fast, laddie."

"Papa was a Biscuit Eater too," she said proudly, using the men's own euphemism for those who survived voyages on hardtack and raw courage. That small truth about her heritage shouldn't be an issue.

"Really now?" he replied with interest, as he piled his version of salmagundi on a silver plate before dousing it in lemon and oil. "What'd 'e go by, yer Paw? I might 'ave knowed 'im; I met a lot of sea dogs over the years."

"Uh..." she had to think about it, but decided it was safe enough to tell. "Tall Tom. Tall Tom Johnston."

Rat Stew Andy almost dropped his pipe on the Captain's plate. His one good eye opened wide. "Ye don't say lad! Be ye tuggin' me pegleg or be that the 'onest truth?"

"You knew him?" Jez asked uncertainly. He nodded vigorously, making his earrings and the beads in his beard jangle.

"Aye, I knew of 'im, and seed him in ports more'n oncet. Tom Johnston was a rangy fella and kinda real lean, like yer gonna be; but fair skinned and with yaller curls." He paused, considering her a moment. "Chin's the same too, sorta sticks out it does, but ye got some darky blood in ya fer sartain."

Jez picked up the plate and her eyes grew hard. "My mother is a freed slave," she said with distaste, and turned to leave. Andy stumped past her, and made sure the way was clear. He grabbed her arm.

"Jez lad, it don't matter none aboard if yer colored or not. Ye know Jengo, that big black lug? Strong as an ox, best fighter I ever seed, but all smiles wit' the Company when they tease him about having a hard lick of the tar brush. These men call 'im brother, and fer good r'ason, too. 'E's fearless, and saved many a life wit' 'is blade. Ye're a right smart lad Jez, and ye got spunk; ye'll earn yer way in time. We's all equal-like, out 'ere."

She gave him a quick wink and then hustled up the hatch ladder before Dandy Dan started hollering again.

Several more days out and they were just luffing along with the fair weather. Ships were spotted, but nothing worth chasing after. One mid-morning they were in sight of Jamaica, but since they were flying a British flag at the time, passed by unmolested. Dan Abrams had no qualms with raiding their ships, but there were too many of them about here. By late afternoon they had left English territorial waters, and so that jack was struck and the *Devil's Handmaid* sailed without colors. They were headed southerly toward the Spanish Main when someone spotted the first potential target.

"Sail!" came the call that had men scrambling all over the decks, a few climbing the ratlines into the rigging in preparation to trim canvas, some to the larboard rails to peer out to sea. It was no more than a speck on the horizon, and gradually moving away. By sunset, it would be out of sight.

Dandy Dan stood on the quarterdeck with his spyglass extended. Gully stood next to him.

"Portuguese," the captain announced. "An older merchant vessel. Not a big one mind you, just two gun decks; but low in the water. She's alone, likely coming back in after a stop in the Indies, loaded with trade goods for one of the coastal colonies." He glanced down over the main deck waist and forecastle at the many eager faces turned his way. "What say you lads, are we going after this one?" he called out to the crew as he shut his spyglass and leaned on the rail.

Calls of 'aye', and raucous cheers came from all around as men who had crowded the rails pumped fists in the air.

Abrams smiled. They were a doughty and eager bunch. He turned to the white haired man at his side.

"Well, that settles it. We'll take her, Master Gulliver, but we need to close in. Run up that Castillian rag so we don't spook them too soon."

"Hoist the red and gold jack!" Gully shouted. Two men ran to retrieve a slightly tattered Spanish flag and send it up to display. It was a calculated ruse to allow them to approach without being challenged, though no doubt the Portuguese captain and his crew would be suspicious. The odds were in their favor of catching up while they had good wind and weather. While the galleon had two gun decks and at least 40 cannon, it was lumbering along and would not maneuver very fast. With a Spanish flag flying and the approaching dusk, the *Devil's Handmaid* might get near enough to use the cover of night to do her dirty work. Darkness was always the buccaneer's best friend.

"Bring us up on her starboard and somewhat athwart," Abrams said with a half-smile. "We'll want to cut her off from slipping past, before we run into one of their gunships. Close haul if you must. Just keep her well in sight until we can pull ahead."

"Come about now, Master Ping," Gully shouted to the mostly silent half caste Chinese helmsman with the straggling dark hair, wispy mustache, and stringy beard. Ping nodded as he gradually but expertly worked the wheel. Men on deck hastened to pull pins and loosen clewlines and buntlines while others were adjusting the travelers. Sails flapped and stiffened as they caught the wind anew. The *Devil's Handmaid* heeled hard and began to pick up speed, cutting through the waves, throwing up foam as she began pursuing her quarry like a big cat stalking prey.

The sun was going down once they got within sighting range. The Portuguese ship had spotted them chasing and added sail, but the pirate vessel was running eight knots to her five, and rapidly catching up. Even considering the way she was loaded down, the small galleon had a full complement of cannon, yet had not decided to stand her ground and demand to know who was pacing them.

For all he appeared a fop, Dan Abrams was an experienced marauder.

"I doubt they fell for our ruse. Something is amiss here," he complained. "Their captain is either inexperienced or a blithering idiot. All those guns and he's never challenged us. They're not making enough headway and there's barely any men a'deck. For all the sheet she has up, she has yet to show us her heels."

"Aye, it sure don't seem right," Gully agreed uneasily. "P'raps they be expectin' someone te meet up with 'em?"

Abrams called up to a small but agile, red haired Irishman in the lookout perch on the mainmast. "Master Duffy, are there any other ships in the area?"

"Nay Cap'n," came down the reply.

"Can you see anything unusual about this prize?"

"Naught I can make out at this distance, 'cept they're short handed," he called down after a small pause. "No one I've seed looked very lively either."

"Well then; by God we'll take her tonight if they're going to invite us aboard. Master Gully, strike that flag and run up our own colors. Let us see if we can't put the fear of death in them." Down came the Spanish flag, and up went the black flag with the red-eyed skull chewing a bone, with crossed cutlasses behind it.

The Portuguese galleon seemingly refused to strike her colors.

"Ah, so they need further convincing, do they?" Abrams smiled sardonically, and called out, "Close in…we'll send them a salutation with the bow chaser to soften their mood. Main deck gunners, man your stations, and make ready. Send a ball as initial warning, and if they don't strike their colors, chain shot to the sails once we're within range. I want the blasted ship stopped but left seaworthy if possible, so boarders, make ready."

Devil's Handmaid was a hubbub of activity, as everyone hustled to his tasks. Both upper and lower decks were cleared and unnecessary items removed as gunners and their support took over. While the long barreled bow chaser was readied and armed, men were scrambling all over to prepare for the encounter. Expert setters and trimmers ascended the rigging, in case of emergency adjustments. Seawater for putting out fires was hauled aboard in buckets, sand from barrels was spread on deck to improve footing, and grappling hooks with lines were brought out. Only a small crew was left on the sails, and men skilled with muskets took the place of lookouts. Those not involved with the gun deck below manned the topside guns or prepared to board, girding themselves with pikes, pistols, cutlasses, daggers, boarding axes and the occasional blunderbuss.

The main deck cannons were two 8 pounders in the stern and that special long barreled 9 pounder in the bow, though small swivel guns could be quickly put in place if they were in danger of being boarded. The gun deck held a dozen sturdy and serviceable 12 pounders, six per side. All stood pre-loaded, but the tompions covering the bore from moisture had to be removed and the lead plates covering the touch holes pulled. Racked tools were taken down, ready to put to service. After a quick inspection, shot garlands were raided for sail wrecking chain or bar shot, which got tamped in with wadding. Once loaded, bracing lines were loosened and men grunted and strained at moving the heavy guns and carriages by dragging on the tackle and forcing them along with levering handspikes. For the present, only the larboard guns were carefully trundled forward to project through the now open gun ports, as the captain believed in an economy of firepower when they weren't under active attack. Once the guns were run out and bracing made fast again, the quoin blocks in the rear of the carriage were roughly adjusted for elevation, the guns were ready to prime and fire.

Jez ran from the galley, where she'd been helping Andy put out his stove and clear off the scarred preparation table to use for possible surgeries. They had no true surgeon aboard, but the ship's carpenter, McNeal, known mostly as Mac, had the saws and strength to cut off damaged limbs, while Walter Armitage and Andy Boone made do for the rest. Ping knew some herbs that occasionally helped, and he often had badly wounded men smoke ganga…dried hemp seeds and leaves…which eased their suffering. It was a stomach churning thought, having a limb cut free, but Andy reassured her that it was better than the stinking black rot that set in when shattered bone and pulverized flesh mortified.

"A good lot of 'em lives through it, if'n we ketch it soon 'nuff. They took me own leg off when I was mebbe less'n twice yer age, laddie. Damned grenadoe tossed by a Frenchy got me. Lucky I di'n't bleed te death. I 'ad te get rip-roarin' drunk te deal with the pain, and mercy me, took four strong men to 'old me down when the surgeon come at me wit' that saw. I chawed right through the 'andle of the wooden spoon they shoved in me mouth te keep from bitin' me tongue in two, and lawd 'o'mercy when they was done sewing me stump, it seemed I'd bled nuff fer three men."

"How did you deal with... with losing a leg," she asked rather squeamishly as she smothered the fire with seawater and sand.

Andy sighed, as he put all but his two biggest knives away. They might need those.

"Ah, those were black days, Jez me boyo. I got drunk plenty and often, so's not te think too 'ard on it. 'Ad te larn meself all over agin 'ow te walk; but I soon adjusted. Ye be alive, ye still got 'ope; and the port town whores don't care whatcher missin', long as they gits their coin." He threw a one-eyed wink in her direction. "Weren't no good at boardin' parties after that, but I 'ad a dead eye and was a crack shot, so I did me part with a musket. Clumb the riggin' and everthin', I did! I would pick a likely officer and take 'im out. Nothin' dis'eartens a crew more'n losin' their Cap'n or Mate. If'n that last shot I took 'adn't blown back and took me eye and fingers, I'd still be up there shootin' teday, I would!"

Just thinking about all that Andy alone had lived through made her stomach lurch. Suddenly, pirating didn't seem like such a lark anymore. It was a deadly dangerous business.

Jezebel Johnston forced it out of her mind while loping past full shot racks, dodging men rolling and tying hammocks out of the way or moving the tables where the crew ate as others were readying the guns. She headed directly down past the armory to the magazine, which was low in the stern, behind water soaked canvas curtains. Neville and Pakke were already there, awaiting their loads. Behind the wet curtains, an experienced gunner's mate was standing over an open barrel, loading hastily stitched shut hempen cloth bags filled with sifted powder into leather pass boxes.

"About time you got here, slackard," the thin blonde boy said with a curl of lip. He still looked pale and ill, but at least he had put aside the puking long enough to be of some use.

"I had to help Andy get the table ready for the wounded," she retorted, carefully taking the handle of a filled box that got handed through.

Pakke's command of the bastardized English spoken aboard was still rough, but he made himself understood. "Me hab dis," he said, taking a second packet. Because all three of them were past the age of children, they could safely carry two charges at once. Six packets…two apiece for the three powder monkeys…would reload the six guns on the fighting side. That left more experienced and able men free to man their stations. With both hands filled, the native boy cautiously headed back out and up the companionway to the gun deck. Neville was not far behind him, hunched over under his own load, but his parting comment drifted back. "You're as useless as a girl, you know; always sniffing the bunghole of that old sea rat." Jez glared at him, fuming.

The bow chaser fired somewhere overhead, the sudden roar of its explosion and fierce kickback rattling the decks above and scaring the daylights out of her. Even though it was somewhat muffled, below decks it was still loud enough to make Jez jump as the ship rocked and timbers groaned. Her comeback to Neville died in her throat, and she almost lost her grip on the handle of the packet she'd been holding. It was just a warning shot she knew; something to make the other ship's crew think a little so they'd perhaps surrender quickly. There were shouts, but she couldn't make them out as she hurriedly grabbed the next pass box and some cloth that came through and trudged off.

She had to pass the arms locker, where Walter Armitage and two other men had come down to collect additional weapons for the boarding party. There was no time for talk, as all of them were busy. Jez had her two filled charges and a bunch of wadding tucked under one arm, and was heading up when Armitage stopped her. He reached out and shoved a dagger into the sash she had taken to wearing at his suggestion during arms practice, to disguise her budding breasts. "Keep that close by, *boy*; you might need it," he said quickly before going back to passing out pistols, cutlasses, and boarding axes. She nodded with a carefully cultivated blank expression, though a small, warm thrill coursed through her as she continued climbing up, being careful not to snag the charges. She stopped and waited off to the side, where Pakke and Neville were standing.

"You know why they put us down here, don't you?" Neville said with a face that was paler than before.

"We don't have the experience for boarding parties and manning sails, or the strength for hauling guns," she retorted.

"No, you stupid idiot," he said, rounding on her, "It's because we're expendable. If one of us dies, no big loss. Less company to share with. They're trying to get rid of us!"

Jez shook her head over his paranoia, but she couldn't shake off her own fears as easily. She kept focused on what was going on around them. Neville was always worked up about being unwanted. His mother had been an English indentured servant whose services were purchased by a wealthy and well-to-do French plantation owner, who fancied her. When the boy was born, his father took some interest in him, and taught him to read and write. The jealous, pampered wife of the planter had not wanted her husband's illegitimate son underfoot, and so had made their lives miserable. She eventually got her way. When Neville's mother died of swamp fever, the bastard boy was turned out on some trumped up reason, while the father was back in France. Buccaneering had sounded far better than begging in the street.

"Look Neville, you have as good a chance as anyone of getting through this. Just keep your head down and do your damn job."

"Blow dem up!" Pakke said with a toothy grin and she smiled thinly. They would if they must, but the idea was to cripple the other ship and force a surrender, not sink them. The native boy's understanding of the process was still fairly simple; but then, he hadn't had a father who was a privateer and spent his leisure days regaling his wide-eyed child with stories of his adventures asea.

Trying to show she was ever conscious of her duty, Jezebel leaned forward and looked around. Someone had brought in the priming quills and there were buckets of water for swabbing barrels between shots. Master Gunner James Reuben stalked by, also noting all was in readiness. He stopped and considered the situation, and then stumped back toward his inexperienced youngsters. He gave Jez a speculative look before he spoke up.

"Johnston, I'm thinking of sending you up to the main deck. I can make do with these two bilge rats down here, but I need a fast runner up there, so men don't run shy of powder or shot. You're long legged and careful. Are you willing to work topside?"

"Yes sir, I'll do that," she said quietly, handing off her pass cans to Pakke and Neville, who groaned at the extra weight. Gun loads were specific; she had learned that much. James Reuben frowned at Neville's complaints and the skinny boy went white and silent.

"Good man! Walter says you are already a fair shot, so take a pistol for yourself, if you can wrangle one from the armory. Remember though, you're a bit tall for your age, and that makes you as much of a target as any man up there. In other words, don't get cocky. If you hear incoming, make sure you keep your head down so you don't lose it. I don't need you getting yourself blown apart in such a pitiful exchange."

"I'll be careful Master Reuben," she promised before turning to leave. Wouldn't Walter be impressed she'd been given special duty!

"They really must want rid of you today! You'll find out the hard way that I'm right," Neville shouted after her. Jez threw back at him a particularly vile epithet in French, which most of the crew couldn't understand, though Neville undoubtedly would, and then otherwise ignored his sputtering as she raced back down the deck and took the ladder to the powder room two steps at a time. They'd be wanting their charges and perhaps some grapeshot once they closed in, and she didn't have time to trade insults with the foolish boy.

When the smothering fog of the bow chaser cleared, it became clear the ball fired in front of her beakhead hadn't encouraged the Portuguese galleon to strike her colors. The pirate ship had sailed far closer, so the order was given to edge ahead and present the larboard battery for a high broadside as the other ship passed. That volley fired almost simultaneously, with a thundering roar and brilliant flashes that shook the deck, lightly heeling the ship to starboard on the recoil and wreathing everything in thick and choking smoke.

Aiming on even a calm sea at dusk, with the rocking motion of the ship and its forward movement taken into consideration, was imprecise at best. Two of the shots went true, one of which chunked a mast and took out the galleon's mizzen sails, and the other a goodly bit of main rigging. Several hapless Portuguese sailors, upset from their high perches, dropped shrieking to the decks with sickening thuds. A dead man sliced partway through by flying debris tumbled down more slowly, raining a gory gush of innards until his body hit the water below with a resounding splat. Three other shots dropped short, though one nicked the hull. The last one blasted through the small galleon's starboard rail and rebounded along her deck, sending up a spray of splinters and blood, eliciting shrill screams and foreign curses.

The Portuguese ship slowed considerably, a quarter of her sail and rigging in tatters. That seemed to convince her crew they'd have to surrender or fight. The ponderous ship began to come about.

Everyone aboard *Devil's Handmaid* tensed for the expected barrage as sail and tiller were adjusted to sweep her away and circle for a starboard volley.

It was with confusion that the pirate crew on deck watched what happened next. The galleon's gun ports never opened. Down came the Portuguese ensign and up went a quarantine flag instead.

"Bloody hell that!" Abrams swore.

"Tis an old ship, naught somethin' ye'd do much trade in. Ye s'pose they could have the black death?" Gully asked uncertainly. Something was keeping the merchant vessel from responding normally, let alone fighting back, and having most of the crew sick or dead would certainly explain it.

Abrams seemed to mull it over, as he stalked the rail.

"No," he said decisively. "Not this far from Lisbon. They would have had to freshen supplies at least halfway to the Indies, and at the first stop for food and water, they would have been booted out and fired upon until they left. No one allows a plague ship to dock up close. Neither would they be bringing in the pox to spread amongst their Spanish trade allies, whose native slaves are always so decimated by it. It has to be something more... *localized.* Unless of course it is a ruse to put us off until they rejoin their fleet or make port. I am most curious about what might be aboard that wallowing tub," he added, with a speculative look. "Ready the longboat, Master Gulliver; we're going aboard to find out!"

Gully sighed and stomped off.

"Hold yer fire! Reef the sail! Lower the longboat!" the quartermaster sang out and men hustled back to work.

"Boarders, to me; smartly now," rang down the deck once the smaller vessel was carefully lowered to the water below. Dandy Dan Abrams girded himself with pistols and cutlass before clambering over the side. As Jez stood by with others remaining aboard, the arms master and his chosen men made their way past and went after their eager captain, going down the rope and wooden cleat contraption they called a 'Jacobs ladder' to the tackle tethered, double banked rowboat below. Jengo gave her a big toothy smile as he went by. Once they were settled and the bow and stern lines cast off and drawn up, with Abrams at the fore and Walter Armitage at the tiller, the dozen well armed men with them bent their backs to rowing. With just a light churning of the oars to mark their passage, they headed around the mostly dark bulk of *Devil's Handmaid* and out toward the lantern lit galleon drifting aimlessly by.

Men aboard the pirate ship crowded the rails again, watching their companions go, wondering if they were heading into a trap. Nothing was a certainty in these turbulent times, when alliances were made and broken, often independently of what was happening amongst the continental powers, so far away. Jez stood amongst the rest of the deck crew, half holding her breath, her sharp-eyed gaze fixed on the long, lean back of the man she could not get out of her thoughts. She prayed for his safety, that he would not come back minus a limb, or worse; remain behind mortally wounded and after having fallen in battle, his lifeblood soaking the enemy's deck, his organs falling free like a slaughtered pig. Walter was just too handsome and alive to die like a dog kicking on the end of some soldier's blade, or dropped with a musket ball soaking his shirt crimson.

The boarding party reached the Portuguese vessel and clambered aboard just as true darkness set in. There came a single gunshot, and everyone held their breath, and then... silence. A short while later, someone stepped onto the forecastle waving a lantern, which was the agreed upon signal that all was well.

"Master Ping, bring us alongside," Gully's voice called out promptly. Men who had been gawking hustled to their posts again as the tiller was manipulated and sails were adjusted once more. They continued around to the larboard side of the slowly moving ship until lines with attached grapples could be tossed, drawing the bigger ship close. The gangplank was laid across, and more well-armed men went aboard, though a couple lookouts with muskets at the ready stayed behind.

As eager as she was to join them, Jez was ordered back below. Now that the big guns were no longer being manned, space must be cleared in the hold for possible plunder.

"What'd we git lad?" Andy Boone called out curiously as Jez passed the galley on the way to the cargo area. He handed her a wooden mug of watered rum, which she gratefully accepted, gulping half of it down to slake the dry throat of breathing in cannon fumes.

"A two deck Portuguese galleon I'm told," she said, wiping her mouth with the back of her hand.

Andy snorted in disgust. "Bah, that's an old timey ship. I bet they be slavers, the lot of them," he said dismissively. "Capn's not in for any more Afrikay crew, and Dandy Dan's not a one to sell another man, no matter 'is color. What be our current sit-chee-ai-shun?"

"We're boarding now," she told him. "They didn't stop when we shot across her bow, but then the larboard guns took down a lot of sail, along with a... few men..." She almost retched at the thought of the carnage, which even from a distance was still horrifically graphic. Another long draught made the awful memory of it fade away as the rum did its magic. "Then they raised a yellow jack," she added with a puzzled look, handing the wooden mug back to the stooped old man.

"That be the plague flag. There's sickness aboard 'er, no doubt, because the Portugee, they normally look over their slave stock careful-like. I'd naught take a chance, 'twas up te me. We'll all soon be down wit' sumthin ugly, ye mark me words on it..." Andy's voice trailed off as he limped back into the galley, and Jez hurried off. There was too much to do to stand around listening to an old man's ranting, and they'd be wanting her help below. If she hustled, she'd have time to hit the bilge and relieve the pressure on her bladder before anyone noticed. There was no time to run for the pail...not with men stowing things all over the ship!

Unfortunately finding a lonely spot in the dark wasn't as easy as she hoped, with men moving barrels around and wedging them. She almost wet her breeches in fright when a voice drifted by in the dark.

"Sum bodee here?" Pakke's voice called down uncertainly. The native boy had been sent to find her.

"Be right up," she said quietly, fumbling with the buttons in front. The sash had made it tough to half disrobe and squat. She had almost dropped her dagger.

"Jez piss like gurl," he said derisively, only his smile faintly visible in the Stygian blackness as they made their way carefully back up the ladder.

"Just don't say that in front of Neville," she groaned and he laughed.

"Pakke no loud mouth lubber," he promised. That was when she decided she trusted him best of all aboard.

They did not see Neville watching them from the shadows below the gangway, where he had followed Jez down to the lowest deck. He had seen what Pakke had not, that this so-called 'boy', Jez, had no male organ within his breeches. It was something to hold onto; a knowledge that might serve him well later on.

Both ships were a hubbub of activity that night, as Captain Abrams wanted to be rid of the Portuguese galleon by dawn. That meant all hands to the unloading. Even the youngest members of the crew had a chance to go aboard the other ship, and help carry away the prizes...which turned out to be mostly spices, indigo, rum, and tobacco. There were still approximately 75 slaves aboard, many of them ill with fevers and bowel fluxes. Their chains struck, they huddled miserably on the main deck with what was left of their captors, and watched with haunted eyes as whatever was portable and worthy of trade was carried off by what appeared to be their latest conquerors.

The captain and any officers aboard were dead, and only a pitiful, sickly crew was now manning her; the Portuguese sailors looking almost as feeble as their human cargo. The slavers had all been disarmed. Dandy Dan was determined to leave the ship to whoever wanted it. The below decks were so completely fouled it was a floating sewer, and it was far too leaky in the rotted seams to bother repairing.

"Tis a miracle they dinna sink on the way over from Africay in this hulk," Gully declared.

On questioning the sailors in halting Spanish, Walter Armitage learned that their ship was the *São Félix*. They had recently delivered 137 live souls to the French plantations on western end of Hispaniola, but the auctions would not accept those who were obviously ill, unusually unruly, or marked by pox. Hence what was left of that slave shipment was considered its dregs, and so they had been headed for Panama, where the Spanish were far less fussy, and those who survived could be traded high. That was when the illness struck, and so many crew died. The rest had mutinied, and the captain and his men had been knifed and thrown to the sharks. A lesser man, who was no less cruel, had taken command, until Dan Abrams had shot him. The survivors were now on their own.

"What are we doing with them, Cap'n?" Walter Armitage asked quietly. He gestured mostly at the slaves, a pitiful bunch of sickly men squatting nearby.

Abrams looked down disdainfully. Most of them were covered in filth and crawling with lice.

"Well, we're full up, and they reek, so we're not taking them. Have their oh-so-splendid overlords," he indicated what was left of the Portuguese crew with a dismissive wave of one be-ringed hand, "dip up some seawater and sluice them off. Leave them some lines and sail, and whatever water and foodstuffs they'll need. I'd not want much that this cursed ship ate or drank anyway. Take all their powder and shot, and any weapons you find though. We can always use those."

"You're not going to do way with the Portuguese slavers then," Armitage questioned.

"What are we doing with them, Cap'n?"

Abrams removed his hat and ran fingers through his long, waving hair, hoping he hadn't picked up too many more lice and fleas aboard. "No," he said with an arch look in their direction. "Let those who survive this wretched voyage sort things out on their own time once we're well away. Oh, and we'll want their blasted flag as well. That could come in handy."

Armitage nodded without taking his eyes off the men he was guarding, and issued orders in broken Spanish to one of the crew to bring forth the Portuguese jack. They were completely cowed and a nervous man nodded and ran off to collect it. He handed the carefully folded bundle over with tears in his eyes, and then sat down heavily. Crossing his arms on his drawn up knees, he sobbed.

"A high strung bunch, these Portugee," Sol commented as he leveled a pistol at another man, who sat up and was glaring at him. "They could do with some sense being knocked into them."

"Just leave them be," Walter Armitage said in a low voice. "Captain says we're not to molest them unless they give us trouble."

"They have cannon. If they trade for powder and shot, they could come after us," Sol warned with a defiant curl of lip.

"With less than a dozen men and sails to patch?" Armitage said with derision. "Sick as they are, these Negroes outnumber them several times over. With a taste of freedom, I doubt very much they are going to go back down into that hold as docilely as before."

"You bloody know everything, doncha?" Sol said under his breath, and Walter pretended not to hear him. Sol was always a troublemaker, but he worked hard and was a good sailor and a fair shot.

"Master Gulliver," the captain called out imperiously as he stalked toward the stern, "I want all hands that can be spared hauling plunder out of here. I'd prefer to be shut of this floating deathtrap as soon as we're able."

Gully made sure every man who was not assigned to a duty came aboard and carried out his share…including the three boys. The only things Dan Abrams took for himself were some bottled wine, an assortment of maps and charts that might be useful, a rare brass ship's speaking horn, and a cast metal mask that he found in the captain's quarters. It had a long face and horns of a goat all inlaid with gold. Since he fancied the evil looking thing, he declared it part of his normal share.

Two men of the Portuguese crew, under the direction of Walter Armitage, heaved the body of the ship's unfortunate second captain overboard just as the three youngest members of the pirate crew came over the plank to help carry off the spoils of their victory.

The first thing Jez noticed when she set foot on board was a putrid stench that assaulted her nose as it wafted up through the open main hatch. It became intense enough to gag her as she went below decks, and like many others she tied her scarf around her nose and mouth to protect against the foul humors. As she helped the other men to carry bundles and barrels up and out, Jez thought the bilge on *Devil's Handmaid* smelled like perfume compared to this stink of filth and death that permeated the creaking old vessel. Evidently others did too, for there was much disgust and complaining. Someone had tapped a barrel of rum, and mugs were being passed around. She took a sip, readjusted her scarf, and passed it on.

The middle hold was a chilling sight for the mixed race girl, for it looked like a warehouse for people. There were shelves dividing it into extra levels, and because of the sickness aboard, the putrid mess smearing them was unbelievable. Each upright support was studded with fasteners for the chains and fetters that every male slave wore, while the women and young children had been sitting loose in the middle aisle. Those deck divisions doubled the cargo space, allowing people to be packed in tightly, one row above another, like cattle and swine.

The sight of those desolate faces on the main deck and the putrid mess below where they had been confined reminded Jez that her own mother had been born the daughter of slave parents carried thus from some dark coast of Africa. Monifa's words about making her own way in the world came back to her, and the girl disguised as a boy became all the more determined to escape that sort of restrictive plight. As she bent her back to her tasks, she purposely carried as much of the captured cargo over to their ship as she could manage, young muscles straining and burning with the heavy burdens.

Piracy was a hard life, but she enjoyed far more freedom and had status aboard well above any a woman of color would have gained ashore. Even if Walter Armitage didn't approve of her presence, and continued to refuse her clumsy, girlish advances, Jezebel Johnston didn't care. She steeled her will and plucked up her courage that day, for she was never going to live as a slave to anyone!

CHAPTER THREE

All sailors are superstitious by nature. It's part of being at the mercy of the vast and watery element they must depend upon as provider of transportation and livelihood. So much can go wrong when you are surrounded by nothing but waves and sky, that you want all possible odds in your favor.

Just before sunrise, with all the valuable non-living cargo of the Portuguese ship snugly stowed aboard, and the galleon having been released, *Devil's Handmaid* was headed away to the north. Watches were set, a minimal deck crew assigned, and weary, drunken men grabbed some shuteye wherever they could find a quiet spot. Many went below to sling hammocks and get some rest. Even the ship's officers retired to their respective cabins in the stern quarter or below the forecastle.

Unlike most of her adult companions, Jez had not drunk herself into a stupor to put aside all worries of illness after the gruesome sights of the night before. Consequently she was still running on nerves and adrenaline when she made her last trip back on board their own ship. Shortly afterward they had cast off the lines hooking them to the unfortunate Portuguese slaver. Wide awake, she had volunteered for the early watch.

By mid-morning, it was obvious a storm was coming in, as the ship was pitching more than normal. Many an experienced seaman awakened by pure instinct to stumble onto the main deck for a quick piss and a long look, blinking and rubbing bloodshot eyes. Clouds were piling up in the southeast and the waves had risen quite a bit from the night before. The trade winds, which had been so gentle, now blew with noticeably more force. The day had started clear, but as the noonday sun climbed into the paling sky, an ominous gray squall line darkened the horizon to stern. The old timers grumbled that they were in for a blow. The master's mate reluctantly banged on cabin doors to wake the captain and quartermaster, and report the change in the weather.

They had been perhaps a third of the way between Cartagena and Port Royal when they parted ways with their Portuguese prize. With the wind and heavy seas coming in from the south, Dan Abrams wisely suggested they run before it and seek a well protected moorage inside the newly acquired English port on Jamaica. The problem was getting there before the storm overtook them, and not being turned away by being fired upon by the fort guns.

A bleary-eyed Duffy came clambering up to relieve her once the news of the impending storm went around. Rather than snatch a couple hours of sleep, she elected to stay up longer and assist wherever she could.

They didn't want inexperienced lads on deck, so she headed down below to help Andy set up for feeding whomever he could before things got too rough. As the storm grew closer, the fire in the galley stove would need to be put out again, and the main deck hatches secured against rain and spray. Those in the lower decks would basically be shut in down there until it was over. Only the most experienced hands would be working above in such weather.

By afternoon, it had turned into a whistling gale, and roiling masses of slate hued cloud shrouded the horizon behind them, indicating a very large and powerful storm was coming in. More sail was cautiously raised and the ship put on speed, but the foul weather was gradually catching up. They were being buffeted around sharply, and with all the drinking done overnight, all but the most experienced sailors became seasick. Buckets were passed round, and gray faced men heaved as they must, wiped their mouths, and went back to their tasks of fastening things down in the hold.

On the upper deck, two dark skinned crew members from French Saint Domingue muttered of bad juju in leaving the slave ship un-captained and taking aboard that accursed mask, which had obviously doomed the *São Félix*. Others of a more Christian disposition claimed the mask was actually a heathen representation of Old Nick, and best given to the sea before the devil himself manifested to claim them. Those listening into the subversive innuendo became concerned, and a foreboding sense of unease began to infect all the deck hands.

Gully scoffed when a worried group approached him, upset and spooked to be caught in a storm during what was supposed to be the quiet season. He had to shout to be heard above the wind.

"Come now lads, where's yer cullions? Yer not aboard the *Devil's Handmaid* fer only fair weather, ye know!" He shook his head and spread his arms wide. "Be ye turnin' into a bunch of squealing wenches on me 'cause we're in fer a bit of a squall? 'Sides," he added in a conspiratorial tone, "who best te treat directly with the devil himself but a bunch of rummy freebooters like us?"

When a couple of men crossed themselves and looked at him reproachfully, Gully scoffed and waved a gnarled hand in dismissal.

"Fine then! If yer all fired on repentin' yer sins and prayin' the rest o' yer days away, I'll be happy te put ye ashore after the storm and split yer share o' the take of this excursion with the real men as stays aboard when things gets a little rough. I assume ye be givin' up drinkin' and whorin' while yer at it too?"

There were a few raucous laughs and several blistering rebuttals, which made Gully smile ruefully. "Well then, git yerselves back te work, ye lazy arsed bunch of scalawags, and don't be bendin' me ear with yer papist nonsense."

The quartermaster waved them off, and they went back to their duties, but not without some additional grumbling.

The three green lads were working on deck, helping secure lines and batten hatches as the seas grew wilder and the wind began to blow fierce. Neville was spending as much time puking over the side as he was working, and as he hung over the edge, a particularly vicious wave swept him overboard. The boy could not swim, and was unable to reach the line the men tossed him.

"'E's as good as dead," one man spat and walked away. Others shrugged and went back to work. Men overboard was no rarity when the wind and weather became rough and the water was fast.

As much as the whining and complaining boy bothered them, Jez and Pakke were not about to give up so easily. Both were excellent swimmers, though these seas were heavy with swells. Jez tied a line around her waist and Pakke and a few others watched her walk down the heaving sides of the ship's hull, before she waved that she wanted more slack. She turned and let go, arcing down into the foaming waves where she had last seen Neville's head and arms as he flailed and called out in fear.

It was colder than she expected, and the shock of hitting the water almost drove the breath from her, but she cut into the waves and dove underneath the way her village's divers had taught her, and stroked out hard. She stayed under as long as she dared, lungs bursting, trying to peer through the tumult and bubbling of the water around her, but she couldn't see him. Surfacing for a quick gulp of air, she cast frantically around, and caught sight of his head barely breaking the water not ten feet away.

Down under Jez went again, and she struck out boldly, hurrying to where the floundering boy was feebly trying to right himself. His eyes were glazed with fear and air bubbled from mouth and nose as she dragged him up to the surface. He looked half-drowned already as she made the line fast to him under the arms so that they could pull him in without his face being under the surface.

"I got him!" she yelled, frantically waving her arms and was satisfied to hear a roar of approval from on deck as men began to haul Neville along. Jez struggled to stay alongside; wanting to be sure Neville's nose and mouth stayed above water, but a rip current had caught her and was sweeping her out of reach. Jez was a strong swimmer, but she had her limits, and she was tired already. She lost her grip of Neville and was being swept away from *Devil's Handmaid*, when a body leapt overboard and cut quickly out to her side.

"Hold Pakke, Jez," a familiar voice called. He had a line around his waist, and he waved to the ship. She was able to right herself and catch her breath while he made sure she had a secure loop at the end of his line to cling to. "Pull in!" he shouted and then they both had to gulp air and duck as another spume of frothy water broke over their heads. Grabbing the loop with one hand, Jez sculled sideways as Pakke kicked and windmilled his free arm, trying to make headway against the current.

Inches and feet at a time, they made their way back to the hull, and were unceremoniously hauled up amid cheers and jeers from the rest of the crew. Neville still lay face down on the deck, retching and coughing up his lungs, but he was alive, and that was a minor miracle in itself.

"Damn foolish thing ye done, nearly wastin' three lives fer the sake o' one," said Gully with more gruffness in his voice than his eyes showed. "Yer a brave coupla laddies, I'll give ye that," he added and stomped off as the two dripping bodies collapsed on the deck in exhaustion.

The storm strengthened and gained speed during the day. The wind had become fierce, rattling lines and blowing about anything loose. All unnecessary hands were sent below, before heavy tarpaulins were securely fastened near the coaming edge of the hatchways, with battens nailed over the edges, tying them down. Lightning forked in the distance, brilliantly illuminating the darkening sky, followed by the rumble of far off thunder rolling like cannon balls down the deck of the heavens above. Rain could be seen falling in great sheets that advanced rapidly behind them.

Nothing sobers a man faster than knowing his life and livelihood, as well as that of all his boon companions, are at stake. Dandy Dan called out for more speed, and the ship and crew responded. Men worked feverishly at doing whatever it took to right the ship every time she heeled too far, and many a prayer was muttered amongst the curses. One man lost the first joint of his big toe to a tangled line that popped it free, but ignoring the pain and the blood that oozed continuously from the wound, he wrapped it with a strip of his shirt and kept working, tying down the flapping end of a sheet before it could tear free.

Instead of cutting cleanly through the waves, they were being thrown up violently on their towering crests before dipping deeply into the troughs between them. The decks were often awash. The scuppers wept copiously each time *Devil's Handmaid* lifted free of the sea's relentless embrace. Eventually the winds became so strong that all but the storm sails had to be reefed to keep them from broaching too far windward and capsizing, sending them all to a watery grave. Even men who normally laughed at safety measures were tying themselves fast to the masts and spars to keep from being pitched off their lofty perches, down into the churning waters below.

The sky above became blanketed with the undulating folds of dark clouds piling up, as the leading edge of the storm fell upon them. Rain started as huge splattering drops, and then the heavens opened and poured a quick and noisy deluge as a prelude to the torrents yet to come. The rising wind began to moan and whistle, rattling the lines until they sounded like hordes of angry bees. It was blowing the downpour in sideways, swirling streams of it crazily to slap against bodies and walls with the force of a giant's shove. With all this heavy weather, in fast and rough water that tossed the ship upward like a bobbing cork and slapped her down again like stone, they weren't going to be able to fight their way to the safer harbor. They'd have to ride out the storm at sea, and it would be a miracle if they didn't get driven up on unseen reefs or coastal rocks and break up.

Some of the men began to pray in earnest.

Dandy Dan wasn't praying though; he was cursing. He stood on the quarterdeck trying to peer through the curtains of bedlam and get some sort of visual idea of where they were. In spite of the weather, he remained steadfastly in place, determined to save his ship and crew. Drenched to the bone and clinging one handed to the starboard rail, he alternately shook a fist at the skies to dare whatever god might be listening to do his worst, and clamped his hat in place every time it threatened to blow away. His plume drooping, and water running off the wide brim in rivulets that cascaded down onto his already sodden velvets and lace, he appeared very much like a bedraggled preacher exhorting his flock. The shrieking winds whipped his curly locks around, plastering dripping tendrils to his face and neck.

One rainstorm ended just before the next band came rushing in. Lightning forked overhead for a moment, announcing the new arrival, before a booming explosion of thunder vibrated the very boards he stood upon. Dan Abrams laughed like a madman, for he had caught a momentary glimpse of the Jamaican shoreline between showers. It was enough to know they were too far north to turn and make Port Royal, but might yet find a safer place to ride out that maelstrom. He knew these waters well.

"Master Ping," his voice rang out loud and compelling enough to be heard above the storm's raging, "round this cape wide enough, and you will find a partially sheltered bay where we won't be battered on rocks and reef, or run aground. We'll weigh anchor there and wait this one out."

"Aye Kep-ten," came the thin articulated reply nearby, almost stolen away by another loud rumble of thunder. All hands were called down to the deck, so that any headway they made now was at the mercy of the turbulent ocean and the violent winds filling small, heavy sails. Their course was adjusted and corrected only by the tiller and the skill of the expertise of the pilot manning it. Silent and determined Ping now held the entire fate of the ship in his long fingered hands; his mind, heart, and instincts their only connection between safety and shipwreck. With great difficulty, the experienced navigator fought the tiller for control as the ship tossed and tilted crazily at times, decks awash, threatening to founder. Ping methodically steered through each pitch and roll, heave and yaw, as they struggled through the wildly cresting waves.

The ocean was a savage mistress, but the *Devil's Handmaid* lived up to her contrary nature, and she responded in kind. Resolute and unflappable, Ping managed to wrestle them by increments around the barely seen neck of land, remaining roughly parallel to the coast but far enough out to avoid grounding in the normally shallow waters. The wiry Chinese helmsman bravely maintained his critical position in the worst of the weather yet, his slight form tensed and shivering, drenched to the bone while he gradually adjusted the tiller in minute increments to keep them from drifting too far toward the shoreline with the storm surge. While the brigantine was a shallow draft ship for her size, they did not want to impact any obstructions lying hidden beneath their hull by the towering breakers.

Once the promontory jutted behind them, its presence tempered somewhat the water piling up, though the wind and waves continued to batter at land and ship alike. Rain sluiced down sideways in stinging lashes that blinded the few saturated men who climbed like ragged monkeys and then fought feverishly to furl the last of the sails and secure them. More than one almost slipped and fell from his wind-rocked perch, only the safety lines keeping them from certain death. Men on deck below labored to drop the big anchor with muscle tearing turns at the capstan. Bare feet slipping on decks often tilting from one side to another, they trod ankle deep in rainwater and spray, grunting and muttering expletives, struggling to find purchase and not fall to be trampled by the plodding of their comrades dragging the next bar, or be swept along in the deck wash.

Finally, the great bulk of iron anchor was lowered and one huge fluke caught seabed. The grateful captain gave the order to 'heave to'. Ping made sure the ship was angled properly to take the worst of the battering without breaking apart, before he lashed the tiller fast and made their way down to the stern cabin to wait it out. No sooner had they done so than the full fury of tempest winds howled like demons around them, rocking *Devil's Handmaid* like a toy in the hands of giants. Dan Abrams stopped long enough to shout in his quartermaster's ear.

"We've done what we can for tonight. I'll not be sending a longboat out with a backing anchor in this mess, and risk losing them out there. We'll take our chances that we don't swing enough to bottom out. Bring the officers into my quarters, and we'll have a drink and decide where we're off to next."

"Aye," Gully yelled back before he turned to cup his hands and issue the final orders. "Get yerself to cover mates; we've done all we can fer this fell day," he called out wearily before trudging over toward the stern quarters. Most of the men headed to the cramped forecastle berths to sit out the worst of the storm. A select few were invited to join their captain in his own accommodations.

Streaming oiled cloaks were removed and hung on wooden pegs. Rum, from a barrel brought up before the storm's full fury hit, was handed around along with wine from the Portuguese ship. Overtired men slumped wherever they could find room to rest their weary bones. The talk was hushed and spirits low. This storm would pass eventually, and with some luck, they'd not breach the hull on something to founder and break up in the meantime.

As the battle to bring *Devil's Handmaid* to safety went on above her, Jez remained below decks with Andy Boone and the rest of the crew. It was a wild trip, with those who had taken to their hammocks tossed about to the point where they had to hold on tight for fear of being flipped free. More than one man was retching before the anchor was dropped, and slop buckets stunk up the crew quarters on the gun deck. Likewise was the case on the orlop deck, where Neville's puking and moaning bouts drove both his companions away, leaving him to his misery. A few of the hardier men huddled at the opposite end in the glow of a single lantern, sharing a bottle and bragging of women they'd known.

While the ship still rocked and tossed, the anchorage in the somewhat sheltered bay made the motion a bit more tolerable. Most of the crew settled down to sleep or pass the time drinking and gaming. There was the sound of singing to a fiddle and skin drums, with some reedy pipes thrown in now and then. Plenty of raucous laughter covered up the wailing winds and pounding of the rain.

Everyone was apprehensive about surviving a big storm, but experienced men did not dwell on such things.

Jez and Pakke sat in the galley with Andy and a handful of others, listening to the old man's tales of voyages past and famous pirates he had known. It was a way to pass the time while the timbers around them creaked and groaned, waves lapped the sides, and the storm-tossed ship threw them about. The galley stove was out, but it was musty and humid in there, with only a single small lantern in a rocking ball cage gimbal overhead to light the gloom. The contrast of light and darkness deepened the crags and wrinkles in the one-eyed old man's weathered face, giving him almost netherworld appearance. Andy was a good story teller, and never was he as happy or in his natural element as when he had an audience. His squeaky old voice rose and fell in cadence with the lashing waves and howling wind, and his two-fingered hand gestured wildly to illustrate each point. The drink slurred his voice, yet it loosened his tongue so that he spoke expressively and at length.

"Aye, and fer sure lads, I've seen some sights in me time," he said at the end of another story. He'd spoken of how a Spanish soldier in armor fell to his death off the stern of his galleon and got his breastplate caught in the rudder, crippling the ship's steering, which the raiders exploited. It was a tale well embellished with rum-drenched wits and a fading memory that filled in the blank spots with its own creations. "Ye kin asks me anithin' and I'll tells ye what I knows. There's not much as gits past me, e'en wit' jist the one good eye." He pointed to it with a gnarled and shaky index finger. "I be familiar-like wit' most o' the 'istory o' this here en-*tyre* region, fer sartain." He slapped the palm of his mangled hand down for emphasis before grabbing his tankard, which had started sliding off the table at the end of a particularly nasty roll.

"What about our captain; Dandy Dan?" Jez asked curiously. It was a prelude to picking the elderly pirate's brain about Walter Armitage, though she had to be subtle. "What do you know about him, Andy?"

A couple others echoed her sentiment, and Pakke looked up eagerly from his work, which was picking old rope into oakum fibers to be used with tar for caulking seams. The native boy, with his nimble fingers always occupied somehow, idolized their dashing captain; though he could never quite bring himself to meet Dan Abrams' hawklike gaze.

"Waaall now, that be a right int'restin' tale," the old man began, scratching his stubbly chin with broken fingernails. He picked off a louse, and smashed it under his thumb on the table. "Dan Abrams, 'e came from gentry, ye know. Bein' a younger son, 'e was not gonna in'erit much udder'n an empty title o' some country lord, so 'e decided te go te sea and seek 'is fortune thar. Some years past, our Dan was a midshipman wit' the Royal Navy. The way I heared it, 'e din't like that too much. All them reg'lations, the floggin's, and so on. Men dying more broke than when they come in; some of em nabbed right off'n the streets, straight outta their mama's or sweet'eart's arms. Boys cryin' in the night fer a sight of land agin; men achin' fer a bit of good food an' a woman's soft body, and none o' that 'llowed too often... Dan Abrams loved the sea, but 'e din't much cotton to bein' treated like some tool, te be used up and tossed aside. So 'e rebelled, 'e did."

"What did he do?" Jez asked, genuinely interested now. Pakke sat up with eyes bright and eager, his work forgotten in his lap.

"The story I wuz told," Andy said, leaning in conspiratorially, "Was our Dan got 'imself in a batch o' trouble over assaultin' a drunken officer. The dirty bastard was buggerin' a young lad in his own quarters, with the boy whimperin' and carryin' on that 'e was being gored te death. No other man woulda been bold enough te bust in thar, but Dan Abrams was." At their shocked and black looks he continued, "Oh b'lieve me, they all done that te the li'l laddies, them pow'rful men, 'cause most o' the wee ones was orphans, and e'en the lower officers was treated like gods, they was. A cut 'bove the rest o' the rabble seadogs, they thought themselves. None dared say naught 'bout it neither, lessen they wanted the kiss of the cat te reminds them o' their place."

Pakke sucked his teeth and winced. He knew Andy was referring to the cat o' nine tails, the vicious little multi-stranded whip that laid flesh open. The Spanish don whose plantation he'd worked on had an overseer who took great delight in whipping slaves. An arrow through an eye had ended that, but made the boy a fugitive.

"Well, our Dan din't take too damn kindly te someone 'urtin' a young un, an' this lad barely past clinging to his momma's skirts. He yanked that officer right off the poor tyke and gived 'im what fer! Luckily the boy ran out a sobbin', wit' his britches down to his knees and his tiny be'ind a raw mess. They din't hang Dan or keelhaul 'im 'cause o' that sight, but they striped 'im sumthin fierce, they did, fer assaultin' an officer. 'E's still bearing them scars te this day, all bunched and ridged on 'is back."

"How'd he quit the Navy?" asked a man called Kendry, who had a big nose as red as the bandana tied around his bald head. He sat propped up against the wood bin, his stubbly chin supported by elbows on his knees. His arms were full of tattoos, one for every new port he'd sailed to.

"Meh, the us'al way!" Andy answered with a shrug. "Ole Dan, 'e deserted at Bermuda. Leapt right over the rail as they was warpin her in te dock, then took te 'is 'eels and run off. That be a busy place, and any man can 'ide 'isself, iffen 'e knows where 'zactly te go te ground. They 'ventually give up huntin' fer him and left, after sendin' word to the guvner te be on the lookout."

He laughed and so did several others. Jez, Pakke, and another mostly silent man they called Gabby, looked confused. Andy explained.

"English and French Guvners out this way as wants te stay in office mostly don't give a tinker's dam who or what ye be, long as ye stay outta trouble and slide 'em some nice bits and bobs now an' then. Men is allus desertin' them Navy ships, an' ye cain't find 'em all. Most o' 'em winds up pirates, and pirates make better allies than enemies, iffen' ye want yer holdin' guarded aginst the Spanish. Lookit Port Royal…our brethren keeps them well-heeled planters and pol'ticians safe in their beds o' night. Tobaccy crops warn't gonna support no'un. Wit'out us freebooters te trade wit', they'd've all starved and be taken o'er, 'cause Bermuda had a whole lot o' mouths te feed, and 'ungry people gives up easy-like."

"So when did Dandy Dan became a pirate?" Jez asked eagerly. She had forgotten all about wanting to know more of Walter Armitage's life, Andy's story was so interesting.

"Right off; soon as 'is ship set sail. Me good ole cap'n, Gentleman Geoffrey Bones, took 'im under 'is wing," Andy answered, and a couple of the older men grunted and lifted their tankards to the man's memory.

Geoff Bones had been well known as a fairly successful buccaneer, hide trader, and salt raker turned full-time freebooter. He had a fairly long career, as pirates go; almost five years at sea. Unfortunately he had been hung when Jez was just a young girl. Her father had told Monifa about it in hushed tones one night as the adults lay together in her mother's bed. The little girl had shivered through the tale of the defiant man's final rebuke of his captors before he was hung, and how his tarred body had been suspended in a harbor gibbet as a warning to all other potential pirates that they would eventually suffer the same fate. She had begged Tall Tom not to leave them the next day, until her mother cuffed her into silence.

"Leave the bold Papa to his business, and mind your own," her mother had warned their young daughter after he kissed them both goodbye and took his leave. "Dis world is dangerous no matter where you work. A man must be a man, and make his way as he knows best. There are plenty of men to choose from; you lose one lover, you take another. They miss you most when they are away so long, and they demand less from you too. Learn to live without them constantly underfoot, and you'll always be free..."

Monifa might have said more but Jez couldn't recall exactly what. Her head was too foggy from grog and lack of sleep. Andy's voice droned on a while longer, and Pakke snored by her side as she finally settled down and closed her eyes. Even with the storm raging around them and the ship shuddering and rolling as it was tossed about on its moorage, sleep overcame her, and she curled up and rested her head on her arms on the floor near where the barrels of galley staples were lashed.

The next morning dawned cloudy with some lingering showers, though the body of the tropical storm had passed them by. Once the ferocity of the waves had abated, the water level began dropping rather rapidly in the bay as the ebb tide ran out. The ship had drifted just enough to ground itself on a sandbar built up by the storm surge, and more sand piled against it so that it canted slightly starboard, toward the lee of the storm winds. There it stuck fast, the tiller useless in the shallows. The wind off the back of the storm was from the wrong quarter, and to set any sail would only push them farther over.

Stranded as they were, the ship and crew were vulnerable to any passing enemy craft with either a shallow draft or longer range guns. The plan was to quickly winch *Devil's Handmaid* off the shoal, using the capstan and line on the still imbedded anchor to help pull her free. After a skimpy feed of biscuit and sops, all available hands were called on deck. Because they were at a bit of an angle to the deeper water in the middle of the bay, the longboat went out, pulled by a crew of oarsmen headed by Gully. They were dragging a warp line fastened to the kedge anchor to help steer them in the proper direction once the larger craft was righted and at least partially freed. The lighter weight anchor could be easily lifted aboard and moved ahead as the growing slack allowed.

Her head still pounding slightly from last evening's grog, Jez joined the men at the capstan. She stood beside Pakke in the gloomy morning mist as the bars were fitted into the pigeon holes, waiting for the call to start rolling in the messenger cable that would draw against the main anchor. Using that massive iron weight as leverage should gradually move the ship forward along the tightening chain, sliding the hull through and off the obstruction.

The young master mate Sébastien Bellanger…usually referred to as 'Sebby'…was busy directing the sail setters, so James Reuben, acting as bosun, stood by with the capstan crew, his eyes trained on the quarterdeck. One man dumped sand from a pail while another spread it underfoot with a few quick licks of a besom. That would improve footing, as the wet and likely mucky cable was pulled in. Men who would not be pushing the bars around stood by below deck at the lower spindle, with hooks and other devices designed to smooth out the windings. There would be chain attendants at the hawse hole, making sure that the heavy links didn't kink and foul up as the great length gradually came aboard to be stowed.

Gully signaled that the longboat was in place and the kedge anchor dropped.

"Man your bars! Heave taut and haul 'round lads!" came the call. That started the weary process where men grabbed a bar and trudged around two abreast, shoving forward with their backs bent to the task, feet pushing off against the deck. Jez was about average height amongst the crew, already a head taller than Pakke, Duffy, and Andy Boone. Yet she didn't have their years of hard work or the brawny upper body strength of a man, as serving customers in a tavern wasn't anywhere near as strenuous, and women tended to build muscle far more slowly. She was at least used to being on her feet all day, so her legs could take the strain, but her back, shoulders, chest, and arms burned with the effort. She ignored the discomfort and doggedly kept pace with Pakke and Walter Armitage, dragging the bar ahead of her. Jengo worked next to her, having been put on her bar to even out the strain for the thinner 'lad'. He likely could have worked it alone and done as well.

"You boys be building big muscles today," he told them with a gold toothed smile, the scars on his dark skinned face crinkling with the delight of a child. Jengo had a smile for everyone except whoever the enemy was, at the moment. His furious appearance in battle was as legendary as his prowess as a hunter, and men said he curdled the blood and turned bowels to water with his demonic scowl. Yet he generally was the most relaxed and fun-loving member of the crew.

Jez only nodded, saving her breath for the work as the upper spindle began to turn. With a mixture of envy and innocent desire, she watched the interplay of muscles underneath the skin on Armitage's bare back, bronze and already slick with sweat. The morning air was thickly humid, and the tropical sun was beginning to break through the cloud cover. If not for the wind, it would have been oppressive.

Pakke, far less breathless than she was, grinned back over his shoulder. "Make man strong for ladees!" he boasted.

Jengo laughed uproariously. "I'll take both of you to a whorehouse, next time we hit port. Set you each up with some fat-assed woman with big teats. You need to work on your shore muscles too." He winked and Pakke nodded eagerly.

Several men behind them joined in the ribald laughter and made comments while Jez's face flamed in a scarlet blush. Thankfully, they had no idea she actually *was* female.

Walter Armitage knew though, and he snorted derisively. There would be no port to laze in anytime soon.

"Belay the small talk and put your backs into it mates," he snapped. "We've got to raise that anchor to get back under sail soon. We're the perfect target, stranded out here," he added, and leaned in harder on the bar, almost dragging a protesting Pakke along before the shorter native boy caught his stride.

As they plodded in endless circles winding the capstan, the arms master's mind raced ahead of him. If he understood Dan Abrams' plan, proposed to his officers between rounds of wine while the storm raged around them, the captain was putting it to a vote once they were back at sea as to whether they'd be heading up toward the Straits of Florida. It was an area through which galleons of the Spanish Flota, wealthy with gold, silver, and trade items, often passed. Those lumbering treasure-laden vessels would be escorted by multiple well-armed ships through what was considered Spanish colonial waters, and the weapons-heavy chaperones' only duty was to protect their mother country's assets at all costs. The idea was to hole up somewhere in the tiny uninhabited islands and lay in wait, using the cover of night and the speed of *Devil's Handmaid* to cut one of the loaded galleons out of the group. They would hit it quickly and cripple the ship, and then sail off to find another prize…perhaps even further up along the coast of the great northern continent, where merchant ships from European ports were reputed to be easy pickings.

In theory it might work; but as a practice, no raid was ever that simple. Piracy anywhere was an extremely dangerous business, continually affected by vagaries of weather, crew, and other circumstances beyond the captain's control. Like the majority of his peers, Dandy Dan was a small time buccaneer, and this change of venue would take them much farther out of their comfort zone than they'd ranged before. They would be encroaching into the haunts of the more famous and celebrated pirate captains, and those desperate, greedy men did not willingly share their more bounteous territory with what they considered lesser rivals. The big name pirates also had the might of ship, crew, and gunnery to back up their claims. Yet with the dwindling prizes in the immediate area split amongst far too many small time competitors, and the increased presence of European warships protecting their respective colonies from raids, the Caribbean waters were not as profitable as they once had been. Men grew restless when the money and the good times ran out well before the next season of freebooting began, and word spread fast. An unsuccessful captain found it hard to sign a decent crew.

Sailing out of the local area could be a far riskier business, as friendly, sheltered island ports within short distances were reportedly far less common. Armitage didn't like the idea, but there was no way to object to it without raising eyebrows. These experienced men would willingly risk their lives all through a longer voyage to live like kings and princes for a while. They could take care of themselves under fire, but the lovestruck,

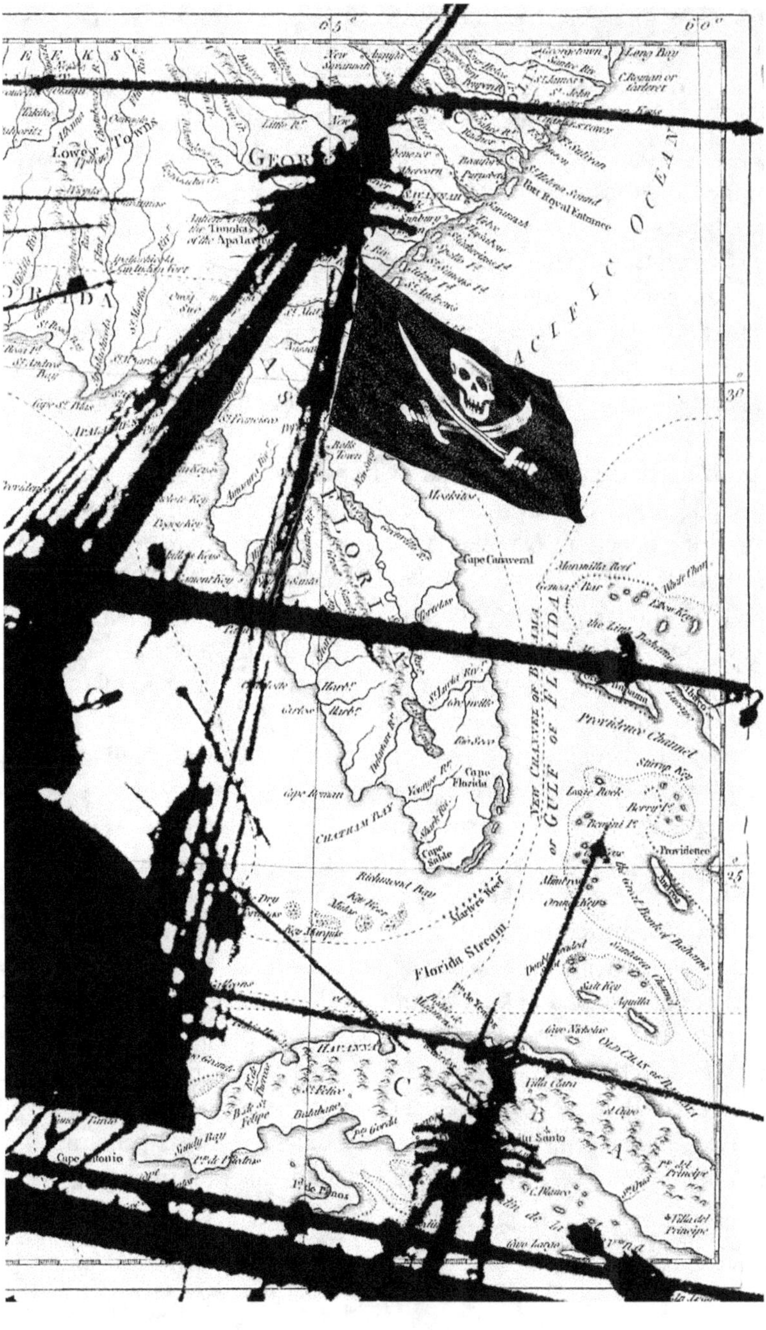

"...they'd be heading up the Straits of Florida..."

mixed race girl who had followed him aboard would be at a distinct disadvantage, unless he taught her to fight well and defend herself. Until now he had been only halfheartedly coaching her to shoot and use a blade, in hopes of encouraging her to leave, but if they sailed out of friendly waters, he'd have no choice. Whether she fought in a boarding party or remained behind to help man and guard the ship, the girl would be in danger and so would anyone depending on her. There would be no safe harbor town to drop her off in once the ship left these tropical islands and their stew pot of ethnicities.

He should have alerted Dan Abrams immediately of her presence and been done with it. At first he had hoped she'd quickly grow disenchanted with all the backbreaking work and constant peril amongst rough talking, quarrelsome men. But if anything, Jezebel Johnston seemed to thrive on pushing herself to the limits of human endurance. In addition she uncomplainingly did all that was asked of her...certainly far more than that puking lay about Neville! He could hear her joining in behind with some bold and bawdy song to which he was certain she didn't understand the full meaning to most of the verses. Certainly, her maidenly advances had been rather innocent, though she was damnably persistent. Her warm and willing arms and soft lips found him whenever they had a few precious moments alone together, and were getting harder to say no to. When he roughly pushed her away, reminding her in sharply whispered tones of the risk, she would fervently protest her undying affection. She begged him not to send her away, saying she couldn't live without him.

He had too often given in to Jezebel's puppyish appeals for affection, while warning her that she was going to get him booted from the crew, once they discovered her gender. That was not something the handsome, dark haired man with the striking blue eyes could afford to have known. He was genuinely fond of Jezebel, and she doted on him, but piracy was his life now, and the last thing he wanted was to be dismissed and marooned somewhere on her account. So far he had held back from deflowering the maiden altogether, and kept their secret to himself, hoping that something would come up to intervene and see her safely ashore. In the meantime, she would have to be treated and trained like the other two lads.

Winding heavy lines was tedious and exacting work. As the messenger cable began to run around the rollers below, bringing the anchor line and chain aboard, the nippers that attached it to the heavier parts of the rig had to be quickly moved. That would allow the draw to continue without forcing the men above to stop and strain to hold the immense drag of ¾ ton of iron, keeping it from reversing the capstan spindle and slacking what had already been reeled in. The ship used heavy hawse line between the chain attached to the anchor itself and the capstan. The reasons were simple…rope was cheaper than chain, it weighed less, and in the event of a possible capture, the line could be cut or burned away, the anchor abandoned, and the ship sailed off immediately. Not an inexpensive proposition, but it saved lives.

Once the initial length of line came in, the chain rattled aboard with a deafening grating noise. The ship lurched forward a bit each time it tightened. Excess line was fed down a nearby hatch to be safely stowed. On the main deck, the yellowed and silt splotched hemp from the kedge anchor began to wind in too, mere feet at a time, adjusting her angle so that the ship would eventually hit deep water. Devil's Handmaid slid forward at a snail's pace. It was necessarily slow going, for the bow was taking the brunt of the strain and that was the weakest part of the ship construction. Hurrying the process might pull her apart.

Since this was destined to be a long haul job, someone started a multi-verse sea chantey, and gradually voices filled in. Singing kept the men on task, and they moved with the rhythm. A crew member they all knew as 'Blackhair Dougie', for his bushy dark beard and hair, was a fine hand on a mandolin. With a leg mangled and missing an ankle and foot, he wasn't as apt on the capstan, but he tapped his peg in time and his playing kept the job lively. The men sang *I'll Take Their Spanish Gold And Silver*, *The Innkeeper's Naughty Daughter*, and *Heaven Don't Want Us And Hell's Afeared*. These were long, ribald songs with a lot of verses but easy, repetitive choruses that anybody could learn fast. Once she caught her breath, Jez joined her rich alto in with the others on the parts she knew. Music passed the time, for between the kedging and hauling, several hours of work crept by. They had shortened the distance to deeper water perhaps by half, but still were somewhat grounded.

Just before midday, a new crew of men gradually took over, giving the first group a break to eat, rest, and relieve themselves. The sun had become baking hot once the clouds moved away, and the reflection off the lightly rippled shallows was blinding. There was an urgency to their work as the winds had calmed and should be changing direction later that afternoon to a more favorable land breeze. This would allow sail to be put on, which would help push them out of the shallows they were wallowing in. In one respect, it was fortunate that they'd not taken on more plunder, for with the ship less weighty, she moved easier in the meager depths, and they needn't dump ballast to lighten the load.

Jez was just heading down to the galley when a call came from above that stopped the voices of good humor abruptly. "Sail Ho!" sang out one of the lookouts, a skinny runt they called Boneyard Bill with a reedy, high-pitched voice. The music died immediately.

"Friend or Foe?" Dan Abrams boomed in query, from where he was taking his own turn at the capstan with the second crew.

Ping, who had been told to stand by the tiller, snatched up the spyglass. "Man-of-War," he called out quickly in his precise and clipped tone. "English and changing heading. They have spotted us."

"Damn!" said Abrams with a scowl. He left his position after motioning another man over to take his place and admonishing everyone to keep working. Bounding across the main deck planks, he took the steps up to the quarterdeck two at a time. Even without music, the capstan pace was picked up and the chain began to rattle loudly into the hold below.

CHAPTER FOUR

Dan Abrams was a quick thinker. He put down the spyglass and leaned on the rail for half a moment.

"We are effectively trapped, and cannot afford to raise any suspicions. Hoist the French flag, hail the longboat in, and get Master Bellanger up here immediately. We shall claim to be no more than just an inter-island trader passing through when we got caught in the storm."

The appearance of another country's ship near an English colonial island might be taken as an affront if not a veiled threat, yet in a storm like the one they had just experienced, vessels were often blown off course. As long as they could pass for French…currently allied with the English against the Spanish…they might be allowed to leave unmolested. It was a chancy ruse. The larger, heavier craft that was coming about just beyond the shallower waters of the open bay, could not sail in close enough to board and inspect them. They would likely send out a longboat of their own to investigate, which would be the pirate vessel's undoing. The warship's far bigger guns were mostly 24 pounders on two decks. They had the reach to take on the stranded ship and do some serious damage. The warship also possessed the manpower, as well as additional small craft aboard, that could be launched in raiding parties. It would be wise to hail them first, explaining away their situation, and reassure the British captain that they would be gone as soon as possible.

That was something neither Dan Abrams nor most of his officers could pull off, as many of them were British expatriates or deserters. They'd be taken for pirates immediately, and would garner no leniency as they might find in Port Royal. An elaborate subterfuge was quickly concocted, involving dressing Sébastien Bellanger up as a French captain and sending him over to the British vessel with a couple bottles of wine and a Negro crew of oarsmen. When the crew was canvassed for anyone else who spoke French well enough to accompany him, or at least pass as indigenous to that nation's colonies, there were few who knew more than a couple words or phrases, mostly learned from dealing with tavern keepers and brothel owners.

Jez, whose mother spoke fluent French with an island patois, stepped forward as a volunteer, one eye on Walter Armitage, to see if he acknowledged her bravado. She had often watched her clever mother deal with tax and tariff collectors, and was used to negotiating with tradesmen in both French and English. "I understand more than I can speak, Captain Dan," she admitted sheepishly.

"But you do actually speak French?" Dan Abrams queried sharply. A lot of lives were riding on these two crew members being able to feign being representative of the crew.

"Yes I do," Jez answered eagerly, and then rattled off the first thing that came to mind, which turned out to be a long list of explicit brothel terms. It would have gotten her ears boxed at home, though only Sebby understood. He busted out laughing, holding his sides and snorting. Dan Abrams glared at the guffawing Frenchman until he fell silent, while others looked on curiously.

"I take it, Master Bellanger, that you understood that rather lengthy oration?"

"Aye sir," he said, wiping his eyes, "and it sure tweren't no sermon! The boy is from Tortuga, but he speaks well enough to pass as a native to

Saint Domingue or any of the other French colonies," a half dressed Sebby reassured him.

"Continue adorning yourself then." Dan Abrams frowned deeply as he considered both of them; his eyes holding a speculative look. He was concocting a plan as he waited for his erstwhile alter-ego to array himself in the fancy outfit he'd chosen to best represent a French merchant captain. He turned back to reward Jez with some rare praise.

"You're a brave lad to volunteer, but I warn you, this is no simple mummery. We need you both to convince them that we are who we claim to be, or we will all die here. We shall be sending you over there to pose as the interpreter when Master Bellanger meets with their captain. His English is far too common sounding, as is the case amongst us rogues; and yours is still very precise and flavored by your home port. So he'll not speak an intelligible word to the man, because that will give away his station. I would have you translate whatever he tells you to say to them, and do the same with whatever they say, as if your captain had not understood what was said."

He wagged a finger at them. "Both of you *must* be mindful of your words though, because your safety, as well as that of the rest of this lot," he spread his arms wide to indicate the entire ship, "depends on the impression you make. Hopefully there will not be anyone aboard that floating battalion who speaks French. Now let's get you dressed for your part as well."

When the longboat came in and the kedging crew clambered aboard, they pulled up the smaller anchor and stowed it. Then the chosen oarsmen including Jengo, as well as Sebby and Jezebel Johnston, clambered down to take their places and set up the universally acknowledged white parley flag before rowing out quickly to the larger ship, which bristled with guns and seamen who were well acquainted with naval warfare. All of the men aboard the pirate longboat were lightly armed, and for safety's sake, two small deck guns were concealed beneath the benches. If necessary they would fire upon the hull of the larger ship and try to cause her to founder. Jez had donned a rather ostentatious looking jacket, her own boots, and had jammed a floppy knit cap called a 'toque' over her curly hair.

The *Ramsgate* was rather modest as English fighting ships go, but she loomed huge compared to *Devil's Handmaid*. Thirty guns were available on two decks and she carried almost twice the crew. As they pulled alongside, mooring lines were dropped down and well armed men crowded the rail above to get a glimpse of these foreign mariners who had requested a peaceful audience. Uniformed officers whose rank was unknown stood back at a cautious distance, posturing with swaggers of self importance and disdainful looks on their faces. Sebby swore under his breath as he grabbed a hold of the Jacob's ladder to clamber aboard.

"Likely a bunch of gentleman lubbers who bought their commission. If our ship was free, we could sink this tub." The Frenchman was already in a foul humor. He did not like wearing wigs, which made his balding head itch, and this one was a bit ratty, so they had tied it back with blue ribbon and set a plumed hat on top. His crimson silk lined cloak was fastened with a fleur-de-lis pin that had been nabbed off a past raid and hastily scrubbed free of the blood which still encrusted it. The fancy buckled shoes he was wearing were a size too small for his normally bare, flat feet; giving him a mincing gait and the trousers were long and baggy. He had doubled them over at the waist and tied them in place with his belt. Hopefully, no one would notice his discomfiture.

Jez said nothing as she climbed up behind him, hoping his grumbling would not be overheard. It seemed to take forever to get to the main deck of that towering monstrosity. Jengo came quickly behind them, minus his cutlass, but with a brace of pistols concealed under his hastily donned coat.

Fortunately, once they were aboard, Sebby went right into character. He looked around with evident contempt at the men assembled there, and crossing his arms, said something to Jez in rapid, fluent French. She caught the gist of it, but did not repeat it all.

"Bonjour Messieurs. This is, ah... Capitaine Bellanger of... um... *La Rouge Dame*," she made up the name on the spot. "He wishes to know if you have any men who speak his language amongst your crew," she related nervously. Sebby had suggested they find that out up front.

"We've no frog eaters aboard; and if that's all he's come to ask, he can right well leave immediately," said a man in satin and lace with long dark hair and a little pointed beard. His mustache curled up on either side around a red lipped mouth and a rather hooked nose. He looked down it at these ratty French sailors in obvious disdain. "Yet before he goes, we demand to know what one of your vessels is doing moored right off our coastline!"

Sebby growled a warning in an undertone.

"We meant no harm Monsieur," Jez answered hurriedly, hoping her voice would ride over the scathing curses from the man beside her. "We are simple merchants, and had the misfortune to be caught in the storm that just passed. It swept us into the bay. Fate spared us, though overnight our ship grounded on a sandbar. We are working to free it now, and humbly request your patience for a while longer."

A few men behind the English captain shuffled their feet and nodded agreeably. It was not uncommon to have to moor anywhere safe in a sudden storm. Their captain waved them to silence though. "I see no good reason for French merchants to be sailing nearby, unless it is to scout for the interests of their mother country. You do realize that for whatever reason I choose, I can confiscate your ship for trespassing in English territorial waters?"

"I will inform my Capitaine of this," Jezebel said hurriedly. She put a hand on the arm of the infuriated Frenchman at her side, who was spitting obscenities and whose fingers had strayed to the hilt of his be-tasseled ceremonial saber...another war spoil of Dandy Dan's. "S'il vous plaît, calme-toi," she said very quietly with a smile and a nod as if explaining something, though it was meant as a warning to let go his anger. This was a dangerous game they were playing, and Jez could not forget the stories of pirates who had been hung for less reason.

"*I need to tell them why we were sailing nearby,*" she warned him in low-voiced French.

"*Tell him I said he can go to hell, and take his precious ship with him!*" Sebby spat back in a vicious undertone. As she turned to face the frowning Englishmen, Jez had to find a way to make her companion's words more diplomatic, and still have them match his all-too-obvious ire.

"My Capitaine is an honorable man Monsieur, and he is insulted that you will not believe his words," she related evenly, though her legs were trembling. "We have come to you in peace before there was any misunderstanding to explain why we are here, and now we are treated as criminals."

The other man laughed. "How tragic!" He leaned forward a bit, like a schoolmaster reprimanding a child. "So, you were on your way back from exactly *where*, when you entered British Waters? I don't recall any current French Colonial holdings on this side of the islands that you could possibly be trading with, so I'd have to suspect your business was with the Spanish...which we are currently at war with!"

Other sailors were closing in, and the atmosphere amongst them was becoming uncomfortably ominous. Jengo had a menacing snarl on his face that gave several of them pause, but he was only one big man, and they were an entire crew of well-armed fighters.

Sebby had partially drawn his saber, and was spewing a long line of invective about what he'd like to do to with it, to whom, and where. Jez gently but firmly stayed his hand, and reminded him that if they died here now, their own ship and crew would suffer for it. He jammed the blade back into its scabbard and shook his head, telling her she better think of something quickly, because if the pompous ass in the brocade coat kept running his mouth, Sebby was going to spit him like a suckling pig and be done with it.

Jez knew it was up to her to smooth things over. She had never felt such pressure before. All their lives depended on defusing the situation. The English captain was hankering for a reason to blow them all to hell. She had to say something.

Just exactly *what* to say was the problem! With what little she knew of the area, telling a grand tale that immediately rang false would only make things worse. The French held Tortuga; and there, the Spanish were hated. She capitalized on local news she had heard bandied about the tavern to concoct a plausible story. Word from Europe reached the colonies so seldom, no one knew when a war was started or ended until months after the fact.

"Monsieur Le Capitaine, we are peaceful and loyal French! We never support those Espagnol dogs, for they have long harassed our colonies. It is as we have told you; we were blown off course on our way back to St. Domingue. We came to pay ransom for a... how do you say it?" She needed a moment to think, remembering that all of the French settlers on St. Domingue reviled their oppressive neighbors, who often came seeking to kill off peasants and capture wealthy hostages... "The son of a powerful man who had been kidnapped in a raid," she finally answered. "He was beaten and flogged, and lies feverish and near to death in our hold. We must get him home to his family."

Some of the other officers commiserated, for most of them had lived in the area long enough to have experienced ongoing invasions. High level prisoners were always ransomed. If this man didn't believe her, they would have to fight their way out, and even Jez had little hope for that.

"What do you think of this lot, Watkins?" the erstwhile captain asked his far more experienced ship's master. With a lift of his pointy-bearded chin he indicated the three strangers.

The other man spat on the deck and shrugged. "Tis the sort of thing we see a lot of around these parts," the weathered seaman said with a shrug.

With a bored expression, the dandified commander gazed indifferently down his nose at the small, poorly dressed captain fuming up at him before giving an exaggerated sigh of exasperation. Crossing one expensively leather booted ankle over the other, he leisurely pulled off a matching calfskin glove, and put his hand out for a snuff box. Several delicate pinches made him sneeze very loudly before handing it back to a junior officer. "So what exactly is it you expect from us?" he asked around another explosive sneeze.

Sebby rattled off a string of anatomically impossible feats involving randy bovines and splintered spars. Jez choked back a shocked gasp before she warned him to please be patient a moment longer, and then turned back to the Englishman.

"We request nothing but your leave to work our ship back out to sea so that we may not trouble you any further. Also, my Capitaine reminds me to say we have brought you a present of wine for your patience." She offered the hastily handed over bottles from an equally frowning Jengo, who while he could not understand a word of the French, had caught on that things were not proceeding very smoothly. She thrust the bottles out toward the sneering men, and winced when they glanced at each other in amusement.

"Spies bearing gifts. How... very... quaint," the English captain replied haltingly as he took them, handing them off to another man. "Tell your captain to get his wreck out of our sight by sunset. Now begone."

"I will inform him, and I am sure you have his gratitude, as well as that of the governor of St. Domingue. We will mention your generosity to him, and I am sure our beloved Père Sébastien will pray for your souls."

"Oh joy, I shall be lauded by a papist," the English Captain said with a wave of dismissal.

Sebby muttered in French, "*Oh, I'll pray all right! I shall beg the Almighty that the ocean opens up and swallows you and all your arrogant, conceited, gutless companions, and that some devil fish will bite off and not choke on your tiny little, dried up...*"

"With your kind permission, we will take our leave now," Jez cut in smoothly, steering her sputtering 'captain' back toward the ladder.

"Please do go away! Mister Curtis, see that they disembark safely," he ordered a junior officer. He grabbed the wine greedily enough though, holding it out at arm's length to squint and smile at the foreign vintage, not even noticing it was Portuguese and not French.

While the English watched them closely, hands on their weapons; first Sebby, then Jez, and finally Jengo climbed back down and into the waiting longboat. They cast off the mooring lines and quickly rowed back, not daring to show any sign of the triumph they all felt. That had been a close call, and if not for the quick thinking diplomacy of the young crewman...

who unbeknownst to them was actually a gangling girl disguised as a boy…a lot of lives would have been forfeit that day.

The effort to get *Devil's Handmaid* through the shallows and into deeper water had been ongoing while their erstwhile emissaries were aboard the British warship. All hands pitched in to free the craft once the longboat came back in, but it still took the rest of the afternoon to get the main anchor aboard and stowed. Once she was partially afloat they used only the kedge anchor and minimal sail to gradually move her into deeper water. It was late in the day when they finally raised all sails and began the journey back out to sea again.

As they started to move under the wind once more, Dan Adams prudently ordered the bow chaser prepped and ready to fire if necessary. The English had monitored them most of the day, but had finally set sail and headed off back toward Port Royal. He didn't trust them; not after the hard time they had given his people. Everyone breathed a sigh of relief when, at sunset, they moved into open water, and no sails were visible on the horizon.

The pirate captain had a private word with each of the daring crew members who had pulled off such a perilous but ultimately successful ruse. He spent an extra-long moment congratulating Sebby for his performance as a French captain.

"I hate to admit Cap'n Dan, but I was so spitting mad at that self-important braggart, 'twas the boy who did all the thinking. He has quite a way with words of negotiation, too."

"It seems we've all underestimated you," Dan Abrams said with a smile that made his eyes crinkle when he came down to the galley to confront Jez, who was helping Andy get some food going for a tired and hungry crew. "You're uncommonly canny for a mere boy, and yet I have seen you working as hard as any man. I'm going to find a special position for you aboard. I can use a smart lad when it comes to trade and treaties, and so much of what we do these days depends on brains and ingenuity as well as might and weaponry. I shall inform Master Armitage that I want your arms training stepped up immediately. While you're welcome to help my old friend Andy when you're able, we'll not waste your talent on the powder room unless we're short handed. Master Gully will show you around the treasure hold as well. I want you brought up to speed on what we have aboard and where best to offer it."

High praise from a man who seldom offered much in the way of compliments. When word got around that Jez had been singled out by the captain for special training, certain members of the crew were jealous... Sol and Neville more so than others. Yet most shrugged it off. The majority of the company was in the mood for a celebration after beating the storm and the English threat, and Dandy Dan promised them a right proper bash as soon as they re-provisioned at the next likely site. A feast and general bacchanal would be planned then, with food and drink aplenty for all. For now though, it would be best to put as far out to sea as possible, lest the British warship's haughty captain change his mind and come back after them.

That night, unable to sleep, Jez curled up on the forecastle deck out of the way, and with her hands behind her head, watched the stars sail overhead. She was stuffed from Andy's sumptuous dinner, which she had carried up to the captain's quarters, and then been asked to join them at the table, as had Sebby. Recounting their tale for all the officers again, she had not missed the speculative and rather appraising looks from Walter Armitage, and his hearty promise to see that she immediately received proper weapons training. Gully had also suggested she be allowed to come ashore and tag along with him to learn the art of trading, since she could also read and write, as well as do figures. Even James Reuben had added that he knew this was the most capable lad he'd seen in some time, and was glad not to see him wasted as powder monkey or bilge rat.

"Never shirks his duty, does as he's told, looks out for others...you can't ask for a better freebooter than that."

Drunk on high praise and good wine, she smiled up at the moon as it kept pace with them, slipping through the night sky just as quietly as their ship cut through the gently lapping waves. For the first time in her life, Jezebel Johnston felt like she truly belonged somewhere.

CHAPTER FIVE

The following days were a blur for Jez, for she was busy learning much of what she needed to know to move up amongst the crew. She still did help Andy Boone whenever she could, but alternately Gully or Walter Armitage would take her in hand to teach her the basics of what they each specialized in.

Gully brought her below decks to the area of the hold where their prizes were stored. He explained to her what each bale, bundle, or barrel held, where it would trade best, and what condition it must be kept in.

"The dampness be bad enough down here lad, but worst be the mice and rats...the vermin get into everything," he related pragmatically. "Tis why we trade often, and turn over the most easily ruined goods into needful items. Only when we have prizes that don't spoil, do we hang onto them, and then just so long as it takes to find the right buyer. Otherwise we'd lose half our cargo before it was sold."

"How do you know when and where to find the right buyers?" Jez asked curiously as they edged past men moving barrels which had been emptied of their food or drink contents. She was learning now that the world was a far larger place than she could ever have imagined, and the best way to see a lot of it was aboard a ship.

"Well now... that takes some knowledge of the different ports and what the locals might be looking for; as well as who won't say a word in the wrong ear. Ye don't want to be selling tobacco where they raise plenty of it, or skins to a place where the cattle roam free. Neither do ye want trouble with the law. There are some towns that cain't pay as high, yet they'll take just about anythin', 'cause it's far cheaper to buy without government taxes and tariffs. So ye do the best ye can. Even if what ye has trades low, yer still makin' a healthy profit; and they'll be all satisfied and feeling like that they got the best of ye. It sort of evens out."

She nodded thoughtfully. She was finding out quickly that piracy was more than just swashbuckling fights and canny raids. She was actually very excited at the trading aspect, because negotiation was something Jez was good at.

"There's a lot to learn," she admitted, glancing around with a speculative eye. "Don't you write any of it down? It would be easier to share that kind of information if there was a ledger." Her mother kept a tally book for each business, with pull out pages that had the real numbers, which got stored in a locked chest beneath her bed. Only the official book was shown to any tax collector who asked for it.

"That would be suicide Jez, were we ever defeated and boarded," Gully explained, "Because it's hard evidence against us in a king or governor's court, it'd kill any pleas for clemency we might make. Naw, I keep it all up here," he tapped the side of his head for emphasis, "That protects both the company and our trade partners ashore. Seems difficult now, even when we've naught much aboard, but ye'll pick it up fast enough. Let me explain more about where to trade what goods we already have."

They talked of possible cargo and likely ports for the rest of the afternoon as the ship sailed toward the Caymans, where they would gather some fresh food and meat. Sea turtles were abundant there, and they made excellent soup. The cleaned shells also traded well in some places. The three islands were mostly uninhabited except for a few people…chiefly deserters from Cromwell's army in Jamaica and their young families… who lived there year round. They might not have much to offer other than food, but they were easy going folk and not likely to turn anyone in. True pirates had no allegiance to any government, nor any other reason to raid so tiny and poor a colony. Consequently, contact from any ship passing the Caymans and not displaying a national flag was welcomed.

Jez was back in the galley early enough that evening to help Andy turn out dinner. While they worked together, he asked her questions about her day, and she chatted amiably of all she had learned. He smiled his toothless grin as he sucked at his pipe, while she laid out the bowls and biscuit, and then ladled stew for the men who came looking to eat.

"Oh fer sure, yer becomin' right handy all 'round. I said from the get-go, our Jez is a bright lad, and this jist proves me opinion. Ye'll become a master or somethin' if'n yer careful like, and lives long 'enuff. Maybe e'en cap'n o' yer own ship some day."

Jez shook her head and laughed, but it made her puff with pride. To think of having her own ship! That would be far more important and exciting than being a tavern keeper and brothel owner.

Walter Armitage called for her earlier than usual. Jez hustled through her morning routine with Andy so she'd have plenty of time with this man who had previously remained so elusive.

"We will be making landfall sometime tomorrow," the arms master said lightly, not acknowledging her puppy-like eagerness and overconfident air as she strode jauntily by his side. "You've shown some aptitude with a pistol and so I'd like to work on that today. I plan to take you with the shore party to learn how to hunt and help guard our encampment."

"Then... I'll be able to leave the ship?" she asked in a surprised tone.

"That's what a shore party does," he answered candidly, but with a thoughtful look. Perhaps the young hoyden would take a fancy to one of the striplings of that colony, and she'd opt to remain behind. It would solve a lot of problems.

"Oh, thank you Walter!" Jez was fairly dancing around him in delight. Several crew members they passed eyed them strangely. A couple of them jeered and one grumbled under his breath about playing favorites.

"Keep your voice down and your reactions under control," he snapped in a loud whisper. *"You're drawing too much attention to yourself!"*

She was abashed, but at the same time an inherent rebelliously playful streak raised its head. *"You're just worried someone will see us together and think I'm your catamite!"* she hissed back in far too loud of a tone.

He rounded on her immediately, and his fist struck with far less force than he would have used had she been a smart mouthed male youth. It still snapped her head up and Jez bit her tongue as she reeled backward with a split lip, which bled profusely before the cut swelled shut. Her cheek would show a bruise for several days. She held her face in one hand and staggered away from him, eyes wide and glittering with unshed tears. The sudden brutality hurt more because it came from this man she so adored.

Walter Armitage met her shocked and reproachful look with a fixed glower. His aggressive stance spoke volumes as he stood with his hands balled into fists at his side. His eyes darkened to indigo pools of fury in the shadowed hollows beneath jutting brow bones. This was an important discipline lesson for any impulsive youngster, so he hardened his heart and showed no more trace of emotion than a hungry raptor would to the tattered prey beneath its talons. The rage he'd felt at her scoffing insult made him clench his jaw, which stretched the skin over his cheekbones, forcing that long scar to become all the more prominent while a vein in one temple pulsed.

The frostiness of that unending glare went right through Jez like ice daggers…it was entirely cutthroat pirate, without a hint of compassion. She had to look away, and that is when he spoke, his words low, clipped, and harsh in reprimand.

"Don't you *dare* jest with me of such things. I am a man grown, far older than you; and I've seen sights that would have you on your knees retching and clawing your eyes out so as never to look upon the world again. You are but a child yet; and while you've earned yourself some status aboard, you remain only one small part of this rough and ready company. You'd get far worse from any of them. From now on you do as you're told, and you speak with greater care. We've no room aboard for cocky, loudmouthed shit-stirrers." He turned to stalk away, and she dashed the tears from her eyes, and hurriedly followed.

"M-my apologies, M-master Armitage," she said in a halting voice made thick by choked-back tears and a sore tongue. "I was wrong to s-speak with s-such… impertinence."

He sighed with frustration, and pushed stray strands of waving black hair out of his eyes. Walter Armitage had struck her not in anger, but to remind her of her tenuous position in a life that offered no mercy, and also so that any of the crew who were covertly watching them saw that no one member was more important than another. He had hated to do it, but the sooner the girl learned her place, the better. He was reasonably sure that striking Jez thus had re-secured his position amongst the other men.

They were both standing at the forecastle rail now, her looking up at him with a half-beseeching expression, while he ignored her and gazed out to sea. The lines of his face were still hard, and he appeared far older than his eight and twenty years. There was a long silence between them before he spoke. Men all around busied themselves with their work in the rigging above and on the deck behind them, so no one paid them much attention.

"You don't belong out here," he said in a barely audible tone. "I should have turned you in that first day."

"But you didn't," she answered quietly, almost hopefully.

"No, I did not," he admitted with unemotional candor. "I kept hoping you'd leave on your own, and spare me the drama."

"Are you going to turn me in now?" she asked with far more bravado than she felt.

"It's too late for that." His voice sounded strained as he turned his head toward her, and the look he gave her was frank and appraising. "You've made a damn hero out of yourself with Dan Abrams, Gully, and Jamie.

"It's too late for that."

You also showed them that with the right sort of persuasion, we can sometimes get out of a fix with our brains instead of always resorting to violence. No one else aboard could have pulled that off so well. You saved a lot of lives, but more importantly, you taught these rummy seadogs there are better ways to do business than at the end of a sword or with the blast of a cannon. Things are changing out here, and they need to embrace that."

"Then... I can stay." It was more statement than question.

"Until someone discovers your secret," he reminded her.

"No one ever will," she said flatly. They both went silent again.

Walter Armitage knew better. A ship at sea is a small, cramped place with everyone minding each other's business, and the girl was on the budding edge of womanhood. It was just a matter of time before someone else noticed one of her less than masculine traits.

Voices called back and forth around them. The wind filled the sails and the water around the bow hissed, bubbled, and foamed; waves slapping the planking. It was a few uncomfortable moments before he spoke again, still keeping his voice down low so they might not be overheard.

"Listen to some good advice then, since you're so determined to remain aboard. Watch what you say, and to whom. Never trust anyone. Keep your own counsel. There are no landed gentleman or government officials on this ship to bow to Jez; in fact, most of these men are the lowliest drunkards, guttersnipes, debauchers, killers, and wastrels you'll ever have the misfortune to meet. And this is a pretty decent crew! Yet amongst them is a sort of informal hierarchy, and some pretense of civility, though that's not solely what this matter of how you act out amongst them is about. It's about giving and gaining quiet respect; the kind you would show to family; because for better or naught, we are your family now. Here we are all brothers, every one of us freebooters, even when we look out for our interests."

"I understand," she said quietly.

"I wonder if you do," he countered with a mocking tone, "Because with all this recent praise, I think you've forgotten who you really are. Well I haven't. Jez, you bragged to me yourself you are the child of a privateer. That's just a pirate with one government's sanction to take prizes from other nations, and a letter of marque doesn't make their life and death any different than ours. Yet while you willingly decided to come live this way, many of us were given no other choice. You will face resentment and reprisal if you keep basking openly in any glory you've earned, and I've seen that tear a company apart. You'll live far longer and with less animosity if you remain inconspicuous. You don't want the notoriety you're gaining now."

It was Jez's turn to sigh. This seemed like the opposite of what Monifa had drummed into her about a woman making her way in a man's world. "So I'm supposed to just go about my business and never attempt to be any more than what I am now? That seems rather...dull."

He snorted. "Dull is good. It's safer. A pirate ship is no place for romantic tomfoolery. This is a bleak life at best. Keep your head down and you'll live longer."

"You sound so bitter," she said sadly.

He gave her a sardonic smile. "I suppose I am. I've already seen far too much of this world, and you've barely left home yet. This is a game to you right now, a lark asea; but a pirate ship is no place for such juvenile rubbish. The dangers are boundless. Even without the killing and the stealing, which will eventually get you shot, run through, or hung; the ocean is vast and deep, and when you spend endless weeks and months in her clutches, she woos a man away from his wits like no flesh and bone woman can. I can tell you from my travels that water covers much of this world. Love it long enough and it will show you how small and insignificant you truly are. The men you've met here all belong to her, and some of them are half mad because of it, but they are still depending on you to do your part and not cause them any more grief than what they bring on themselves. They have no idea who you really are at this point; so for now you are just one of the lads and you have to act the part at all times. If and when they ever find out, you'd best be able to defend yourself."

"If it's so bad out here," she asked him earnestly, "then why do you do this?"

He looked at her pointedly, catching her eyes in a way that made her heart pound in spite of the sudden brutal streak he had shown her.

"My fate was fixed years ago, when I came back from the war and killed a man for deflowering and then driving away a woman I thought was waiting for me. She was so ashamed of believing his empty promises and betraying me, she hung herself..." He turned away.

"I'm sorry," she said simply.

"I've made my peace with it," he said with a sigh. "Unfortunately, his family has not. He was the son of a high ranking nobleman with a long reach, and their outrage followed me wherever I went. If I'm too long ashore, I will be recognized; and if caught, I'll hang. So there's no safe life on land for me. You have more options, yet you chose piracy anyway. I would not have wanted this life for any man, let alone a mere girl." He said that last part very low.

She did not tell him that she chose to come aboard solely to be with him. Not now, when his feelings were so raw. "So you can do nothing else in this world but attack ships and kill men for their wealth," she said flatly, recalling the Portuguese ship they had raided before the storm.

"It's what I know how to do, and I'm no saint anyway. Jez, I have been a soldier as well as a seaman, and I had killed my share of men long before I came to this brotherhood. I know the kind of bitterness about life that makes these filibusters turn their backs on the world and go raiding, and why they spend every coin they make. I've seen it up close; I've felt it inside my own heart." He thumped his chest for emphasis. "While I did not set out to be a pirate, here I am; and I can tell you from first hand experience, a pirate's life is a short and hard one, and basically hopeless. Yet that's what you agreed to do when you signed the articles, and your name on that list has to mean something. Any ship is far too small for your wise mouthed, poorly thought out quips, and if you speak out of turn to one of them as you did to me," he inclined his head back to indicate the various crew members in sight, "You will get far worse a punishment than a quick blow from a pulled punch. You might get a knife in your ribs or have a sudden accident above that sends you hurtling down to smash your head on the deck, if you don't drown. So if this is truly what you want to do with your life, you'd better learn to speak wisely or not at all. In the meantime, use that sharp tongue and ready wit where it will benefit us all, as you did with the English."

She wanted to say, "I love you," and throw her arms around him, begging forgiveness and thanking him for sharing his thoughts, but there were too many eyes on them. So Jezebel Johnston nodded and pulled herself up straight.

"Let's get to that shooting practice then," she said with resolution in her voice.

Walter Armitage smiled sadly as he pulled one of a pair of pistols from his belt. He went over with her the loading and priming, how to cock it and when, and made her do it by herself the last time. Then they had to find a target. They made do with a small cask tied to a line and tossed well out overboard. It moved and bobbed with the waves, but the arms master managed to hit it solidly twice out of three times.

"Now you try," he told her, handing her a loaded pistol. She had a little trouble cocking it, as the hammer was rather stiff. "This one is not well broken in, but I gave it to you for a reason," he said, reaching around her shoulders with both arms to ease her hands into a better position. "Less chance of you accidentally shooting yourself in the leg." The warmth of his body against hers was somewhat stirring, and she had to force herself to concentrate. He steadied the gun and then showed her how to pull the hammer back to first half and then full cock position and a bit about sighting. Then he let go. "Pull the trigger when you're ready," he told her, stepping back.

Jez sighted down the barrel the way he had showed her, lining the hammer up with the top of the bobbing cask. The trigger was a hard pull and when the flint struck the frizzen, the priming flash down in the pan was a bit blinding. The puff of white smoke as the lead shot discharged didn't allow her to see if she'd actually hit the barrel.

"Did I get it?" she asked eagerly.

"Not even close," he said with a laugh. "You jerked upward as you pulled the trigger; it's a common beginner's mistake. You have to practice more often to develop a steady grip. In a battle situation, you won't have time to line up a shot, so aiming has to come naturally. Let's try it again."

Powder and shot was precious, but they made a dozen attempts. By the time they were done, Jez's arm was tired but she could load the weapon reliably and had nicked the top of the barrel three times.

"You've done well," Walter Armitage told her with pride. "Most of the shots after the first four were close enough to disable a man or take down game. You have a good eye for this. Once we develop that skill, you'll be a dead shot."

High praise again. This time though she fought the urge to gloat and swagger, which had gotten her into trouble earlier. The sore tongue and lip, and her swollen and bruised cheek, were strong physical reminders that she always needed to respond with discretion. So Jezebel Johnston buried her feelings and paid close attention as this man she idolized showed her how to clean the pistol, making her sit on the deck to disassemble and rebuild it several times.

"Always care well for your weapons, and they will take good care of you too," he admonished her. He collected both pistols when they were done, as most of the firearms were kept in the armory room. The crew was often drunk and rowdy, and on longer voyages, the tedium would wear on everyone. Fights over virtually nothing would break out, so whatever knives and small weapons they had readily at hand were danger enough.

"Thanks Walter. Now I have to go help Andy," she said reluctantly, looking at the position of the sun in the sky. "He wants to make souse before the rest of the meat spoils and he'll never be able to handle all that work alone."

"Go then; we'll practice again tomorrow…mid-morn before we make landfall," he told her. "Send Pakke and that laggard Neville up if you see them. Might as well get in some practice with them as well."

She touched her forehead with her fingers in a sign of deference before loping off. Walter Armitage watched her go, a practiced unreadable look on his face. He was truly fond of the girl, mainly because she was so different from the majority of young women he'd trifled with lately, whose favors he had gladly accepted without a second thought for their feelings when he left. Jezebel Johnston might be thoroughly infatuated with him, but she didn't simper and bat her eyes, or act the tramp to gain and hold his attention. Her unfailing affection was like that of a loyal dog; one minute gazing at him with adoring eyes, and the next snarling at the nearest intruder. It was… refreshing. Even for a man who no longer trusted women.

She's not out here just for me, he realized as he turned back to gaze out at the sea with a morose expression. *She truly wants to be a pirate. It's in her blood.*

Something about that was very enticing indeed.

By the time they reached the bigger island, which Dan Abrams called 'Grand Cayman', Jez was already proving herself to be a fair shot. Most of the company was buzzing about that, so no one was surprised when the tall boy became part of the shore party that rowed out from *Devil's Handmaid* in the longboat, which was filled with bales of tobacco and empty casks for food and clean water. They'd had aboard less tobacco than anything else, and here it was highly prized, so it would trade well. Jez pulled hard at the oars like the others. She was growing more accustomed to strenuous work, so that it no longer tore at her back and shoulder muscles. They needed room for the trade goods, so there were fewer men than usual in that group that Dan Abrams and Walter Armitage lead. That meant every man aboard was considered necessary.

Once they reached a crescent of sparkling white sand beach fronting a lagoon and surrounded by thickly dark jungle foliage, they set down the oars and dropped out into the shallows one by one, leaving the weapons and anything else that should not be gotten wet aboard. In water up to their waists, they pushed the boat ashore. A few barefoot boys in mismatched and raggedy clothing came running to help them draw their vessel up above the high tide line. These were a mixed group of youths of various ethnicities, at one end of the spectrum fair-haired and blue eyed, the other mahogany skinned with ebony curls. Most spoke at least some broken English, and a slender boy was fluent in Dutch. The youngest appeared to be at least part local Indian. When Dan Abrams told them, "Someone go find Papa, and tell him we have come to trade," the Dutch boy nodded and ran back down an almost unseen trail through the tangled wilderness that brooded over the hot and sparkling sand. They picked up their weapons and girded themselves properly. Pirates never went anywhere unarmed.

Grand Cayman was the biggest island of the three, and it was where most of the local settlers lived. They were a mixture of military deserters, former pirates, escaped slaves, and local hunters, along with a handful of women and a gaggle of children of various ages. There was one Irish priest trying to save a few souls in between bouts of delirium after long drunken nights. Their unofficial headman was a balding and fat, jovial expatriate Spaniard named Papa Juan Molina. The former conquistador gone native spoke reasonably good English, and when he saw who had hailed him, he laughed until his sun bronzed belly shook over his raggedy loincloth and jingled the shells and beads on the thong around his neck. Two women…a smiling and freckled brunette with the slight swell of a new pregnancy, and a dour older mixed race woman with a toddler in arms, her bare abdomen distended by a late term baby…stood behind him. They were his wives, and the five children with them were the beginnings of his dynasty, he joked.

"How have you been Juan, you old rascal?" Dandy Dan greeted him with a hardy handshake and true affection.

"Terribly busy!" the fat man said with a gap toothed smile and the noticeable accent of his former land. He spread his hands in an expansive gesture, indicating the thickness of the jungle growth beyond the simple beachhead. "My family is growing faster than my colony, it would appear. I may have to marry another girl; if I can find one I'm not related to who can please me. With two of these rounding out at the same time, a man could starve for want of affection." He winked, and all the other men laughed. Jez just looked down. The younger wife was only a few years older than she was, and stretch marks on her bare breasts and belly said this was not her first child.

"How many do you have now?" Walter Armitage chided him. He glanced more than once at the younger woman, but he'd already noted less men amongst the villagers than in the past, and some wary looks from the remaining ones. Not everyone here was as happy as Juan Molina would have you think.

"Wives?" Juan asked with a shrug. "Just the two. But if these babies live, they'll make seven that I know of, though I might have a couple more I haven't seen yet on the smaller islands. A man does have to get out fishing now and then."

More laughter.

For some reason, that candid response upset Jez. While she had been raised on pirate tales, and understood well the role of a woman in a man's world, these women were no more than servants and playthings to this jolly, fat foreigner, who was acting as if he were king of the three islands. Brothel talk had always been crude, and their licentious activities often spilled out into the street. With the harbor at Tortuga being full of men at leisure with coin to spend, the lewder facts of life were something Jez had learned early in childhood. Yet such crudity just seemed out of place here in what should be a paradise. Grand Cayman was a peaceful place, along with a far more successful melting pot of diversity. This was how she wished her home island had been.

Walter Armitage's hungry stare did not improve her mood either. There was covetousness in his eyes that she hadn't missed, and she resented his participation in the chiding everyone was giving Papa Juan for his success at populating his island home. She wanted to hold Walter to a higher standard than most pirates, the majority of whom only longed for strong drink, loose women, and the coin to buy them both.

The big man was urging them to follow him.

"Come! Feast with us, and we shall have great talk and much liquor. Maybe we find you a nice plump woman to keep you awake all night. Let's go!"

Later that evening, after the most odd yet satisfying meal of island delicacies that Jez had ever tasted, the rum-infused talk ran high. They lounged around a cheery fire, sprawled out on the sand or seated on sections of tree trunks and old crates.

"So why do you grace our bay with your presence, my filibuster friend?" Papa Juan asked Abrams around a belch.

"We've come to trade some tobacco for food and information. I also plan to do a little hunting for fresh meat before I take my lads up to the strait and liberate your former countrymen from some of their ill-gotten gains," the pirate captain related casually as he picked food out of his teeth. He waved a hand holding a carved mug and a girl came over and refilled it. "We thought you might have a bit of information to share as well," he added just before quaffing another long swallow.

"Way down here?" Papa Juan scoffed with a casual wave. "How should I know what the Flota is up to these days?"

"Oh, so they don't pass through these waters anymore?" Abrams said with an obvious note of sarcasm in his voice. "I would think a year's worth of pipe fill would buy more loyalty than that from an old friend."

To Jez, watching from the sidelines, things seemed to get a bit tense between the two smiling men. She caught Walter Armitage and Gully both eyeing Juan Molina with wariness.

"On occasion, yes it can," the fat man said evasively, "but times are changing. These big convoys never stop to consult me about their route. So other than how many ships are involved, what else can I possibly tell you?"

"That number would be a good start," Abrams countered, and his eyes took on a crafty, speculative look. "Along with how long ago they passed through. And what about the condition of the ships? A wise man can tell a lot about what a ship holds by just watching it. For instance, how many of them were low in the water, which means they were well loaded with something heavy? How many gunships accompanied them? Did any ships lag behind or list as if they were taking on water? These are things an observant person would note, and this island has many such eyes now."

"Those observant eyes... they can be popped out by a turn of the screw," Papa Juan countered, referring to the head crusher of the Inquisition tortures. "I have no wish to have my glorious face turned into putty because I helped someone get himself tortured after unsuccessfully taking on a galleon of the wealthiest nation of the European continent."

When the pirate captain made a sound of exasperation, Molina waved a chubby hand. "Oh, I know you would protest your loyalty to me, but every turn of the rack brings new revelations to light. Each flaming brand applied to tender flesh can cause a name and location to slip forth as part of a scream of agony."

Dan Abrams sat upright, and his face twisted into a scowl. "You're assuming of course I don't know what the bloody hell I'm about and would instantly get caught," he countered, using his dagger to viciously spear another slice of spicy roast goat. He looked it over, found it rare enough and free of parasites, and nibbled it delicately right off the blade while Papa Juan looked down at his own bare and callused feet as if deep in thought. Finally, the big man spoke up.

"Soothe your temper, my proud and bloodthirsty friend. It is not that I do not believe in your marauding prowess on the high seas. It is just... well, we are all running from something out there," Papa Juan swept his hands out in a dramatic gesture to indicate the world beyond his island home. "I have found my peace here. I wish that to continue beyond my generation." He pulled two of his children close, and kissed their heads in a show of affection. "No one bothers us, and I've no desire to undermine that. As much as I love a good smoke, it's not worth even an entire year of it to divulge such information without some... how would you say it? 'Insurance protection' for our people. I might have to move them suddenly, if those gunships full of soldados come back looking for poor, foolish Juan of the big heart."

"Pay close attention here lad," Gully leaned in toward Jez and whispered. *"You're about to learn how to bargain with unprincipled men."*

Abrams gave him a jaundiced look as he reclined backward into the lap of a giggling island girl who had been combing through his hair and picking out nits. "So just how much more 'incentive' must I offer to win your confidence in me, and loosen your tongue a bit further?" he asked in a mocking tone.

"Hmm, as to that," their host began, a calculated look of thoughtfulness on his face, "A certain percentage of the silver or gold might go a long way in buying us some firearms, a cannon or three, and perhaps a suggestion spoken into the correct ears that any part we might have played in local raiding be overlooked. You understand how it is, I am sure. I have a lot of women and children to think of. We have so little here for them."

Now the hard bargaining began. Jez watched carefully as Dan Abrams nonchalantly said, "Five percent after the crew is paid."

Juan Molina shook his head. "If the take is small, that would be a pittance for what we risk. Twenty five percent of the overall prize would be much more fair."

"That's bleeding robbery!" Abrams protested hotly. The chunky Spaniard held his belly and chortled.

"This coming from the man who intends to steal whatever amount we're talking about in the first place. Twenty percent then."

"Ten percent after the crew expenses!" Abrams shot back, getting up to pace around the fire.

They went on that way for quite some time, but finally settled on 15 percent after the crew was paid. The deal was sealed with several bottles of the Portuguese wine that Abrams had hidden in the longboat in case he needed extra incentive. He had no doubt that Papa Juan knew it was there already, because the children had likely reported everything left behind.

"A toast then, to a fine partnership," the Spaniard said heartily after they all were given a splash from the first bottle opened. They drank to the health of the company, to the health of the island people, and the health of the Spanish Plate Armada. The rest of the imported wine was reserved for their host to enjoy at his leisure, but there was almost boundless rum and some island brewed rotgut aplenty to drink. By moonrise, every adult and some of the youngsters were well past inebriated. A few had already passed out. There was music and dancing, bawdy talk and laughter, as men began to slip away with women and sometimes younger girls on their arms. Dan Abrams staggered off with two of them, as Gully was too busy having a sniffling, off key, and wistful singalong with the Irish priest, who still recalled the melancholy tavern ballads of his misspent youth. Papa Juan bid them goodnight, and was escorted back to his own hut by his younger wife and one son, while he cradled his three remaining wine bottles like babies.

Jez lurched to her feet, just barely eluding the grasp of a plump girl with budding breasts and wide hips, who obviously thought this was another lonely pirate lad in need of company. She staggered past the disappointed island maid and moved as far off into the brush as she dared go without getting lost, not stopping until she was positive she was alone. With great relief Jez emptied her bursting bladder in private before wandering groggily back toward the settlement.

On the way she got a bit turned around and wandered more toward the shoreline. Getting her bearings again, she passed a small clearing that fronted another short section of beach in a sheltered cove, idly noting that two youths had built their own bonfire. They sat behind it, passing a rum bottle between them, gazing out to sea and muttering in low voices.

They certainly had enough rum on this island! She reeled away from there before they could see her, and headed back toward the settlement again. What people did on their own time here was the business of the islanders.

Eventually Jez stood outside the hut where the men were supposed to sleep. She was swaying on her feet, yawning so hard her jaw made a cracking noise. She stumbled inside and pulled the cloth back down over the opening.

It was pitch black inside, and her eyes seemed to refuse to adjust. She took a few tentative steps within and stopped again, confused. At first it seemed like she was alone, but then she heard light snoring. She took about six steps more and then tripped over a pallet of palm fronds and branches holding what turned out to be a pair of legs. She wound up sprawling right on top of a man, whose last snore cut off in a snort as he reached out with strong arms to steady her, before he pulled her close to him. His rum laced breath made her giggle as his lips found hers.

"I knew you'd come looking for me Mia. How did you get away from your husband?" he said as he stroked her face and shoulder.

"Iz tzhat yoo Walter?" Jez answered in a slurred voice. She giggled a bit and hiccuped once, and sort of slumped into his arms. His body was very warm and sweaty, lean with muscle and he still smelled faintly of gunpowder.

"Jez?" he said with growing incredulity as he held her out at arm's length, though he kept his voice low. "I thought you were somebody else." He set her carefully aside, and when she tried to snuggle closer to him, pushed her roughly away and sat up rubbing his hand over his stubbled face. "What the devil are you doing in here?"

"I comed inshide ta go ta shleep," she said thickly, "But mebbe I'm not sho shleepy now..." She tried to drag him down, but he got to his feet. "Not scho fasht!" Jez said, and in spite of her inebriation she was able to grab his ankles. "I gotz ya now, thiz time yer not getting' awayz from me."

She dragged him down and smothered him in kisses. At first he protested, but Walter was just as lonely and almost as drunk as she was, and the alcohol had taken the edge off his natural wariness, baring a man's desires that had gone unrequited far too long. Jezebel Johnston was a stubborn young woman, and not one to take no for an answer. She also had grown up in a port town that featured bordellos as a main source of income, so her knowledge of the carnal act went far beyond her personal experience. It did not take much more encouragement to get him into the spirit of the tropical night in paradise, and the fact that she had come to him a virgin only made his ardor for her grow.

Still, he had been a gentleman in what now seemed like the dim past of his life. "Are you sure this is what you want Jezebel?" he asked in a voice hoarse with desire, holding her away from him long enough to catch her dark eyes in the dim moonlight that filtered through the fronds of the hut wall and roofing. "Your future husband might feel cheated."

"Ah wull nevah mawwy!" she declared, tearing at his breeches. "Now lub me or ahm gonna get mad at you!" She growled and nipped his ear, while he laughed and pulled away.

"As you please, my fierce Pirate Princess," he said with a chuckle, and rolled her on her back, stifling her giggles with hungry, demanding lips.

The predawn hours found them still partially clothed, but collapsed in each other's embrace, sated and fast asleep.

CHAPTER SIX

The frigate *Harrier* was just rounding the western end of the island when the captain of the privateer vessel was awakened. He was informed that shortly after the night watch had struck the second bell; a signal fire had been spotted. He came out on deck to verify it for himself before issuing orders to change course and head for the bay where he knew a pirate ship would be moored. It should be one of the renegade captains who had refused to ally with the authorities at Port Royal, Jamaica. A letter of marque allowed the Welsh commander of *Harrier* to take prisoners and confiscate ship and cargo of all unauthorized freebooters in the area.

When they spotted *Devil's Handmaid* lying at anchor in the bay, *Harrier's* grizzled old captain smirked. The Spaniard had done well, and he'd be duly rewarded. Dandy Dan Abrams, that deserter turned freebooter, was going to swing at last. There was quite a reward for turning him in, since Abrams had the audacity to prey upon even his own countrymen, along with their allies. He was also rumored to have aboard the wanted man Walter Armitage, who had killed the son of the Earl of Abingdon. There was an even greater bounty on the famed sharpshooter's head. It would be a feather in anyone's cap to bring them both in at once. Perhaps he'd be given a knighthood, like Francis Drake had earned under old Queen Bess; or a governorship of a quiet colony in a warm climate. Ah, the possibilities...

Before they had left their moorage and sailed off, the privateer launched a cutter filled with well-armed men. They would be landing on the nearest beach and marching inland toward the settlement, to round up any of the pirate crew that might be ashore. They would meet up with their comrades stationed within the settlement, and capture them all.

In the wee hours before dawn, *Harrier* slipped into the sheltered bay unnoticed and turned broadside, ready to pound the pirate ship before the crew aboard awakened.

One thing that made Dan Abrams hold onto men like Liam Gulliver and James Reuben was their determination to maintain some semblance of order aboard. Unlike many of their brethren, the crew of *Devil's Handmaid* had never been captured…mainly because they weren't all allowed to all get drunk at the same time. Regular watches were kept aboard, and men slept or drank in shifts. Pirates weren't noted for their orderly conduct, nor did they take well to regulating their behavior, but men who lived by stealing and killing other men could be made to see the worthiness in at least occasional bouts of temperance and self-discipline. It beat sitting in a jail to rot until the hangman came for you.

So that night in the safe harbor of Grand Cayman, there were plenty of drunken men aboard sleeping off their stupor, but also sober watches posted who were well alert. One of those was Pakke, who was not fond of liquor, and had volunteered to take Duffy's turn in the crow's nest.

"Light come round da bend," he called down to the deck watch, a sour faced old man everyone called Milt. "Mebbe big ship!"

"Mought not mean much, but I'll let Jamey know. Keep a weather eye out, boy," Milt said and stumped off to awaken their acting captain, who was primarily sober and only catching some rest before the morn.

Even with his hearing being somewhat affected by years of roaring cannons, James Reuben came fully awake at the first quiet call. He stumbled out on deck, swiping at his bleary eyes. The enigmatic Ping had already manned the helm, and he handed his current commander the spyglass. James ground both eyes open, and then set it to the left one and squinted into it. There was still enough moonlight to make out the contours of the ship slipping into the bay, effectively blocking their escape.

"Damn it all!" he swore aloud. "A frigate…British by the bit of jack I can make out. She's moving fast to block us in. Has to be a privateer or a pirate hunter. Wind's against us, so we can't outrun her. We'll have to take a stand. Get that anchor up immediately and come about for a broadside."

All around him sails were being unfurled, and half besotted men were hurriedly hauling away. Below decks, some were scrambling to move tables and hammocks while others readied the larboard battery. These men may not always be tractable or cooperative, but they knew their business. Everyone aboard would die one way or another if they didn't bring their own cannons into play first.

It was fortunate they'd only dropped the lightest anchor to keep from drifting too far into the shallows or a reef, knowing that if they were to do any hunting, the ship would need to be moved soon. This one was strung with hawse line, so it came aboard far more quietly.

The one thing *Devil's Handmaid* had going for her was the recklessness of her crewmen and the savvy gunnery experience of her acting captain. They understood a threat when they saw one, and no one aboard wanted to be taken alive. The frigate was just as well defended from the look of her, but she was slow in bringing her own guns to bear. The captain must be an overcautious man...a quality the more ruthless pirates could exploit.

"They want to board us and take prisoners, or they'd have fired at least a warning salvo by now," James Reuben said with a smirk. "Must be a glory hound running their ship. Fine with me; we'll let her get just close enough that we have the advantage, before the dratted fool realizes his folly."

The first round took the privateer by surprise. A tremendously resounding series of explosions reverberated off the jungle growth, accompanied by noxious clouds of smoke. It heralded a whistling load of chainshot which ripped through the frigate's sails, knocking men from the arms and slowing their speed considerably. The pirate ship had barely made it about and was beginning to circle like a wolf when Reuben gave the order to open fire. The entire larboard battery was emptied as soon as they were in position, and with sails now filling, and Ping's expert handling of the helm, they were racing in and nosing around with the bow chaser ready to fire and the starboard side battery after that.

While the frigate yawed a bit, she still came tacking in drunkenly for a starboard round of her own. The reason for her captain's caution in wanting to be closer became noticeable as soon as her guns boomed a reply. The pirate hunter bore mostly light cannon, 8 pounders on the gun deck, and nothing heavier at the bow or astern. They certainly had more guns, and fired wisely, they would have wreaked havoc. They likely carried more powder and shot as well.

"We have to make this next battery count," James Reuben said with a grimace as he and another man shoved the now loaded the stern chasers out of their ports, bracing himself as *Devil's Handmaid* came around just in time to avoid two thirds of the frigate's hastily fired response. Most of their opponent's shot missed because of the quick maneuver, but one ball hit the starboard bow rather hard. There was an explosive crunch and the screams of injured men, and the ship shuddered and heeled a bit. That was far too close to the powder room!

If they could just get close enough to cripple her, they could take the frigate out. "Ping, get this old lady about so we can lay into her, and then get me a good clear shot with the chasers. We're sending that bastard son of a Crown bootlicker down to parley with Davey Jones tonight!"

The first reverberating cannon barrage woke both Walter and Jez, who were closest to the bay where they had all come ashore. When there were several more in rapid succession, she almost shouted in surprise before Walter clamped a hand over her mouth. He whispered in her ear.

"Hold your tongue and get dressed. There's some treachery afoot here." They hurried into their clothing. A low voiced disagreement outside in the clearing accompanied the sound of tramping feet.

Jez winced and ducked instinctively when a pistol cracked nearby, and a woman screeched in terror. There was the sound of a scuffle, with blows falling heavily amid oaths and shrieks of defiance. Above it all, Dan Abrams' besotted voice was raised in fury, mixing with the angry retorts of other men. Walter handed Jez a loaded pistol.

"Use that only if you need to," he warned her in a low tone.

Jez stuffed the loaded pistol into her sash and slid her knife into her boot sheath with shaking hands as pounding feet and shouts were heard all around.

"We need to get away...quickly now!" he hissed, and dragged her arm. Torches were being lit outside as they scrambled to the back of the hut. Walter pulled his blade and slashed at the palm fronds and Jez helped him pull apart a hole in the light framing.

They had just crawled into the darkness when a blinding bright light accompanied by an ear-splitting explosion blew apart much of their hut, sending them both sprawling. A grenado! They had just gotten out in time.

Slightly dazed and partially deafened, they were just cautiously regaining their feet when the click of a hammer being drawn back and the flicker of a torch announced they had been discovered. Someone grabbed Jez roughly, yanking her upright. She felt the cold steel of a barrel pressed against her throbbing temple as another hand relieved her of the pistol and stuck that in his own belt.

Walter's remaining gun was up in a flash. It wasn't any use.

"Throw down your arms pirate, or this boy's brains will be splattered all over you," he was warned as the man holding the gun to Jez's head tightened a finger on the trigger.

"What makes you think I give a damn about... *him,* when I can shoot you dead afterward anyway, and be out of here?" Walter Armitage said with an edge to his voice. He avoided Jez's questioning eyes, keeping his ice blue gaze emotionless and locked on the man with the gun pointing at her. Someone else answered.

"Tsk tsk! You fool no one, my friend. In fact, you would do well, Señor Armitage, to put your hands in the air," an all too familiar voice added. The man holding Jez prodded her along and stepped closer, and they could see who followed behind him. The one with the pistol pointed at her head was a professional soldier by his look, and seemed perfectly at ease with a firearm. His other arm wrapped around Jez, pinning hers to her side. Their erstwhile host stood behind the man, holding no more than a torch. He was smiling sardonically.

"We could hear your foul fornication for half the night! I thought perhaps you had decided to best your captain and take three women to your bed. I see you prefer other pursuits..." He let it dangle there, hoping that Walter would take the bait and make a false move, for Juan Molina knew this was the most dangerous man aboard the pirate ship, better dead than alive in his mind.

Armitage was also no fool. The tall man lowered his gun. "You, who befriended us, now betray us?" he asked angrily.

Molina shrugged. "I apologize to you and the boy, but these men seem to think you're worth a fair bit of gold if taken alive. As I tried to tell your most stubborn and greedy fool of a captain, gold is something I need right now, to build myself a fortress and purchase cannon. It did not move him...in fact, he sought to cheat me! Now, he finds he cheated himself instead. You understand the consequences, I am sure?"

"I understand that you're a coward who sells out to the highest bidder!"

"You, who befriended us, now betray us?"

Armitage all but spat at him as he slowly laid his pistol down and then came to his feet with his hands out, showing he had no intention of making trouble. "We could have made you very rich, but you show nothing but false loyalty." He was trying to buy time; hoping to catch a break of some sort.

"It is simply a business proposition. You would do the same in my place," Molina answered frankly. "And besides, my little Mia longs far *too* much for your company, Señor Armitage. That I cannot allow...that she would so readily bed a murderer."

"I never touched her!" Armitage snarled. "She's only a child."

"So I have heard," Molina said brightly. "She told me herself, begging my forgiveness for her folly right before I took her maidenhead. No matter...I will now tell her that you prefer the favors of boys. That should cool her ardor for you." Juan Molina's big belly shook with hearty laughter. He seemed to think that was a great joke, though his eyes remained hard. Even the soldier smirked.

Jez's nimble mind was already racing through the possibilities, taking in everything around them. There had been only a handful of able-bodied men on the island, and not all of them were soldiers, so those few had gone after the captain and Gully first. That only this one had come for Walter and her without any backup other than cowardly Juan Molina meant there was no one else available. That was a distinct advantage.

She noted Walter tensing up as Molina boldly shoved past the man holding her and put out his hand. "Your sword Señor. And no heroics or this man who has two pistols at his disposal will kill your paramour and then you. He does not love me enough to care if my blood is shed needlessly, I fear."

"That makes two of us," the angry pirate said as he slowly withdrew and then handed over his cutlass, hilt first. A smirking Juan used it to hook Walter's second pistol away, so that it was well out of reach. The Spaniard looked each weapon over with an appraising eye before dropping the blade nearby. For whatever reason, he did not take one up against them.

That was a mistake that could be exploited. Juan Molina, the former Conquistador, was no longer much of a fighter at his age and size. The fat man did not move very fast at all and he seemed quite inclined to avoid violence. Managing to catch the gaze of the only man she trusted, Jez remained silent, but she winked twice, hoping he'd know to be ready.

With the men well separated, this was her best chance to free them both. She acted quickly, feigning a swoon and as she slid down, yanked out the knife she had stuffed in her boot, and jammed it upward, into her captor's inner thigh. He let out a howl of pain as blood gushed forth, and the bullet meant for her head clipped her shoulder instead. Before he could draw his blade, Walter had shoved Molina away and leapt at the more dangerous of the pair. Amid curses, they were rolling on the ground, fighting for control of the man's saber and the second pistol.

Juan Molina was so bulky, bending over was hard for him. Tossing the torch aside, he was trying to grab Walter's other discarded pistol. Jezebel Johnston saw her chance and lunged at him, snatching up Walter's cutlass. With a grimace and a wild sweep, she threatened the big man, nicking his forearm. Molina's head snapped up as he stumbled backwards, ponderously sidestepping her bold charge while holding his bleeding arm in shock. On instinct she went for his neck but only managed to slice into his voluminous chins. Blood ran copiously down his neck and chest anyway, and that frightened him so thoroughly he screeched and wet himself before lumbering heavily away into the darkened forest, babbling in Spanish.

She turned back to the combatants, just in time to see Walter Armitage punch the other man one more time before he ran a knife across his throat. A bubbling cry was cut short as a gush of dark blood spewed into the predawn air, spattering him with some of the gore as he rolled away.

"Let's get the hell out of here before the rest of those bastards find us," he said, coming to his feet before grabbing up as many weapons as he could carry. He robbed the dead man of all his powder and shot, and they set off together into the night.

The starboard broadside of *Devil's Handmaid* fired just as *Harrier* lumbered into a turn to aim at them. The barrage was not as close as Reuben would have liked, but several balls hit the mark, low and on the waterline. The frigate began taking on water, listing so badly, her larboard guns were pointing downward. That was a trick the savvy man who had started his career as a fourteen-year-old gunnery mate had learned well. Cripple the enemy's ability to sail, and then take out access to her arsenal.

Before her frantic crew could get their barely responsive frigate turned about, a recklessly precise Ping had brought the stern sharply around and *Devil's Handmaid* showed her heels. The stern chasers fired immediately, their payload landing right onto the bow of the crippled frigate with deadly accuracy. Since both were loaded with hollowed balls called carcasses that spewed explosions full of lead balls and powder, men either fell with shrieks of pain or scrambled out of the way, unable to put out the fires before they set the ship ablaze.

"Send her to hell, with my regards lads!" James Reuben yelled, as they came broadside once more. That last barrage was almost at point blank range, and the blazing frigate began to break up and capsize as *Devil's Handmaid* pulled past, sailing out to sea again, with the intention of rounding the island to search for further trouble before they dropped anchor somewhere safe and assessed the damage.

Several men had been injured; two critically, and one had died of blood loss from a severed leg. There was a crack leaking into the bow that would have to be patched, and already the carpenter and his mate were hard at work with tar and oakum. It could have been a lot worse.

"We got lucky this time," Reuben told his second in command, a weaselly little man the crew had nicknamed Brazen Bill. "I hope our captain's party fared as well."

Dan Abrams was not a large man, but he was a scrapper, and he could fight. Even dead drunk and literally caught with his pants down, he was not easily subdued. It had taken several men to corner and disarm him. By then they all had their share of bruises and cuts, and one lay bleeding out with a sliced open gut. *Devil's Handmaid*'s captain had given a fair accounting of himself, having brawled on with a self-inflicted gunshot wound to the foot when he attempted to pull his pistol and it went off prematurely; a broken nose, both eyes blackened, two missing teeth, several cracked ribs, and a huge knot on the head that left him seeing double. It wasn't until reinforcements joined the three men still left standing to assail him that he was finally brought to bay; and then only because a club to the skull had temporarily scrambled his wits.

As intoxicated as he was, Abrams had not missed the point that these men wanted him more or less alive, and he knew what that meant. Someone planned to make an example of him, by hanging him publicly. Most likely the new governor of Jamaica, since these men were primarily English. *Devil's Handmaid* and her crew had spent the last raiding season thumbing their noses at British authority; robbing both the newly minted Republic's merchant ships along with those of their allies, whenever the chance presented itself. Abrams considered himself an expatriate of the realm, and therefore he owed allegiance to neither Crown nor Commonwealth.

He slumped sullenly in his fetters like some tattered slave, his head pounding, his foot throbbing, barely able to draw a healthy breath without nearly blacking out. His face was a swollen mask of contusions and dried blood. But there was still the fire of defiance in that raptor-like glare, that made men who were far larger than him, skirt well around where he was shackled to the trunk of a palm.

That Juan Molina was behind this betrayal rankled him to no end. He had trusted the Spaniard, who had spoken prettily and at length about being fed up with the constant warfare waged by his own countrymen. To turn traitor on a benefactor, and invite soldiers in to waylay them, was a capital offense in the pirate code. Abrams mentally kicked himself for not realizing the man's avarice far outweighed his cowardice. It was Molina who had actually clubbed him over the head to end the fight. If and when he managed to work himself free, that fat turncoat would pay for his treachery. They had been lulled into a false sense of security while that smirking Castilian Judas had sold them out to the highest bidder.

Abrams had not missed the sounds of the battle in the bay, and knew that his ship was under siege. He hoped canny James Reuben had somehow escaped, but he couldn't see the harbor from where he was being held, and no one would give him the news. One of the ships had gone down, of that he was certain, for the bombardment had ended abruptly. The sudden quiet was interrupted by the raw and ugly sounds of his remaining men being brutally subdued and questioned by torture, now that the pirate hunter's soldiers' ranks had swelled. At least a dozen more well-armed men had come hiking in to join with the few who had been sprinkled throughout the settlers. That disparity in numbers was the only reason they had captured him and most of his meager shore party alive, for all his lads could fight.

Only a few men were left to watch over him and whomever was left alive of his own hearties, while the rest of the soldiers were out scouring the jungle growth. That gave him hope. He had not seen Armitage or Gully yet, so at least one of them must still be at large.

We shall get out of this mess somehow, providing either Walter or Liam still lives.

As far as Liam Gulliver, he had been sleeping it off in the priest's hammock, his loud snores rocking him gently back and forth. The good Father slumbered head down on folded arms upon his own roughhewn table top. They'd had a grand night of drinking and reminiscing about the old country, Father Molloy being from Kilkenny, and Gully himself hailing from Kinsale. The priest's hut was a fair distance from the others, nestled in a small clearing where he had a little garden, a hand dug well with a sweep, and a view of the bay.

When the commotion started, both men rose groggily. They stumbled out to relieve themselves and see what was happening. The pirate quartermaster snarled angrily as he hitched up his trousers and stomped back inside to retrieve his weapons while Father Molloy watched the entire confrontation between *Devil's Handmaid* and *Harrier* with bloodshot, disbelieving eyes.

"What in God's Name is going on out there?" the priest asked in slurred consternation.

"Be ya daft? They fired on our ship, so we sent them all to watery graves!" Gully answered with a snarl. "Looks like yer friend Molina is a traitorous snake." Already shouts and sounds of fighting...along with a single gunshot...had filtered back through the surrounding vegetation. The quartermaster pulled his pistol, but the priest gently grabbed his arm.

"Go easy now, my friend; there is enough violence in the world already."

Gully wrenched his arm free and leveled his pistol at the priest. "Oh, and so I'm to just give meself up to you, I suppose? Was that the plan then, Father?"

The priest shook his tousled curls, with palms out in an appeal to reason. "I knew nothing of this Liam. Come though; they will be looking for you as well. Let us find you a proper hiding place until this blows over."

Gully frowned ominously and took a lurching step away. "That's a coward's way. My place is fighting at me captain's side," he retorted between gritted teeth.

The priest sighed and looked heavenward, throwing his arms up as if calling down the Holy Spirit as his witness. "Fine then! You'll be captured just as handily and hang beside him too. Don't be such a heroic fool with your life. Follow me, and I will get you safely out of here, and then go negotiate for clemency. They might have survivors to rescue, which will occupy them. In any event, they've no way to sail off with the lot of you, and if 'twas your ship which sailed free, they'll be expecting a rescue attempt. You likely have them out-manned as well as outgunned at the present; so for the time being, they may listen to me."

"Fair enough reasoning, I wager," Gully said with a frown, "But if you betray me Dennis Molloy, ye'll be the first man of the cloth I've shot dead."

As unsteady as he was on his feet, the priest looked the pirate straight in the eye. "You have my word that as I love God, Liam, I've no intention of playing you false. Now let's go or this discussion will have been for naught." He straightened his cassock and they slipped off into the jungle undergrowth just as the sounds of pursuit came down the trail from the little island village.

Jez and Walter were making their furtive way through a shadowy tangle of undergrowth, trying to reach the far side of the narrow island, when they heard the sound of someone moving amidst the foliage nearby. *"Down and be ready,"* he whispered in her ear, pressing her to her knees. Touching a finger to his lips to tell her to be quiet, he drew his knife and crept forward.

There was a scuffle, a couple of oaths, and then... *silence.* Jez held her breath until Walter came back, wiping his knife on his britches. He was carrying a wineskin, another powder horn, and an additional pistol. To her nauseated look he frowned and said quietly, "This is no time for thoughts of mercy. They'd as soon kill us on sight, and you'd best be prepared to do the same."

"I... I don't care for all this butchery," she said with a shudder, recalling Juan Molina's gory retreat and the spray of arterial blood from the sliced throat of the man Walter had killed earlier. Her comment elicited a raised eyebrow and a sardonic smile.

"Then you've no business aboard a pirate ship," he replied in a grim undertone as they moved out again.

The island had its natural dangers as well. Already they had stumbled across several large snakes. Both had brushed against some plants that had left raised welts on the skin and black tarry marks on their clothing. The biting insects were fierce in the wet areas with thick vegetation, and they were both covered in itching bumps. It was a miserable dawn on what promised to be a hot and steamy day, when the wanton moments of bliss just a few hours before seemed like they had occurred days ago.

The adrenaline surge of the surprise attack and the ongoing violence since, had sobered them both up quickly. That sudden temperance left

Jez with a pounding headache, and a brooding feeling of dissatisfaction. Nothing about this pirating life was as flamboyantly heroic and enchanting as she had pictured it would be. Walter, for all she had idolized him in her fantasy, was just another freebooter at heart. He stole what belonged to others, killed people without remorse, and eluded responsibility when things got out of hand. He even bedded a woman just as casually as any other man, and hadn't seemed the least bit intrigued or enamored with her since. Any romantic notions she'd cultivated had been shattered quite thoroughly, the shards of her girlish fantasies disappearing along with the morning mist as the bright golden sunlight swept over the vegetation, waking the birds and other creatures to another day of fighting for existence.

She tramped wearily beside her able companion, her mind sunken in a haze of gloom and bitterness. She had thought losing her maidenhead would be a glorious event, not just a sweaty tumble on an itchy pallet with a coarse-bearded man over twice her age whose calloused hands were rough and kisses stank of sour rum! Crawling stealthily through undergrowth to cheat the hangman from stretching their necks was not the swashbuckling life together she had imagined when she set out to join *Devil's Handmaid*'s crew.

Walter was not very handsome in the harsh morning light, either. His blue eyes were bloodshot and sunken, his stubbled face grim and bruised, and his clothing rumpled, dirty, and rank. If this man was all she had run off to sea for, she would have been sorely disappointed.

No, there was more to it than that now. The ship was a community where all sailors were equals and no one asked nosy questions; the ocean, a place where even a woman might find opportunity and respect. She would make her own way, carving out a reputation. But first, she had to survive this day, and get off this cursed sandpit of an island!

As the sun rose and the heat built oppressively, Jez began to wish she was back aboard the ship, somewhere on the water. Out there, the salt air was bracing, and it didn't have that closed in, dank and dismal, claustrophobic feeling she was getting from the thick vegetation that surrounded them. On the open water, you could see for miles, and tacking into the wind was far preferable to hacking and slashing your way through thick and sometimes spiny undergrowth where you couldn't view more than an arm's length ahead. As they tromped along, she kept her eyes roaming, as did her more experienced companion, for any signs of pursuit or dangerous creatures. Not all the menaces they faced were large and bore the weapons of mankind. Centipedes, scorpions, and spiders were all things to be wary of. A bite, once infected, could cost you a limb, if not your life, Walter had warned her.

The island's people had proved just as dangerous in their own way. Because of their treachery, they may not even have a ship left intact...now there was a depressing thought! Certainly the longboat would be well guarded, if not scuttled, to prevent their escape. Their only hope now was to win their way to the other side of this narrow bit of land and either steal a small boat or build a raft, and somehow get themselves to another, less hostile shore.

She continued to fret, and then mentally kicked herself when she almost put her hand on a scorpion while crossing a rotten log. It was dangerous to become distracted in this foreign place, and greatly increased the chance she would be injured or captured. Jez reined in her fears and frustrations to remain alert and wary.

If she were going to survive, Jezebel Johnston would need her wits about her, and to become as ruthless as the next buccaneer.

CHAPTER SEVEN

Morning was nigh. Dan Abrams was drifting in and out of unconsciousness when a verbal altercation broke out. He lifted his head and peered around through blood matted hair with weary, swollen eyes. The village's priest had showed up and he was arguing with Juan Molina over something.

"So tell me Padre, why I am supposed to care about what happens to pirates? They are thieves, rogues, and brutal murderers. One of them...a mere boy...tried to kill me yesterday!" He lifted his head and showed off the crudely stitched slice on his chin, carefully tended and slathered with healing salve by one of his wives. "The less of them we must deal with, the safer we all shall fare."

Father Molloy sighed and shook his head, and immediately regretted the motion. He was still quite hungover, so his brogue was thick that morning. His temples throbbed, his stomach roiled, and his mouth was dry with a persistent aftertaste of soured brine. A sense of duty alone kept him on his feet.

"I'll not excuse their actions asea, but here certainly we should not be setting an example of betrayal! Any man, once threatened with treachery, is going to respond with violence. I find myself saddened that you would involve yourself in such skullduggery. We are not put upon this soil by God to judge one another. We should leave their fate to God and the courts…"

"Or the Inquisition perhaps?" Juan Molina interjected with a raised eyebrow. "I am sure the Mother Church will be much more gentle with these men than the Protestant soldiers of Cromwell."

The priest's face darkened. While he had little love for the Vatican's horrific and misguided investigations via torture and public executions, his motherland had suffered greater atrocities under the thumb of the Protestant policies of the Commonwealth.

"Sadly, that's the way of it these days. We all know life becomes horrifically unpleasant for those accused of heresy by the Holy Office, but I am still a Man of God before all else. Atrocities have been perpetrated all around it would seem, for power corrupts the minds of those who wield it, and the Devil will have his due. I can testify firsthand to the devilry of those English butchers you so admire. In my poor country, they have stolen away our lives and livelihood, turned us out of our own homes, and laughed as our wee ones and elders starve! Yet these things we speak of are far away across the ocean, and we've no reason to transport that madness into our lives here! I left Ireland to do good in this new world, thinking perhaps here in Paradise on Earth, we might all find peace, salvation, justice, and brotherhood without prejudice."

Juan Molina laughed and waved him off. "Bah, you're a childish dreamer as well as a drunkard Padre! There's no paradise here. These men you want to save the souls of are no more than common freebooters. Savages of the sea, they rob and murder the innocent! They are now in custody, so they are no longer your concern. Go back to your cups and your Bible. Say a prayer for good Juan Molina instead; that he may find much profit, sire many strong children, and live a long and healthy life."

The fat man shook all over in mirth as he waddled away. Father Molloy watched him go with some consternation, knowing he'd lost his battle for souls with this Spaniard, who obviously didn't have a conscience, let alone a care for his fellow human being. The priest had done his best to put up with Molina's unorthodox living arrangements and even the taking of multiple child brides, all in order to bring the prospect of redemption to these islander renegades and refugees; but this went too far. While it was true that the captive men were pirates, they were also mostly outcasts who had been driven from their homelands because of various calamities, and that was something Dennis Molloy understood in his heart. He'd taken quite a liking to their querulous but witty captain and his feisty quartermaster, and while he intended to bring the Word to them and save their souls, he'd have to save their lives first.

He caught the eye of Abrams on the way by, and raised a hand with the two fingered benediction sign. Dandy Dan watched him warily, and then gave a slight and shaky nod before closing his eyes again. He was not a Roman Catholic, but educated and well traveled enough to know what that gesture symbolized.

Blessings. Mercy. That priest was up to something! Gully at least must still be alive.

Perhaps the soldiers would be easier to deal with. Father Molloy wandered around until he located the acting leader, and addressed him politely.

"What do you want, Papist?" the man snapped irritably. Injured men, along with the dead and dismembered, had been floating in regularly. The entire business was a bloody wreck, and he had not slept in hours. He had been catching a catnap when the priest interrupted him.

"I come to you as a Man of the Cloth and the Cross." His left hand held up his crucifix and he kissed it to show his sincerity. "I wish to offer these prisoners of yours a chance at redemption. I assume they will be taken away soon…"

"You assume wrong." The man was not shy in sharing details. "We'll not be leaving before we've collected the rest of their rabble and the next Commonwealth ship can be hailed, so I may well be hanging them here. That said, I'm not inclined to listen to your blathering. Mind your own business, and be on your way. Go preach to those who believe your Catholic drivel and nonsense." He turned to walk off.

Father Molloy dodged ahead of him, his arms spread in supplication. He gave the man a sad smile. "My son, I know our beliefs differ, so I only came to offer my services to those who sorely need it. You'd not deny a man his final chance to confess I hope!" He made the sign of the cross, praying all the time for God's intercession on his behalf.

The frustrated man rounded on him and snapped, "Listen priest… unless you can pray us up a ship or make the ocean part long enough that we can walk these cutthroats back to Port Royal for a proper trial before the governor, I don't care much what you do! The rest of their lot are still out there somewhere, and meanwhile, I've a sunk ship, a drowned captain and crew, and what few of our men who have survived are in poor shape at best. So unless you can be of some real assistance, leave us the bloody hell *alone!*"

The priest backed off as the man stormed past.

"I am truly sorry that your captain and crew were lost. I'll pray for you all."

"A lot of bloody 'elp that'd be," said another man, coming up to see what the ruckus was about. Several had gathered, and their mood was overtired and ugly.

"Well, I see that I am not needed here. Yet if these prisoners are to be executed, then I must insist to grant them absolution and a chance to confess." He was pushing it with the harried leader.

The man sighed in frustration, fists balled at his side. "Do whatever the hell pleases you, but get on with it and leave us be! We've England's work to tend to."

Father Molloy inclined his head…slowly this time…and moved off on a roundabout way to speak with Liam Gulliver. A plan was forming in his mind, one that nobody but a renegade priest would dream up.

In the blue and gold radiance of the morning sunrise, *Devil's Handmaid* was rounding the northwesterly tip of the larger island of the group. Not a ship was in sight, which was fair news enough for an attempted landing, and to the best of anyone's knowledge, the island had no large gun defenses. Yet with their only longboat still ashore, they would have to moor somewhere close to land and wade in.

So far, they had encountered numerous reefs. Beyond them, most of the shoreline appeared either white sandy beaches that were far too open for a sneak attack, or inhospitable and insurmountable jumbles of jutting, jagged rock. Much of it was inaccessible from sea because of those reefs. Ahead of them currently was a very large but shallow sound filled with sandbars, with more reef fronting it. If that water had been deeper and sailing close possible, they could have moved in, dropped anchor, and it would have made for a short hike inland. Unfortunately, there was no way to get near enough to actual shoreline without foundering. Ping had the lookouts above diligently watching the surface as men on the bow took soundings. The cautious helmsman expertly steered them as near as he dared with what little information he was getting.

James Reuben was livid as he stood by the starboard rail squinting out over the ripples, and he swore repeatedly. They had to rescue Abrams and company before someone decided to hang or shoot them on the spot…if they hadn't already!

"Master Reuben," someone called out excitedly, "There's deeper water here!"

"Where?" he barked with growing interest as he headed forward. Ping handed the tiller over to an experienced man, and followed his acting captain to the bow, the smaller man's quick and quiet steps easily catching up and keeping pace with the longer legged Englishman. They both watched the sounding line as it was dropped several times from different angles, and they studied the water ahead.

"What do you think?" Reuben asked the experienced navigator.

"A channel must lead to a small bay," the Chinese man said with conviction in his quiet voice. "It is narrow and slopes, so we will have to warp out. It is the closest way in."

"As long as it gets us through this blasted reef and shoals," he ordered Ping, "we'll drop the light anchor at the first likely spot. Start making your way out of it as soon as our lads hit dry ground. Hopefully they haven't scuttled the bloody longboat on us!"

Ping nodded and hurried back to his post. Reuben stomped off too; only stopping to grab Brazen Bill on the way by. "Tell Jengo to put together a well-armed shore party. We're going to go pay that lying, thieving bastard Molina a visit he will *not* forget!"

Father Molloy had been ousted from his home parish for the sin of public drunkenness, but his dedication to his faith had never wavered. In the spirit of the Dark Ages monks who had secluded themselves from most human contact to concentrate on finding God through their quiet labors, he had readily volunteered to relocate to the South Sea Islands and open a ministry. He had come to the biggest island of the Cayman trio along with several expatriates of Cromwell, hoping to convert at least a few of the colonists and help negate some of the abuses perpetrated by both church and state. A restless man, he had tromped every inch of that tropical wonderland in his three years there, memorizing the most minute details of geography, flora, and fauna. He knew better than anyone else— even their self-important leader, Juan Molina—where to weather out a storm or hide a wanted man or three.

While the island was relatively flat and low-lying, much of its rockier shoreline was soft limestone which the ocean had carved into ankle-breaking crags atop and sea caves or blowholes below. Some of those caves went well inland. One of the nearby ones was relatively dry and had a hidden back entrance in the forest, so he had laid in a store of supplies and foodstuffs, including bows and arrows crafted with both hunting and defense in mind, and several private casks of rum. That was where he had taken Gully, and also where he planned on bringing whatever members of the shore party he could rescue. You could launch a boat from the far end of that cave if necessary because it had an outlet to the surf. Unfortunately, the priest had no way to procure any watercraft without raising suspicions, and he knew nothing of boat building or seamanship. He did however have no love for the English government, and a perverse notion that these particular pirates might become useful allies.

A man of peace, yet of great vision; the good Father had plans for starting a mission for the dispossessed and unwanted of the area. He had watched with dismay as the battles of greed and dominance between the European powers spread their poison throughout the Caribbean colonies. It had a demoralizing effect on the local immigrant populations, and devastated the indigenous people. Juan Molina's diverse little community had started out as a place for all to live in harmony, but once elected headman, the Spaniard had become enamored of his position and was rapidly evolving into just another despot with profligate ethics. The priest knew from past experience how the sense of power that is awarded with such titles ultimately corrupts. He was frustrated in watching it happen yet again.

What Juan Molina wanted was to be a king of his land, with all the perquisites that go along with becoming a supreme authority. Because they had so little to trade, the islanders needed gold to set up defenses, and the English had promised Molina handsome rewards for turning in pirates the Commonwealth had not been able to bargain with. Dan

Abrams and his crew were such a prize, for they answered to no one but their own whims. Yet they had always been forthright with Molina, never showing up demanding terms or special treatment, and they had proven themselves trustworthy lads in the past, for pirates.

Someone else needed to take charge before the entire colony collapsed. Never as compliant as his position would allude, the priest understood that small, but well thought-out acts of revolution often brought change to tyranny, as well as led sinners to salvation. Dennis Molloy was not one to befriend others only to betray them, nor was he given to instigating violence. If there was a solution to this situation without further bloodshed or strife, he would find it; but one way or another, things had to change. He bowed his head in prayer.

God would show him a way.

The pirate hunters that had been tracking them through the bush seemed to lose interest in any further pursuit, perhaps because the day was turning fiercely hot. The heat and humidity drained the strength from you, and fresh water was hard to find. They had stopped only long enough to refill their canteens from the only potable natural well they had found, and had to make it last. The limestone base of the island was porous, so most of the ground water was tainted with the sea's saltiness, and any rainwater pools that hadn't completely dried up or soaked in were sickly smelling and full of debris.

Sweat rolled copiously off both of them, and Jez found herself incessantly thirsty. Still, she tempered her drinking the way Walter insisted she must. He was hoarding the little wine they had, adding measured amounts of it to the water. "It keeps you from getting the gut ache and flux," he explained.

They were resting in the late morning in the shade of an ironwood tree that had branches festooned with strap leaved bromeliads when the sound of a party of men making their way toward the interior of the island filtered through the undergrowth. Walter motioned for her to follow him, as he drew a pistol and crouched along to get a better look. She did the same. They crawled to within mere feet of the hastily hacked trail and peered out carefully.

The backs of a raiding party…comprised of perhaps a dozen all told…

were just disappearing into the brush. These men did not move or act like soldiers; in fact they were dressed like pirates. That was all he could say for sure, other than they were mainly Negroes, though there was at least one mulatto and a scrawny white amongst them. They were being as cautious and quiet as possible, carefully picking their way through the undergrowth.

Jez, who had a different angle, grabbed Walter's arm and tugged him close.

"*That last one looked like Sol!*" she whispered excitedly.

"*This heat can play tricks with your mind,*" he hissed back. "*They're most certainly Brethren, so they'll be well-armed. They could be rivals of ours or allies of the Crown.*"

She looked up at him with concern. It was not unknown for pirates to kill each other in feuds over booty or land rights, and some had sold out to the English. What if these were competitors seeking to take over and establish a base of operations here? The two of them would have to get off the island unseen or they'd be captured and forced to swear an oath of loyalty. Still, she had some nagging doubts...

"*They're moving slowly. If we can get ahead of them, we can see who they are and how well armed they are as they pass by,*" she suggested in a murmur. "*Then we'll know where we stand.*" Walter saw the sense in that, and his military experience took over.

"*You're better at this than any woman has the right to be Jez. All right, flanking maneuvers; you're on the left. Quietly and no heroics! There's too many of them to take on at once.*"

They split up to move around the others, and Walter melted into the brush again. Jez's nerves were on edge as she tried to emulate the silent way he moved. It seemed like there was always a twig underfoot, and each brittle bit crackled like lightning. Fortunately, the group they were stalking was making more noise than she was.

The closer she got, the more convinced she was the laggard was Sol. What she could see of his back had the scars of smallpox, and his skinny arms were full of tattoos. She was about to signal to Walter when someone grabbed her from behind, and a hand clamped over her mouth. A knife pressed against her throat.

"*Hold your tongue or lose it,*" whispered a voice with a distinct British accent and extremely bad breath that reeked of rotted teeth and rum. "*I'd as soon slit your throat as bother with you, but there's bigger fish out here to be taken, and you're going to be part o' the bait as reels 'em in.*"

She struggled with him, biting deeply into his thumb, hoping he'd yelp, or let go long enough that she could shout a warning. Not this one though. The man dropped his knife and she kicked it away. He cursed low but quickly wrapped fingers around her slender throat so that she couldn't draw a breath.

Her eyes bulged and she squirmed and kicked as he choked the consciousness from her. Although she fought the whirling blood red stars in her eyes all the way into blackness, Jezebel Johnston eventually sagged into his arms. He trussed her up, shoved a rag in her mouth, and dragged her off.

"But...but... I was promised some gold!" Juan Molina sputtered in protest as he clumsily trotted along behind the men dragging a snarling and struggling Dan Abrams toward a makeshift gallows.

The leader of the group rounded on him. "Your *payment* is currently lying somewhere in the bay, so I'd suggest you go look for it there," he snapped. "I warn you, if you keep annoying me, Spaniard, you'll join this freebooter in a short but vigorous dance, in which case we will be quite delighted to be rid of you!"

"Bah, better to shoot 'im and be done wit' it," suggested one of the injured men who had struggled in from the shipwreck. "That fat lug 'uld break the rope anyway. If 'e 'its the ground 'ard enough, 'e'll sink this 'ere bit o' rock." A couple of nearby soldiers laughed, but the women and children tagging along behind the group turned frightened eyes at each other.

The commander stalked away after his men, who were just setting up for what would be the premiere event of the day. Dan Abrams would swing immediately, along with several of his crew members who were still alive enough to put on a good show. That should draw the rest of the bloody bastards out, including the pirate's erstwhile liberators, who were making their skulking way down toward the settlement.

That freebooter rescue party was heading right into a trap.

A group of older boys and girls had been tracking the progress of *Devil's Handmaid* since she had left the bay. Always paranoid, Juan Molina had small lookout points all over the island's perimeter. Younger children used as runners reported the progress of the ship, and the soldiers knew exactly

He trussed her up and dragged her off.

where she landed a party of well armed crew members bent on retrieving their captain and whatever other men of the original shore party remained. With the few survivors of the sinking *Harrier* having joined them ashore, the soldiers equaled or exceeded in number the ragtag group of filibusters making its way toward them. The pirate hunters already present had been expecting a confrontation at some point, and had brought with them not only plentiful powder and shot, but a small supply of matchlock rifles and two small deck guns filled with grapeshot. These undisciplined sea rats would be met by men armed and prepared to cut them down.

First though, they would hang those pirates already in custody. That would be a great welcome to hell for their potential rescuers; to find their captain and his companions black faced and swinging aloft.

Father Molloy had been busy that morning, ostensibly offering absolution to the condemned. He had managed to take a battered Dan Abrams into his confidence, but had not been able to talk openly to the other pirates, who were tied together hand and foot, and so were being watched closely by the two injured men who were chosen for that duty. Their captors both held pistols at the ready, should someone get out of line.

A cassock worn loosely on such an ascetically thin man can hide a variety of materials. In the process of mending it, the clever priest had added interior pockets for the oddments he carried while trekking around the island. Most of those had been emptied now, after having been filled with purloined or scavenged items such as a couple of powder pouches, a tinder box, wax candle stubs, and several lengths of island made sennit cordage. From these he hoped to create a diversion that would deter the execution and give him and Liam Gulliver a chance to spirit away the pirate captain and his comrades.

The priest trusted no one but the pirate quartermaster to help him, for the locals were all in thrall to Juan Molina, and overawed by the soldiers with their pistols, sabers, and rifles at the ready. The priest had scurried about, putting on a show of blessing condemned men and hearing confessions while he and his accomplice laid a rather crude but ingenious network of explosives. 'Twas a shame to waste so much good rum, but it was going for a worthy cause.

He walked up to the two small cannons, stopping to make an elaborate sign of the cross on the ends of both barrels while small unseen things rolled out of his sleeve and tumbled down inside. Since they didn't have enough soldiers to take up the longer range muskets as well as man the bigger guns, a lone guard sitting on a rock watched over them while the prisoners were being prepared. He had been drowsing, and most of the others were too busy to notice what the priest was up to. Battle nerves served him well, as with a snort of surprise, the lame man opened his eyes, and heaved himself to his feet immediately. Grabbing a makeshift crutch, he hobbled over with a pistol drawn and pushed the priest away, eyeing him with suspicion.

"Wotcha be doin' there, ye blasted bog-jumping drunkard?"

Father Molloy choked back a retort and instead put on his most humble and penitent look. He heaved a dramatically sad sigh.

"Well, since I cannot stop this potential carnage in the Name of God, I have blessed your guns; in hopes that His judgment alone shall decide the outcome of this situation."

"Get yer holier than thou carcass away from 'ere or I'll bless ye wit' a ball 'tween the eyes, ya rummy fool!" the man warned as he leveled his pistol at the priest. The entire area around the robed man reeked of alcohol.

"Rejoice in The Everlasting Light, my son," Father Molloy said before he turned and walked away.

The man made a rude gesture at the priest's back, and then peered down each barrel. Seeing nothing amiss, he clomped back over to his seat and settled himself with a groan.

It was not as much as the priest had hoped to accomplish, but perhaps it would be enough.

The pirate hunters had chosen a spot on a reef-protected stretch of beach that would allow no bombardment from the water. The soldiers surrounding their prisoners were adequately armed and ready for any attack by way of land. The gallows stood well out of range of sniping shots from the concealment of the jungle brush. Anyone coming to the rescue would have to charge out into the open and take their chances with the gunnery aligned against them.

Juan Molina had been protesting something in a whining voice as the execution party approached, but now he stomped off in a huff. A gathering of island people had assembled to watch. The unwitting civilians had been purposely placed between the jungle and the gallows area, effectively screening prying eyes from sighting the sudden barrage that would meet any attempt at heroics. That a few locals might well get caught in the crossfire did not concern the pirate hunters. These villagers were mostly deserters, or runaway slaves and indentured servants who had jumped ship at some point. They stood with their families, many of them foreign nationals like their leader…no one of consequence or value to the Crown.

Executions were something that the people of the small colony had hoped never to see again. Fearful gazes flicked from the well-armed men to the rude pole device fashioned from palm trunks. It dangled nooses above empty barrels each man would stand on before it was kicked out from under him. The four pirates still alive were prodded toward their doom, including the ship's captain and a tall and slender boy who was newly captured. None of these pirates had done anything to the islanders to warrant such brutality; but then, such macabre spectacles had always been the way of the outside world they had thought to have left behind.

The four prisoners' arms were tied behind their backs, their legs hobbled so they could not run off. The sounds of the jungle receded to the point where the slow shuffle of feet and the restless surf beyond were all anyone heard as the condemned were dragged into position. Once each pirate was lined up he was heaved and boosted up atop a barrel by men balancing on horizontal poles in front and behind them that would be removed when the time came for the hanging. Each prisoner's head was shoved through a noose, and then tightened enough not to slip, insuring a quick death.

As the prisoners were brought up, they passed by the priest, who was standing before the makeshift gallows, his eyes downcast and expression both morose and contrite. Dan Abrams knew better; for the cunning mind of the Irish Father had come up with a bold, if rather chancy plan. Its success would depend on timing. While the pirate captain had not been surprised that some of his own lads would come after him, their intervention might arrive too late to save his own wretched hide. The hope was the good Father could pull off his diversion, and buy them all some precious minutes.

"'Ere's a nice lace collar fer yer lordship," quipped the soldier who tugged the noose taut around Dandy Dan's neck. This man was one who delighted in torturing men to make them talk, and their screams had filled the night with dread.

Abrams favored him with a look of cold and calculated fury. "How lovely. Here's a kiss goodbye for you in return," he added with a sneer of contempt before he spat full in the man's face.

The man sputtered and scrubbed at himself, losing his footing and falling backwards off the narrow pole. He hit the sand rather hard, knocking the wind out of him. He thrashed around gasping, before half raising up and shaking a fist at a smirking Dan Abrams.

"Ye scurvy seadog! I'll not tighten that any further, 'cause I'll enjoy watching ya dangling and kicking yer life away." The soldier regained his feet, if not his pride. "And 'ere's 'oping it's a nice and slow-like dyin' ye do, and that ye soils yer breeches in the process."

Dandy Dan rolled his eyes and smiled maliciously. "Let's hope *you* enjoy your bout with the flux as much as I have. Don't fret though…I'll inform The Devil that you'll be on your way down shortly to shake his hand." If he got out of this, that fellow would be one of his first targets.

"I want those guns in place on each end of the gallows. And gag that swaggering bastard," the commander insisted. While men set down their arms to heave and drag the cannons about on their carriages, which tended to bog down in the sand, someone else crawled up behind the pirate captain to stuff a filthy rag in his mouth. It was tied in place with a length of cording so he'd not be able to spit it out. If looks could kill, everyone opposing Dandy Dan Abrams would have died on the spot.

Turning his head carefully, Abrams looked down the line at his three remaining men and willed them to courage. Crazy Tom down at the far end had been so badly beaten he sagged wearily against the rope, waiting for the inevitable. Old Jonas Clegg next to him was trembling, but a longtime pirate's pride kept his head high. All the others had perished of the torture they'd received. The boy Jez had only been captured that day, so appeared no worse for wear, other than some bruises and a bullet graze on one shoulder. In clandestine whispers while they stood next to one another, he had brought hopeful news that Walter Armitage was still at large, and that a party of their hearties were headed their way.

That gave Abrams a slim but persistent belief that Father Molloy's hastily hatched plan of sedition might have a chance after all. He vowed to be ready if the opportunity to escape came in time, or at least to die with as much dignity and fire in the belly as he could muster. That would, hopefully, spike a rebellion in those docile followers of the cursed traitor Juan Molina, who didn't even have the bollocks to stay behind and gawk at him in his final moments.

Walter Armitage mentally berated himself for not realizing that on an island as small as this one, very little passed the knowledge of the Spaniard. In his haste to catch up with what he was sure now was a landing party from *Devil's Handmaid*, he had stumbled across one of Juan Molina's child couriers. The boy had literally run past him as he was slinking through the brush, so with a quick grab, he had the thoroughly surprised and quaking lad firmly in his grasp, a hand clamped over his mouth.

"*As long as you don't shout or try to get away, I'll not hurt you,*" he whispered, "*But I want what news you have. Will you cooperate?*" At the exaggerated nod, he slipped his hand from over the boy's mouth. "*Speak quietly,*" he warned, a hand on one of his pistols.

The boy's eyes were wide and he trembled. "*More pirates have landed. They come through the jungle from the big shallow bay up north of us. I have to warn our village, so Papi Juan can get everyone away before the shooting starts. Papi said the soldiers there have rifles, and two small ship guns loaded with many balls that can hurt lots of people at once...*"

Cannons with grapeshot! Blast it...their rescuers were walking into a trap.

"*Go hide somewhere safe boy, I'll warn the others,*" he said, letting him go. The little one stared at the pirate a bit confused, and then ran off in the opposite direction.

With a quick glance around, Walter hurried back to where he had left Jez, only to find her missing, with signs of a scuffle. A strange knife lay discarded, and from the appearance of the hilt, it was British Navy issue.

He knew what that meant; there had been a spy tracking the progress of the pirate band through the jungle, and now the enemy had her! For a moment he paused, conflicting emotions running through his mind. They'd treat her as harshly as they did any pirate until they discovered she was female, and then she'd get far worse.

A black rage rose up in him along with the memory of another winsome miss who had ended her life while he was off fighting for England rather than face him with the truth of her forced infidelity with the son of her employer. As young as she was, Jezebel Johnston was ten times the woman that silly little Molly Packer had been, and he was not leaving her in the hands of those soldiers of the country he had been forced to flee. Yet his first duty was to his captain and crew, whose lives were also endangered. Fortunately, they were all headed in the same direction.

Walter Armitage set off resolutely to catch up with the landing party, slipping silently as a ghost through the jungle on their trail, grim determination on his face, and murder in his heart.

CHAPTER EIGHT

As soon as the soldiers hauled the prisoners away, Liam Gulliver came skulking out of cover and began setting charges. The village was all but deserted. Juan Molina's people were either watching the proceedings or keeping an eye out for further incursions from pirates or British ships that could be hailed. Since there were only enough ambulatory pirate hunters to handle the prisoners and counter the potential for attack, the entire settlement was guarded by one seriously injured man, who sat propped up with a pistol. The poor wretch had fallen into a stupor from loss of blood and fever, so had been easy enough to throttle from behind; his body dragged off into the brush.

The idea was simple: a few handmade bombs fashioned from empty calabash tree gourds filled with pebbles and chunks of limestone from the cave he had hidden in. They would not do much damage, but should make some loud noises. A charge of black powder was poured within, a plant fiber wick dipped in melted wax, and the hole sealed round with a wax and lime mixture so that the wick would burn down inside before the powder ignited. Those bombs along with piles of refuse and the sides of huts doused with rum would make a convincing amount of smoke and flame to cause a diversion.

Gully had just straightened up from setting the last charge when the click of a pistol being cocked caught his attention. Immediately, his hands went up and he turned slowly. Juan Molina stood behind him, a great big grin on his fat face, and a loaded gun in each hand.

"You very carelessly forgot to check that man for additional arms my friend. He had been issued two more pistols…one hidden in each boot. Now kindly hand over your own weapons, and then you will show me what you have been up to."

Gully stared him down for a few tense minutes before he nodded in his direction and made as if to surrender his weapons. He took two slow steps toward Molina with the pistols extended butt plates first and laid them down, his cutlass across them; then backed off, hands raised again.

"I see you are no fool, and know when you are beaten. Keep those hands up and do not move a muscle." The fat man had just bent over to pick up the additional weapons when he heard a hissing noise somewhere behind him. Eyes wide, he tried to lurch upright but only managed to upset his balance and landed on hands and knees.

Grunting and straining, he was trying to regain his feet as Gully dove for cover. There were several loud explosions, and bits of sharp rock and rounded pebbles sprayed everywhere. Juan Molina took the lion's share of the nearby blast in his broad backside. It knocked him forward on his face, howling in pain as the hot fragments cut and burned through his loincloth and scarred his nether regions with lacerations and blisters.

Walter Armitage stepped from the shadows and held his cutlass at Molina's neck, a pistol in his other hand. Gully rejoined him, collecting not only his own weapons, but the pistols Molina had confiscated from the dead soldier.

"Well done me bucko," he quipped. Walter grinned back. "I take it our lads are landed?"

"They are, Gully," Walter assured him. "They're well on their way to the rescue of the Captain and whoever else is left alive."

"Aye, that's the best news I've had in two days. Now what 'dye want to do with the likes of himself?" Gully asked, nudging a groaning and cursing Molina with his foot while fingering his cutlass.

"He still might have some use," Armitage insisted. "Besides, his fate is the Dandy Dan's to decide. We'll truss him like the pig he is and stow him for now."

He frowned down at the quailing man who was moaning in discomfort.

"Get on your feet turncoat, because while I'd as lief kill you now as haul you along, the lads may think you'll be a good bargaining chip."

"The English don't care about me," Molina protested in between grunts and squeals of pain as he heaved his bulk upward.

Walter smiled maliciously, his face still blackened from sweat, dirt, and smoke; making it look rather like a demonic snarl. "Well, we do," he said with all the malice he could muster. "Your people here are about to be cheated of one execution. Perhaps they'll settle for another." Juan Molina moaned in angst and put his hands over his ears.

Any further discourse on the topic was interrupted by the sound of gunshots in the distance, along with yells of defiance, and screams of alarm.

"The fun be started, and I'm itching to be part 'n parcel of it," Gully said as he and Walter yanked the big man up, and with a gun in his ribs, marched him out of the village and into the forest.

"As am I," Walter said with vehemence. He prodded a protesting Juan Molina along with the barrel of his pistol.

They left the village headman gagged and tied to a tree with strips of his own ruined loincloth, his bruised and bleeding backside full of welts open to the breeze and already covered with flies.

An islander began to beat a slow rhythm on a log drum, and Dennis Molloy knew they had run out of time. With the execution imminent, the soldiers had taken up their arms and stood ready to fire on any intruders, obviously expecting some outside interference. The next to last prisoner had just been secured in his noose; a scared mixed race youth who had just been captured. Probably the lad's first time at sea, for he bore no tattoos, piercings, or scars, and his voice was low toned and respectful when he spoke.

As they boosted up the captain next to the boy, the priest prayed that Liam Gulliver had finished setting up the diversions they had been concocting half the night. It was his task to arrange them around the perimeter of the village as if it were under attack.

So where were the blasted explosions? It was taking far too long.

"Pardon me," the priest began to the leader of the soldiers with the intention of stalling the procedure, "But that laddie over yon has just been brought in." He indicated Jez with a sweep of his arm. "I've not been given the chance to hear his confession or offer him absolution."

"And you'll not get it, Papist," the man answered with a snarl. "This is a secular matter of the Commonwealth, and you've held us up long enough. One would begin to believe you are in league with these rogues and butchers, the way you carry on about them." That last bit was stated more than a little ominously, and Father Molloy got the message. Interfere again, and he'd be joining these pirates with a noose around his own neck, accused of treason. That would benefit no one!

He put on a shocked and insulted look. "My son, you are sadly mistaken. Of course I have no fondness for their deeds; I'm just trying to save their wretched souls before they meet their Maker."

"Take it up with Him later, and leave us to our work," the man shot back, and then turned to address the crowd while the poles were being withdrawn, leaving the prisoners in their nooses standing on barrels.

"These pirates," said the commander, his voice sounding flat in the afternoon haze, "Are sentenced to death for their crimes against humanity in general, and the British Commonwealth specifically. Along with their ongoing thievery and butchery, they have just attacked and sunk one of our good ships right here in your bay, with the loss of captain, most of the crew, and all equipment. This is an act of open warfare, and so shall not go unpunished! With the power vested in me by The Lord Protector, and the admiralty of the British Navy, I declare them enemies of the state, and deem their lives forfeit."

The log drum rhythm reached a crescendo as he spun and pointed at the first prisoner with his saber. Two men grabbed a shorter pole, and swung it around to shove the barrel from beneath him. They did not get far when there was a resounding blast from the direction of the village, and birds flew up squawking in fright. Everyone dropped and ducked, expecting a cannon ball to go whizzing by. Two more explosions followed it from various directions, along with frantic screams of terror.

"Our village is under attack!" someone shouted. Island people ran yelling for children, friends, and other loved ones who might have remained behind, many fearing the worst. They almost ran into a howling group of pirates swinging cutlasses and axes, who under the cover of the general chaos burst out of the jungle and raced toward the gallows.

"Execute those prisoners, you bloody fools!" their commander yelled and raised his saber, just before his throat and chest sprouted arrows. Eyes wide with surprise, he dropped his blade and fell backwards, dead on the spot. Having carried along his only worldly possessions, a crude but effective bow and a mere handful of arrows, jungle-wise Pakke had slipped in quite close, before clambering quietly up the nearest sturdy tree. Since he was a far better shot with a bow than a pistol and it was a fairly silent weapon, at Walter Armitage's earlier suggestion, he took out the leader of the group first. Military men without someone to rally around fought less efficiently on their own.

Pandemonium ensued as men clashed, and weapons began to bark or slash. It was such a brutal, fast, and furiously fought battle; there was little time to react.

No one was guarding the cannons as Father Molloy slipped up and poured something down each barrel.

Jengo, with his bosom pals pounding along beside him, roared like a beast; an axe in one great hand, a pistol in the other and additional weapons stuck in his sash. The huge and angry Negro took a glancing musket ball from a rifle to the upper arm, which tore free a chunk of flesh and sprayed blood down his side, but he never even slowed. He smashed into a group of soldiers frantically pulling pistols now that their muskets were empty, or desperately attempting to reload. Swinging his axe sideways with one hand, he lopped off arms and severed a neck, and then raised it overhead to cleave one man nearly in half. A saber cut to the outer thigh made him stumble, but that man went down with a smoking hole in his chest from a point blank shot before a back swing could bring the offending blade around again. Covered in gore and laughing like a madman, Jengo pulled a second pistol and shot another soldier before running after one who was trying to frantically reload from the cover of a couple of dead bodies. Two more soldiers nearby clashed blades with three other pirates, one of them Sol.

Armitage came running into the fray behind the rest, and his first pistol barked immediately. One of the English combatants who had drawn on Jengo dropped screaming with his thigh spouting arterial blood, and a slash of a blade to the throat ended his suffering. "I'll get our fellows cut down, you concentrate on taking those gunners out," he called. His acknowledgment was a bloody axe waved briefly before it brained one of the wounded soldiers who couldn't get out of the way fast enough.

"Hard heads you English have," Jengo remarked in his deep and accented voice, having to stop and yank his weapon of choice free of the twitching man's skull.

"You've no idea," Walter said as he slipped up behind Dan Abrams and sawed at his bonds.

Another pistol fired nearby, clipping Sol's ear.

"Owww damn ye, I'll gut ye for that," the scrawny man shrieked before he ran the hapless soldier through with his blade and yanked it backwards, taking a couple floating ribs and part of a lung with him as well as getting a face full of red spray. The man's shriek turned into a bubbling sigh as he sank into sand already pooling red. Sol wasn't powerful, but the curving edge of a cutlass at the end of a running charge could do a lot of damage.

"Fire those blasted cannons, ye damn fools!" the soldier who had tormented Dan Abrams shrieked as Jengo and his remaining men bore down on them. He ripped a musket from a dying man's grasp and shot wildly at Walter Armitage, who was sawing away at his captain's noose after freeing his feet and hands. The angle was wrong, and the hastily aimed firearm kicked. Walter ducked as the shot whistled past him and three other prisoners but, unfortunately, took Crazy Tom in the side. In his agony, he managed to kick his own barrel free and effectively hung himself.

Dan Abrams had spit out his gag as soon as the cording was cut. The noose was off his neck now, and he jumped down off the barrel, landing on his burned and broken toed bare feet in the sand without so much as a groan.

"He'll bloody well pay for that! Just give me that blasted blade Walter, and then get Jonas and Jez out of harm's way before they wind up doing the hangman's jig as well." Armitage handed over the navy issue knife he had picked up along with his last pistol, and jumped down to scavenge a saber from the man Sol had killed before running back to the prisoners on the gallows.

"Walter!" Jez called in a high pitched voice full of fear. "They're turning the cannons our way. Set me free and I'll release Jonas. Get our captain out of here, he's hurt and won't run fast."

He cut her bonds and handed up the cutlass, and then turned to look for another weapon. Dan Abrams had waved him off, as he had found another weapon and was about to join in the fight. Father Molloy was herding terrified village women and children out of harm's way, and Gully…with his belt stuck full of firearms, as well as Pakke holding a pistol, were guarding any village men and youths who looked like they might be inclined to join the fray on the wrong side of things.

"I'll shoot the first one 'o ye as makes a move to intervene. This be our fight, and naught any o' yer business," he warned them. They could sort out who was to blame later on.

Of the rest of the rescue party, only Jengo, Sol, and one other man had survived, and they were actively engaged with the last four of the pirate hunters. The remainder of the combatants laid dead or dying, except for the soldier who had taunted their captain and got spit on, and the lame man with the crutch. Each stood behind a small 2 pound deck cannon; both now aimed toward each end of the gallows. It might not be a direct hit, but if they bore shells or grapeshot that would certainly kill most if not all of the remaining pirates at that distance.

"FIRE!" shouted the more able bodied of the two, and he touched off the short fuse as the other man did the same.

The farther cannon made a roar and a dull bang before the barrel simply bulged out. Before its sole attendant could make more than a few limping gallops away, the back end exploded, taking the hobbling man, who was directly behind it, 25 feet across the sand in a long gory streak, and left him blown apart.

The second cannon only fizzled and went out.

"What the blazes ails this bloody thing?" the would-be gunner snarled as Dan Abrams, armed with a bent short sword he'd picked up somewhere, came stalking at him.

"Maybe you should take a peek inside," Dandy Dan said quietly, an unfriendly smile spreading across his face. The man stepped forward, and knowing his pistol was empty, drew his sword.

"I'm no fool, ye blasted sea scum. And I can take the likes of ye in a fair fight."

"Is that so?" Abrams said, as he drew a loaded pistol he'd picked up from another body, and shot the man in the stomach. The distance between them was too far to kill him, but his would-be opponent dropped his sword and grabbed his bleeding abdomen, howling like an animal. Abrams smiled without mirth as he advanced.

"Now, who in the world told you I'd fight fair? Was it one of my lads that you took such delight in *tormenting* until they were sobbing for their mothers? Or was it your bloody commander over there, stuck full of arrows like a lady's pincushion? Perhaps now you understand what it means to *suffer...*"

He walked slowly up to the man, who was groaning in pain, and disarmed him. He picked up the soldier's own saber, looking it over carefully.

"Mercy!" the soldier pleaded in a raw whisper, his face white, his breath coming in gasps. Dandy Dan looked down at him with a sardonic smile.

"Mercy... is that what you want? You, who had none for others, now beg it for yourself? I shall consider it for a bit while I examine this sword you waved at me just a moment ago."

He lifted it before him and studied is closely, seemingly oblivious to the ongoing clashes around him. "Ah, but what a fine weapon this is, and well made. It has a skillfully crafted basket hilt, and wrapped horn for a grip." He tried a few experimental slashes with it, showing graceful form in spite of his own painful injuries. "Very good counterbalance weight in the pommel. I rather fancy it, because it's so totally wasted on you," he pointed the tip at the man's nose, "who have appointed yourself judge and jury as long as you are on the winning end of a situation. Without it, you're just another mewling coward begging for your life."

"Take it," the wounded man whispered, "Just don't... Don't ye leave me to die here like a dog."

"Oh, of course not, that would be quite cruel, wouldn't it?" Abram's eyes wore a faraway look tinged with an edge of insanity. "It would be horrid to have the wild creatures come to feast on you, with you still alive enough to feel their teeth ripping out your guts. Sadly, I'll admit I'm a bit done in and in somewhat of a hurry, so I don't have the gumption to carry you off. Yet we mustn't leave you unarmed..."

At the dawning hope in the man's eyes, Dandy Dan smiled brightly, but without warmth.

"So I thank you for your generosity in the gift of your fine sword, and here, you can have this one," he added, shoving the bent blade he'd been carrying into the wounded man's bloody abdomen and giving it a few slow twists.

The wounded soldier writhed and shrieked in agony as his eyes rolled white, and then he shuddered and went silent, gazing blankly at some unseen world. Dan Abrams' coldly contemptuous stare watched every moment, his slight smile pitiless and cruel. Satisfied the other man was dead; he sheathed the fancy saber and dusted his palms.

"A far faster end than a torturing bastard like you deserves, especially after all the bellowing and begging my boys did. I heard you laughing over them with your companions every night, and I hope this brings their shades some recompense. Say hello to the Devil for me; we're related you know..."

He limped away, sidestepping bodies already bloating beneath the merciless Caribbean sun.

"Come away lads," he called to Sol, Jengo, Jez, and whoever else could hear him. "We have need of food, drink, and medical attention, and then we have a ship to catch."

It had been a costly trip so far. Almost a third of the crew injured or dead, the ship in need of repairs, and their permanently limping captain stood to lose face with his men over the whole bloody business. Piracy was supposed to be lucrative, and while Dan Abrams had always provided well for his crew, some of them were grumbling that he'd lost his magic touch.

When *Devil's Handmaid* was moored once more in the great bay, not an English soldier remained alive and all the dead had been burned on the beach where they had fallen, stacked in a great pyre. Father Molloy became the village headman. Juan Molina, with his broad backside patched up, was taken bound as a prisoner aboard the longboat, where he lay draped across the middle like a beached whale as several men rowed him out to the ship. He was hauled up with tackle mounted on a yardarm, and locked in a stuffy storeroom with a cot and a bucket, crying and complaining every time someone opened the door to toss him some wormy hardtack and a skin of watered rum.

That anything the *Harrier* carried should be salvaged before the storm season started was on many minds, but the wily pirate captain didn't plan to linger in the area. His men wanted real plunder, and so far this trip had been lean of it.

"I've plenty of boys and idle men here to assist me in recovery," the priest told Dan Abrams quietly. "I'll set them to work bringing up whatever they can get from the wreckage. You're welcome to come back and look it over."

"Keep whatever you find of use, but set aside anything you don't need," Abrams told him. "Whatever pittance of gold that was supposedly aboard rightfully belongs to them." He swept his arm dramatically about, indicating the village. "It's not enough for us to bother with in all honesty, because we're after far richer prizes. I will advise you, a wise man would hasten to raise any watertight powder kegs, all the available shot, and especially those cannons. Get them first and foremost, before they begin to rot. The British know where you are, and they will eventually send an envoy to question what happened here. One of the 2 pounders left on the beach is ruined, and the other will be a dangerous chore to unplug, according to my gunnery master. Those ship's guns will be far more powerful anyway, and there are more of them. Working all that back ashore should keep your people busy and out of trouble the entire season."

"I'll make it a priority," the priest promised. To his relief, all working firearms had been confiscated by the pirates, in case any of Molina's supporters decided to rally.

After making arrangements for a future rendezvous with the good Father and his flock of wary expatriates and their families, the pirates set sail for the smaller islands, which, according to the priest, were entirely wild with no known inhabitants. Gully had taken a ball to the shoulder just above his right lung, which had to be dug out with a heated knife. With copious rum he was back on his feet, directing others to their tasks with his left hand while his right arm hung useless in a sling.

They took most of the day sailing around the eastern tip of Juan Molina's island. Dan Abrams wanted to be sure that there were no more British troops waiting over where they had landed before attacking the pirates ashore. The next morning found them moored within sight of the larger of the two smaller islands, which was reputed to have inland fresh water sources. While carpenter and mate more permanently patched the *Devil's Handmaid*, the longboat went out again. Jez and Pakke got to do their hunting along with Walter Armitage and Jengo, restocking the larder with smoked meat of all kinds and feasting on sea turtle soup for days. Turtle shells traded well, which was a boon. After the refitting and hauling food aboard, and refilling the water barrels, they were sailing off again toward the Straits of Florida.

"Them caves on the isle wit' the great bluff, they'd make wonderful fine storage, they would," Andy Boone commented as he and Jez watched the smaller of the three pass away to the rear until it was no more than a speck in the distance. He'd been ashore to boucan the meat, which, properly smoked, would last longer. "Ye could 'ide a bloomin' army o' scalawags in there, and all the booty a man could take in a lifetime. We oughta look into it, dontcha reckon?"

"Might be a good idea," Jez said thoughtfully. The huge stone cliff on one end was a great spot for a fortress, as none could climb it without being seen. It was a place she would not forget, a small island to be sure, but well riddled with dry caves and other interesting hiding places, and supplied with water and a ready source of food.

"Eh, I gotta go feed the pris'ner afore 'e begins a screaming bloody murder about bein' starved. That blasted Neville be allus makin' 'imself scarce these days," Andy complained before he stomped off.

Jez went off to her own duties. She had won more praise for her quick thinking and bravado in the face of danger, and now that he was injured, Gully had taken her on to train as his own Master Mate. It gave her some status amongst the crew, but also gained her the ill-favored attention of those who had been aboard far longer and resented this green lubber youth who was always somehow making himself noteworthy. It grated on some nerves that a mere boy always seemed to be two steps ahead of his far

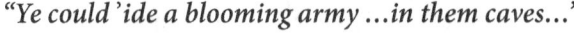
"Ye could 'ide a blooming army ...in them caves..."

more experienced shipmates, and that the captain, Gully, James Reuben, and Walter Armitage all thought so highly of him. Sides were being taken, and Jezebel Johnston found herself ostracized at times, for reasons she could not quite fathom.

"Well, I say it makes no sense. What're we doin' with that damn Spaniard aboard?" Sol asked bitterly one night as he and several others who were fed up with Dan Abrams were passing a rum bottle around down on the orlop deck. "It's not like the blasted bellyaching fool is of any use, other than eatin' and drinkin' enough for three," he continued bitterly, picking at the dirty rag bandage on his mangled ear. "He shoulda been hung from the bowsprit or shot and tossed overboard to feed the fish."

"He spends enough time bendin' our ears wit' his girlish whinin'," Luke the Limper commented as he wiped his mouth on the back of his hand and handed the bottle over.

"Well, 'e'd holler louder iffen 'e thought 'e'd be rescued by 'is mates crost the way," Spike, the wizened man who worked as the carpenter's helper, suggested. He watched the bottle go round with eagerness in his rheumy blue eyes and hands that shook.

"He would," Sol agreed. "Hey Mouse, cain't ye put some of Andy's rat poison in his gruel or somethin'?"

Young Neville shook his head as he put the bottle to his lips, because there was no way he was taking the blame for poisoning a man. Finally over his seasickness, he now sat regularly with the malcontents aboard, and had ventured to take a few small but adventurous sips. Galley helper had been his duty while Jez was ashore, and now that she had proved herself an able buccaneer and was training daily on sails, in stores, and with weapons, he was stuck down there with Rat Stew Andy Boone, who watched him closely, and berated him daily for being slow and clumsy. These men had accepted him, and nicknamed him 'Mouse', on account of his uneasy association with Andy, as well as his small size and timid nature. He didn't like that moniker, but it gave him a way to fit in.

Neville swallowed carefully, letting the burn go down his throat into his belly. "Andy keeps his poison locked up," he answered, "On account of it having killed the Captain's last cat." He shoved the bottle into the hand of Puggy, who was impatiently reaching for it.

"No matter lads; according to Gully, the Spanish might find him most in'erestin'," since he's a deserter," bulldog-faced Puggy countered in his gruff voice before he took a copious gulp and passed the bottle to the silent man simply know as Ezra, who was supposedly a mute.

"Meh, what should they care?" Sol countered with a contemptuous sneer. "He's well past enlistment age, and they'd not find bloody armor to fit his fat carcass."

"Armitage says Fat Juan was a' officer. They'd likely shoot 'im anyhow," Puggy explained further. He was a peaceful man by nature and a good sailor, but had never been popular with the captain for his reluctance to fight. The bottle went on, as did the debate.

"We could have saved them the time and powder," Luke the Limper quipped and they all laughed.

Blackhair Dougie spat on the floor between his bare foot and peg before he took his swig, and he swallowed noisily before he spoke. "Bah... most o' the lads b'lieve Cap'n's somewhat addled from his torture, but I say Dandy Dan was allus queer like this. "E jist favors some o'er others, and there be no rhyme and reason to it. Notice 'e made it back in one piece? By kissin' the arse o' that Spaniard, no doubt. 'E owes 'im a favor, 'e does."

"Gully and Wally come back all right," Puggy pointed out, "And in far better shape, both of 'em, than the rest."

Dougie glared at him under his straggling black locks. "Don't be stirrin' up trouble where thar ain't none Puggy! Gully got shot ye know. At least 'e was willin' te fight, 'cause 'e knew the lads captured were bein' tormented somethin' fierce afore they gived up the ghost, but the priest talked 'im inta setting the bombs instead, and that got ever'one freed. I'd vote 'im cap'n in a' 'eartbeat; 'e's got right more sense 'n the barmy fool we be stuck wit' now. Not so wit' Wally though. Crack shot as 'e is, 'e run right off and left em all te face it alone."

He guzzled his share to let that sink in, and satisfied at the amount of angry rumbling that caused, he handed the bottle back to Sol. Clearing his throat, Dougie continued, "Jonas claims as Armitage spent most of his time hidin' out with that pretty boy, Jez. He di'n't even come out of the bleeding jungle until the striplin' finally got hisself captured."

"Wot's the damned attraction?" a red haired and bearded man they called Rusty said. "Wally was on an island full of half naked women and yet he fancies to run off with a boy?"

"Whatya think, ye damned fool?" Sol snapped. There were winks all around, and a few of them smiled knowingly. Sol accepted the bottle and guzzled the last of it, and then popped the cork on a second one with the tip of his knife and it began making the rounds again.

Neville saw his opportunity to discredit Jez, whom he was beginning to hate. Jez, who was so perfect at everything. Jez, who could sweet talk enemy captains and shoot like a soldier. Always Jez! He took a larger swig of the rum when it came his way, almost choked, and then wiped his mouth before passing it on. This time the alcohol bolstered his courage.

"W-what... what if J-Jez isn't really a... b-boy?" he said in a tremulous voice. The other men looked at him oddly, and a couple scoffed, but Sol's eyes narrowed and brightened.

"What d'ya mean there Mouse?" he demanded.

Well, the cat was halfway out of the bag, might as well pull it free. Neville Felton took a deep breath and blurted, "I seen Jez go down to the bilge to piss one time. Jez is a girl."

There were indrawn breaths all around. "You sure o' that? Might be jist wishferl thinkin'," Blackhair Dougie said with a laugh.

"Yeah, our Mousie's growing a li'l spar in 'is drawers is all," Puggy chimed in, slapping Neville on the back.

"I know what I saw!" Neville retorted with a pale face flushed red from both embarrassment and alcohol.

"Cain't be...that Jez, why 'e's tall as a beanpole and there's no teats on 'im," Rusty interjected.

Neville looked right at Sol. "I'm *positive*," he said with conviction bolstered by rum. "I know what lady parts look like, and sometimes there's been blood in his pail."

"Eh, that could be jist the blinkin' flux," Luke the Limper scoffed. "Gets worse iffen yer bein' buggered."

"I don't think so," Neville countered. "It looked like woman's blood; all clotty." He had been raised in a genteel household, but was regularly left to his own devices. Being nosy, he'd spent his time peeping where he shouldn't. The servants openly gossiped, and often talked about the cruder facts of life. He'd spied on a few trysts as well. Consequently, Neville knew far more about female anatomy than a well-raised boy had a right to.

There was a general outcry for Mouse to hush himself, that no one wanted to hear about such things, yet Sol's smile was triumphant.

"This could right well be useful information you be givin' us tonight Mouse. Lads, we need to keep this quiet for now, but I got me an idea..."

They spoke quietly, huddled together for another hour before dispersing to go sleep it off.

CHAPTER NINE

evil's Handmaid passed warily to the south west of Cuba, still within what was considered Spain's territorial waters. Now and then they would spot an inconsequential sail on the horizon. They kept the Spanish flag up, hoping that at a distance; its raggedy state would not be noticeable. It had been heavily patched at the suggestion of Juan Molina, who advised that if the colors were matched carefully, it would only be up close that the tattered look of the thing would give away their ruse. As a prisoner aboard, the wily Spaniard was more than willing to offer his captors any advice that might make him seem valuable and consequently keep him alive longer.

Days later, they had entered the Straits of Florida, and as luck would have it, encountered their first Spanish treasure ship. A lumbering nao, *Gloria de Sevilla*, had been making her way from Veracruz, headed toward Havana. Once she left port, she would join the rest of the Flota; heading toward the Azores, and then on to Spain. Low in the water, the lightly armed ship was wallowing along, loaded down with a heavy cargo. It was likely silver, considering her route, though no doubt there were other things aboard. She was closely followed by the small war galleon *El Halcón*, which had three masts behind the bowsprit and two decks of cannons. It appeared to be far more maneuverable and seaworthy. The two ships had lagged well behind the rest of the fleet; likely because of the leakiness of the nao.

This was the kind of opportunity Dan Abrams lived for! "Lady Luck smiles on us at last," he said enthusiastically as he shut his spyglass with a flourish. He turned toward Ping to issue his orders. Gully, who had been nearby, moved in closer to hear.

"Stay apart a safe distance, but don't let her out of your sight. I've no doubt we'll find a way to cut her off before she joins the rest."

"That warship might prove a bit of a problem," Gully remarked quietly. He'd had enough of a glimpse of the guns aboard to realize that the small Spanish galleon had been equipped with more than a few 24 pounders.

"She might at that," Dan Abrams admitted, and his look was thoughtful and guarded. While evading or disabling such a nautical adversary was no easy matter, he was also well aware that the crew was restless and some of them had grown surly. Pirate captains who did not produce much in the way of prizes would soon find themselves replaced…or worse. So he spoke with more confidence than he felt, knowing that he would likely be overheard. "Perhaps we can delay her somehow. We've a few days to devise something of that nature. Let us keep pace at a distance, though we shall wait until we have a solid plan of action. In the meantime I will consult with our prisoner, and see if he can offer us some insight as to the best way to approach this." He shuffled off barefooted, still unable to wear anything on his feet with the broken and mangled toes remaining swollen and painful.

While Dan Abrams had considerable experience with raiding the Spanish, it mostly came from the pillaging of colonial towns or taking on regional merchant vessels. He had never ventured very far north of the Caribbean Sea, and normally gave the highly armed ships of the treasure fleet a wide berth. Unfortunately, the local pickings had become thin as more privateers were commissioned, and the competition amongst full time freebooters had risen. The real wealth to be made was in taking on the larger ships, with their hefty cargoes worth a king's ransom.

This season's crew was the biggest and boldest bunch he'd ever had aboard, for the workload and danger they would face was greatly increased. Dandy Dan had no doubt he'd lose more of them before they were through. That was expected amongst all freebooters. As long as they were victorious, the prize was worth the sacrifices, and the numbers of dead and wounded were not too extensive, none would complain.

Juan Molina might be a two time traitor and he was far from trustworthy, but he was a ready source of information. He meticulously explained what he understood of the Flota and the trade system, offering his insight each day in 'just-recalled' tidbits, as a way to continuously bargain for his life. This was what had prompted Dan Abrams to take him aboard, for the wily fat man had a native Spaniard's knowledge of the inner workings of his country of origin's colonial system along with the inevitable consequences of their perpetual cycle of greed and glut. No doubt he'd had some contact with other pirates as well, and talk always ran high as liquor flowed.

A lively exchange existed all through the central isthmus and southernmost of the great western continents that Spain had proclaimed her own. Silk, pearls, spices, and other gems from the countries of the Orient were being transported across the Pacific by ship, and then hauled overland through Central and South America from west to northeast via mule train. A portion of this cargo would trade high locally before the remainder was shipped out. The Spanish colonial ports and their outlying areas were redolent of wealth even in those latter years, though the mother country was suffering from inflation due to the continuing largesse arriving from the New World, devaluing the currency at home. The colonies were only allowed to legally trade with Spain, and in return, they were taxed heavily on any European merchandise they coveted. Since Spain had little manufacturing she was forced to purchase goods from neighboring nations.

Ships that made these transoceanic trips were subjected to all kinds of weather conditions and extensive wear and tear. Yet quick turnaround time was important when there were wars to finance and voyages took months to complete, so they were quickly repaired and refitted, and sent out again.

Without proper maintenance, much of the celebrated merchant fleet of Spain had decreased in number, and the remainder grew timeworn and battered. Many of the ships leaked, and were continually patched to keep them serviceable. It seemed the Spanish Crown had her regal attention fixed on other things, such as spitting in the eye of France, so the demand was for even greater wealth. Saber rattling took a lot of financial impetus, as did the ostentatious public persona of her ruling class. As the sad state of her treasure hauling galleons was regularly neglected, it became harder for them all to remain on a consistent schedule. Some were always lagging behind. Even so, the treasure fleets were still guarded by a few gunships of far better condition, and accompanied by messenger and supply vessels. It would be folly for a lone ship to attack them once assembled, but this laggard was fair game. For a bold sea wolf such as Dandy Dan Abrams, this was a situation that could well be readily exploited.

"So you see," Juan Molina exclaimed as he was brought on deck, his gradually decreasing bulk encased in a sleeveless jerkin of crudely cut and sewn canvas and broad slops of linen duck borrowed from Jengo and suspended with rope to hang below his flabby gut, "You have only to wait and watch, and some opportunity will occur. That ship," he waved a pudgy hand in the direction of the nao, which was well ahead of them, "is not going to move very fast unless someone in Havana plugs up more carefully whatever is leaking."

"Aye but to do a proper job o' that, they'd have to offload first, and then take the time to pump her out and dry-dock or careen her," Gully interjected. "It looks to be well below the waterline. Without removing the weight, they'll naught be in a fat hurry to unstop it to take a better look, lessen they want te founder."

"So we shall for the short term remain patient and see what happens," Abrams agreed, "though it irks me to no end that I can't seem to find a solid second vessel worth hanging onto!" He stomped off in a huff with Juan Molina trailing behind him, imploring that he should be allowed to take a daily turn on deck in exchange for his voluntary cooperation.

Jez watched them go from where she was nimbly climbing the shrouds to tighten some lanyards. She painstakingly reeved them through a couple deadeyes, taking up slack in the rigging, her hands finally starting to callus over from the constant contact with rough cordage soaked with salt spray. From up that high, with the wind in her ears, she could only catch snatches of what was being said below, and the higher she climbed, the less she heard.

She squinted out over the water, noting the position of the two ships that they had been pacing, well off on the horizon. Walter said that somewhere to the southeast was the Spanish colony at Havana. That was where those ships appeared to be heading.

She knew Dan Abrams was not fool enough to follow them into a trap. The wise thing would be to cut them off from one another...preferably at night. The war galleon had a lot of gun ports, and the idea of facing that level of bombardment made her stomach flutter. She could not forget the carnage on the deck of the Portuguese carrack they had taken earlier in the voyage. Men had fallen from rigging to deck or water in pieces, spilling their blood and insides. It was a gory business, this fighting life, and you had to get hardened to it.

For Walter, she could do that. They talked sometimes about having their own ship, with he the captain, and her his quartermaster. They would do things differently, get better crews, and keep them loyal. Neither one of them openly criticized Dan Abrams, but things aboard were not going very smoothly, and Dandy Dan's quicksilver personality and borderline fanaticism with goading and defying the English was making it hard for men to remain steadfast. He could have had a pardon for himself and his crew had he accepted a letter of marque and reprisal.

She wanted to know much more about this latest plan of their captain than what little she had overheard, and no doubt Walter would be in the thick of things. There should be a gathering of officers soon, before it was presented to the crew for a vote. Walter would give her the details. He'd taken to meeting her for quick trysts in odd places they agreed upon ahead of time. Tonight it was behind where the longboat was stowed. They had learned to be quiet about it, but neither one could go an entire day without at least a few quick kisses and some frantic fondling. And, if the rest of the crew were drunk enough, it often went much further.

The decision was made that evening, during the second dog watch, to continue to shadow the lone treasure ship and her single escort at a respectable distance so as not to alarm anyone, but not to interfere with her reaching port. That would allow her bring aboard additional cargo or passengers in Havana, hopefully fattening the prize they'd take. Once she was back in open waters, they'd hit her hard sometime after dark... definitely before the two ships were able to rejoin the main host, which should be amassing well ahead, out in the strait.

Based on the information they were able to wrangle out of Juan Molina as far as what to expect the defenses of the treasure ship to be, James Reuben suggested they send a boarding party on the longboat out after the treasure nao late at night, and then let those remaining on *Devil's Handmaid* take on the war galleon. That would separate the two vessels, and possibly capture them both unawares.

"I don't have to tell you that the crew has been grumbling about how poor the trip has been so far. They've got the itch to cause a commotion in order to be heard, and that always leads to trouble," the chief gunner warned.

"Yes, I understand all that," Dan Abrams said with resignation in his sigh. It had not been a very lucrative trip so far and pirates were not known for their patience. "We shall try it your way then James, and if we do overthrow their escort without seriously damaging the ship in the process, perhaps then we'll have a large enough hold to take all the goods. We could certainly make use of those cannon!"

"I'm thinking ye'll be wantin' Jengo and what's left of his lads, maybe that loudmouth Sol, and the tall boy Jez for the boardin' party, with our arms master a'leadin' them," Gully interjected. He turned to look at the man seated next to him. "Whatcha say to that Walter, ye rascal? Ye up to a challenge?"

Walter Armitage glanced dubiously at the quartermaster. Liam Gulliver was a man he respected, but this sounded like long odds and wishful thinking, and he was surprised the sage and savvy older man had so readily agreed to it. He understood that Gully and Dan Abrams had traveled together for years and were about as close friends as any pirates could be. To renew his status with the crew, Dandy Dan had to act boldly or he'd be voted out as captain and someone else would take over. Gully must be worried about that as well.

"We've done crazier things," Walter admitted with a sigh. "I wouldn't take Jez though, sh...he's still a green youth." He'd almost slipped and given away their most intimate secret.

"Yes, but one who shoots remarkably well, has a decent hand to any blade, is fast thinking, and shows great mettle under pressure. I say you'd be a fool *not* to include him," James Reuben insisted with a strange look at his cabin mate. He knew Walter Armitage well enough to ignore the rumors circulating that he was buggering the lad. They'd spent enough shore time together over the past few seasons for him to be sure that Walter completely relished the intimate company of women.

So why was he always protecting the boy? Perhaps he was the son of one of his shoreline dalliances. If so, Armitage was being cozened. Other than a similarity in height, the boy bore him little resemblance.

The meeting broke up shortly after they'd toasted the adventure ahead, and all went off to their duties or bunks. Quiet and thoughtful at the end, Walter said he'd take a turn on deck; but whatever solace he was seeking was awaiting him elsewhere.

"Well, at least we'll be fighting side by side," Jez reminded Walter triumphantly in a throaty murmur. Something about facing danger together again made her very aroused. She ran a hand down beneath his loosened shirt, feeling the ridged muscles along with a few old scars, and toyed with the front laces of his breeches. They did not dare to completely disrobe for lovemaking, in case one of them was called for. They always faced the possibility of being caught, and so things were done rather clandestinely while half dressed, which to Jez's opinion, added spice to the whole excitement of the carnal act.

Walter knew better than to push her away...that would just make Jez all the more determined to have him. She was a wanton minx for a young woman just barely past her girlhood. He allowed her to do as she willed while his mind wandered to the days ahead. He didn't like taking Jez with him on the boarding party, because he knew he'd be half-distracted in looking out for her, and that could get a man killed. Yet she'd be no safer aboard the pirate vessel, not if they were taking on that war galleon bristling with armaments. Both ventures entailed a terrible risk.

He had to get his mind off that pervasive sense of doom. A man was half dead when he contemplated his own end, and she'd need all her wits about her as well. Instead he slid his hand inside her shirt and cupped a small but firm breast. That elicited a shiver and some rather enticing squirming, making him smile in the starlit darkness.

"This could very well turn out ugly Jez," he warned her in breathless words as she straddled him and began to roll her hips in time with the pitch of the deck. He fought for control, keeping his voice low and even-toned only by sheer will. "Even if our lads manage to keep that gunship at bay, at least some of the men aboard the treasure ship will be armed, and they have a few deck guns. If they see us before we board their ship, they'll blow us out of the water. Once we've made our presence known, you will have to be completely intimidating. We shoot to kill. You can't freeze up, because they will certainly fire first or gut you on sight."

"I'll do my part," she promised in a gasping whisper with just an edge of ecstatic strain in it, and then allowed him to roll her over onto her back again, digging her fingers into sweaty linen and meeting his frenzied assault with equal ferocity, hoping that he'd forget all about anything but her. Life was for the living, love was for the taking, and the devil could have tomorrow!

Pirates, Jezebel Johnston had learned, lived for the moment.

The Florida Straits was a relatively narrow deep water passage off the southeast edge of the North American continent that linked the Gulf of Mexico with the Atlantic Ocean. This was the root of the great Gulf Stream, that warm and swift ocean current that could hustle ships along toward their destinations in Europe or Africa. Here at its very source were many small, rocky islands, where a careful navigator could find a place to hide. Dan Abrams chose one in Spanish territory, northeast of Havana, where they would be able to spot ships going out into the channel but would not be readily noticeable.

A small headland dotted with mangroves hid a tiny bay. They dropped the light anchor to prevent excessive drifting, and set watches out on the point to alert the crew if a sail was spotted. The idea was to remain under cover nearby while staying within sighting and sailing distance of the channel. They would have but one chance to cut this duo off from joining up with the greater convoy that should be amassing somewhere farther north. A quick ship like *Devil's Handmaid* could sail between them after dark and cut the treasure ship off from her escort, the boarding party in the longboat taking the nao unaware, and seizing control before she could fire a distress signal. It was risky, but what in the world of buccaneering wasn't?

These were hazards Dan Abrams understood well, but he also knew the Flota was far less organized than the Spanish would have anyone believe. He prided himself of his ability to stay abreast of whatever news he could gain while in ports or picking the brains of captives and other captains. It had stood him well in the past to be able to see the big picture and not just spend his time ashore after taking a prize wallowing in a drunken stupor until he was broke again, as many of the brethren did. He had a plan in place to take a big haul this time, and then retire for the season someplace where money bought all the good things life allowed. He'd had enough misery for one trip.

It was time for bold action!

They had been biding their time for a six day stretch when the word came early in the morning that two sets of sails moving away from Havana had been sighted, both vessels flying a Spanish jack. It was high time to move in on them, and so all hands worked feverishly in order to get back out into the open ocean before the opportunity passed them by. The anchor was quickly hauled aboard as the shore watch came racing back; the canvas set as additional men took their stations. Ping announced that it would be a foggy night after a warm day, as the weather was going to cool off abruptly, and there'd be little but a thin breeze for hours. No one had any idea how he knew all that, but the Chinese helmsman was a skilled navigator who was seldom wrong when it came to anything dealing with wind and water.

"Then we *must* hit them tonight," Dan Abrams said eagerly.

"Beggin' pardon Cap'n," Duffy said when he came aboard, the sharp eyed little man having climbed a mangrove to act as lookout, "But I noticed somethin' whilest I was out there a spottin' those ships. That nao, she be riding a bit higher, wit'out the list she 'ad. I seen all the gunports on the starboard side o' that old scow be closed up tight, though they still 'ave the aft guns out. I couldna see the bow rakers 't'all. So I'm thinking to meself, well, I betcha they offloaded their bigger guns in Havana port… sold 'em fer a pretty price, and lightened the load fer te counterbalance wats in the hold."

"I'd say that'd be a good bet," Gully commented, and when asked, James Reuben agreed.

"It makes sense, for they have a dedicated escort, which is well manned and properly gunned. You'd only fire the aft guns if you were being chased, and their weight back there adds a bit of low counterbalance to that high sterncastle. If you're going to join a convoy and cross the ocean, there's no sense in overloading that leaky tub with additional heftiness she might not need. There was nothing very contemporary aboard, from what I noted previously anyway." He gave a disdainful sniff, for if there was one thing James Reuben believed in, it was the quality of his guns.

"Well that will make our job a bit easier now, won't it lads?" Dan Abrams said with a devilish smile.

They sailed before midday, making a course north/northeast to get ahead of the quarry, with the intention of circling back and cutting between the two ships as night fell.

All decks were a flurry of activity as more sail was piled on, guns were readied, and the magazine was foraged for weapons, powder, shot, axes, and blades. Grenados and 'stink pots'…an Andy Boone specialty…were assembled, with many passed out amongst those who would comprise the boarding party; the rest stockpiled to be used by the remaining company if it came down to fighting hand-to-hand with the galleon's crew. There was hearty laughter and jesting with a macabre edge to it, as men who regularly faced the specter of death and dismemberment are accustomed to relieving the tension of the impending battle by making light of it.

Jez joined in where she could, but always her eyes were on Walter, and her thoughts strayed toward a future where they sailed together in more peaceful times, maybe having a plantation of their own someday on an island that was not being continually raided by others. By hanging onto those dreams she got through the pre-battle jitters without dwelling too heavily on the possibility of losing her first great love, or her own life.

Racing before wind and tide, the water foaming and bubbling up against the hull, they were well ahead of the slow nao by sunset. As darkness began to fall, a fog did come up and the wind began to drop off. Dan Abrams had Ping change course as soon as they were out of sight. They club-hauled by dropping the kedge anchor to slow and turn the vessel, and then circled well up to the north and west, with the more experienced sailors gradually changing tack from larboard to starboard before the wind died altogether. *Devil's Handmaid* almost stalled dead before she caught a crosswind to full the sail to bring her back around. By dark fall they had come within sight again but kept their distance with the lanterns off, and had begun to sail parallel with the nao, as if seeking to join up.

As the stars became visible, the war galleon spotted that maneuver and closed in with the nao, halving the distance between the two ships, and cutting right into their intended path. Dan Abrams swore, and had them slow up and drop behind the warship as a sign of respect. There was no way to get between the Spanish ships without seeming aggressive and putting themselves in immediate peril.

"What's the plan now? Walter Armitage asked as he stepped up to the quarterdeck after being summoned. Juan Molina had been standing with Abrams, and they'd been in some sort of heated discussion as he approached.

"They're onto us, I'm afraid," the captain said with irritation coloring his low voice as they walked away from an ingratiating and all-too-helpful prisoner. They stopped at the stern and Dan Abrams leaned wearily on the taffrail, looking over the starlit ocean behind them starting to become obscured by fog coming out of the islets and cays. Walter stood half turned to keep an eye on the helm as well as their erstwhile captive. Both spoke in low voices that would not be overheard.

"How good is your Spanish?" Dan Abrams inquired thoughtfully.

Walter Armitage snorted. "I know enough to make myself understood if I want a bed, a wench, or someone to surrender. Why?" He stretched cramped muscles in his shoulders and flexed his arms, clenching and splaying out fingers. He had a very unsettled feeling about what the answer would be.

Abrams sighed. "I suspected as much. That bilge rat of a Spaniard claims the galleon is flying a special jack that indicates an important personage is aboard. He thinks we should hoist the parley flag and then hail her, and claim to have a message from the leader of the fleet. He says that must be obeyed and they will slow down so that we can contact them. He's seen that speaking trumpet that I took from the Portuguese slave ship, and says we should hail them from a distance."

"He doesn't miss much, does he?"

"Apparently not." Abrams turned to catch his arms master's gaze, his eyes glittering in the starlight reflected off the waves. "Of course, he does have a point...one good look at the likes of us and they'd know whom and what they're dealing with. Molina has volunteered to address them for us, but knowing we'd understand no more than a fraction of anything he had to say, I said I would give it some consideration before I made a decision."

He turned and faced Walter. "I don't trust him, but we're running out of time."

"I don't like this idea much at all," Walter said with some certainty, "yet it might work, if we move fast enough. We'd have to let them get terribly close to pull it off though. They'll likely send a jolly boat out anyway, rather than risk their ship, and their guns would be trained on us the entire time. Once they get close enough, they'll know it was a ruse and we'll be food for powder. Better to pull away now while we can," Walter advised.

"Certainly it would be less risky to retreat," Abrams said flatly, "But this might be our only chance to take a large prize this season, and with the crew all fired up, we've got to give them something. The galleon will halt at least until they investigate us, and that could buy us valuable time, if you and your men are up to pulling swiftly, well out in the dark. If you do manage to take over that wallowing scow they're guarding, you could force them to fire on the galleon; they'd not expect *that*."

He leaned back against the rail. "Can you bring this off for us Walter?" he asked, using his arms master's given name for the first time ever. It meant Walter Armitage had earned the respect of his captain, and was accorded the privilege of being one of his trusted few.

"We'll manage," Walter answered against his better judgment. "They're all strong and hearty lads I've chosen, ready to fight or die," he added, though his mind was mostly on Jezebel Johnston. What they were about to attempt was even riskier than he first expected, for they'd have to slip past the gunship in the dark to get to the nao.

Dan Abrams put a hand on his arm. "Stay by me then, just long enough to hear what the Spaniard has to say to them. We'll drop the longboat in the meantime so your company can assemble, and you'll just have to get down and set off quickly.

"This *has* to work," he added, his fingers tightening on the bigger man's forearm, "because even if we somehow survive the night, I fear a mutiny is ahead. You and I are not being spoken of with great affection these days."

"I'm aware of that. So we'll make it work," Walter answered with far more surety than he felt.

Raising the parley flag with a lantern lit to display it seemed to halt both ships. As far as Walter Armitage could understand, Juan Molina's long-winded shouting through the brass horn to the Spanish warship was nothing more than a plea for a conference, and seemed innocuous enough. It at least had bought them the time they needed to get the longboat out into the water. He and his handpicked boarding party pulled well out into the darkness that surrounded the barely moving ships, and took a roundabout route toward the nao.

They'd need to be stealthy and quick in their boarding, and threatening enough once on deck to keep the treasure ship's crew docile in surrender. If there were many soldiers aboard, they'd be walking into a deadly ambush. As soon as the shooting started, *Devil's Handmaid* would be fired upon, and with the guns the galleon had at that short a range, the brigantine would never survive the encounter. Everything had to go like clockwork to pull this off, and he had no illusions about the probability of that happening.

"*Dig in…quietly now lads*," he murmured as they passed out well beyond the starboard side of the galleon, making use of all shadows on this foggy night. The sea gods at least were with them, for the current moved them along briskly, while the sky was moonless and the clinging mist killed noises. As he rowed, Walter watched warily all activity on the galleon. His eyes were riveted on the great stern castle, main deck, forecastle, and especially the gun ports as they passed by, relieved to hear no hue and cry raised, to see no one rushing to the rail, or the swivel guns on the main deck being manned and aimed in their direction.

So far, so good.

Aboard the galleon, a liveried messenger bowed before the 17 year old Hildalga, Antonia Margarita Campos, who had been visiting her tio Don Bernadino Alvarez, at his plantation. She was supposed to be headed back to Cádiz to be married, but that port city was reportedly blockaded by the British, so her thoughtful uncle had put her on a ship he considered safe, and was sending her to Seville instead.

"Why have we stopped sailing?" the narrow faced young woman with the very large eyes asked as soon as the man was allowed entry. Her hair was long and dark, worn down about her shoulders for an evening alone in her tiny but elaborately appointed cabin, for the older woman who was her traveling companion had been brushing it out when the knock came. A voluminous patterned dressing gown had been hastily pulled over her ankle length and lightweight camisa, for the night was warm and humid, and very little air circulated within those cramped quarters.

"Senorita," the man began, "The wind has suddenly died. I beg your pardon for interrupting your repose, but I have been given foul tidings that came from a *patache*...a communication vessel, you understand. They tell us that an English fleet has recently attacked and raided the Flota, which we will be joining soon. The ship that brings this foul news does not look like one of ours, and so our noble Capitán says it may well be a ruse by pirates, though the man who called out to us spoke fluent Castilian. This *patache's* capitán claims they had been fired upon and were forced to commandeer another neutral vessel to bring us this information. We are investigating them now. Would you care to be escorted to our Capitán's quarters, where you will be safer? I fear that if fighting breaks out, the roar of our many powerful cannons may assault your ears."

Both women's faces went ashen at the news. Senorita Campos fanned herself with a long fingered hand. "I would like that, yes," she answered quietly, rising to her feet. "Senora Inez, my guarda, she will pack and move my most personal things. I must take my Bible and all my jewelry if pirates are suspected...surely your good Capitán will protect them for me..."

"Why have we stopped sailing?"

She prattled on nervously as they led her to the more secure cabin. As soon as her overburdened lady companion came in with numerous gowns and boxes of jewelry and trinkets, the women were locked inside without a candle to light the interior, and the admonition to refrain from calling out or making any noise. A single pistol was left on the captain's table, "For your protection," they were told. No one bothered to ask if either of the women could actually shoot. For some reason, the Capitán insisted on keeping her Bible locked in his own sea chest.

Once the door shut, darkness set in. With the guards gone, their pretense at brave nobility ended. The two women sat on the bed in the only spot of light filtering through the aftercastle gallery windows, and hugged each other, weeping silently and praying for deliverance from whatever new evil of the times had sprung up around them.

Even with Neville almost useless on one of the oars, the longboat reached the nao without incident. Pulling just past the towering sterncastle, they found a spot to snub close, making fast so as not to have their own vessel float off. It would be handy for transferring people and treasure.

Jez looked up the towering height of ship's side, and swallowed hard. Her heart was pounding in her ears, and sweat beaded her body, soaking through her clothing and into her hair underneath the dingy scarf she'd tied over it to keep the wild black ringlets out of her face. She laid her oar down across the benches as did the men with her, and stood up. Remembering Walter's teaching, she nervously checked the brace of pistols she had thrust into her baldric, the knife in her boot, and made sure the cutlass rode easily in its hanger before she hefted a boarding axe with a spiked back, which was good for climbing. It was a long way up there, and if she lost something, it was gone for good. She'd need to concentrate on what she was doing to avoid falling to an almost certain death in the dark waters below.

In her heyday, that grand old Spanish vessel would have been a glorious sight, but even in the wan light of the two sputtering lanterns that marked her aft end, it was evident that she had not been well tended in some time. The gilded decorations were chipped and tarnished, some of them coming loose, and all the colorful paint had faded. The wood was old, and considerable spotting of tar and patching showed where she had sprung numerous leaks. It was hard to believe that what should be the richest monarchy in the world would take such poor care of the ships that delivered its wealth.

Even when not actively sailing, a big ship is far from quiet. The night was full of the sounds of slopping waves punctuated by the creaks and groans of old wood, the sawing sounds of wind rattling the rigging, and the fluttering of sails partly furled. A dozen men, led by Jengo and Walter Armitage, clambered up the weathered wood of the side strakes unnoticed, using axes and knives to gain purchase. They moved as quietly as possible along the tall side of that gently heaving hull, before slipping aboard. Keeping out of the light of the sputtering lanterns overhead, which had been all lit this foggy night, they began to disperse.

Jez was the next to last up, only Sol was behind her. As the thin pirate climbed past her, he clapped a hand between her nether cheeks, and squeezed. Jez gasped and looked over angrily at his grinning face, almost losing her grip on the axe handle with one hand while twisting to slap his hand away with the other.

"*Mouse is right, ye've naught fer bollocks,*" he whispered as he climbed past her. "*Unless yer a blinkin' eunuch, yer no lad.*"

A cold chill came over her as she continued her crawl up the side, now well behind him. Sol knew her secret! Who else did?

She didn't have time to worry about it. Wily Sol and his arse-kissing shadow Neville were nowhere in sight as Jez came over the gunwale and slipped into shadows amongst the shrouds and rigging on the main deck. The fitful light overhead was spotty at best, and threw thick shadows, which worked in their favor. Walter and Jengo were already fanning out to clear the stern and capture the wheel, with other men creeping through shadows to access the officer's quarters.

Of the roughly 50 crew members aboard the nao, only a few were active, and with the ship nearly dead in the water the wheel was lashed for the evening. Most of the night watch were all lounging about; drinking watered wine, gambling and jabbering in their native tongue, or gnawing on hardtack. There were few soldiers amongst them, but Jez had no doubt there were more below, for how else would you keep the miserable wretches in the crew from stealing and squirreling away their own share of the treasure aboard? Most of these crews were likely impressed into service or had known no other life, and merchant ships were far from egalitarian in how sailors were treated.

All the soldados were well-armed, but there was no glint of armor.

She'd been instructed to take out any of them she could reach as quickly as possible while Jengo and his mates tossed Andy's stinkpots into the lower deck hatchways to either bring the crew to their knees early or ferret them out so they could be dealt with. Any soldiers below they would handle as needed.

She drew her knife and slipped up on the first Spanish soldier, who had the unfortunate timing of using the scupper as a urinal. She was as tall as he was, and her long arms had the reach she needed when she yanked his head back. Before he could react, a hand clamped over his mouth while she pulled the well-honed blade to slash diagonally across the neck, catching the jugular as well as one of those all-important arteries under the ear, which Walter had taught her would make a man instantly unconscious. With no more than a bubbling whimper, he sank to the deck with his lifeblood spewing from the rent in his throat and his white rolling eyes already sightless.

Her shaking hands and blade were coated in his blood, but Jez quickly wiped them on her slops. This callous taking of life was the part of pirating she detested, but for the sake of Walter and their comrades, nerves were driving her to eliminate every possible point of resistance before someone she cared about got hurt. With their ship and its onboard treasure at stake, these foreigners would eagerly kill them without a moment's thought of mercy, had the situation been reversed.

Jezebel Johnston screwed up her courage and resolve and went on, creeping in the shadows, searching for the next victim.

CHAPTER TEN

The light wind had indeed died down. While not totally becalmed, no one was making much forward progress. Neither the pirates nor the warship had completely halted, but they had slowed considerably, and the hulking treasure nao was barely moving. The Spanish ships seemed to have been considering their alleged news of the fate of the Flota, for hails had exchanged between them as the fog began to rise, but so far there had been no small craft launched, and only one further request for information from the smaller ship following them.

With all sails reefed except the light air sets, *Devil's Handmaid* had maintained a respectable distance behind. The lighter vessel rode high, so the current tended to carry them faster. They'd moved up within hailing distance again. A sweating and protesting Juan Molina was brought forward once more to offer some further explanation, a pistol in his back as he shouted into the brass horn to the ship across the water. No one had any idea how much of what he said was actually heard, but the parley flag was raised once more.

"Tell 'em we've no small boat aboard, and the tiller's damaged and not handling well," Dan Abrams commanded and Juan Molina complied…to a point.

"I have said as much as I dare. The rest is up to the whims of their capitán." Some tense moments went by as the three men standing with him on the bow watched anxiously for any indication of the big ship coming about, which would precede a broadside volley.

Nothing much happened.

"Well, at least they're not gunning for us," Dan Abrams muttered as he shut his spyglass thoughtfully.

"Aye," Gully agreed. "They're still part under sail though, and I've not seen e'en a light anchor dropped. If we don't send someone out, they'll likely run."

As he squinted out into to the darkness and fog at the half seen stern of the warship, James Reuben took a spread-legged stance with arms crossed over his chest. "They haven't fired yet because they don't fear us," he said with edginess coloring his tone. "We have the speed and maneuverability, but their guns have the longer reach, and they've far more of them. Spaniards and French are known for taking down rigging to disable a ship before they attack. If we move in closer, they'll certainly turn and fire. Once we've lost sail or mast, if even one or two of those big guns catches our hull, sinking us would be child's play."

"So now what will you do?" Juan Molina asked in a sharp tone. "Here, I was prepared to volunteer to be… how would you English say it? A goodwill emissary. Yet against my advice, you have declined my offer. Since you have already sent your only boat off raiding, there is no other way to reach this ship but to move closer, which you cannot do without revealing your true nature and intentions. If we do not show more interest though, they will surely sail off. You are like the little fox, trying to outwit the big wolf and steal his dinner." He laughed bitterly.

Gully and James Reuben exchanged some pointed looks. As true as his analogy rang, their erstwhile interpreter had nothing but his own self interests in mind. Of course he was very eager to have close contact with his former countrymen, for with Walter Armitage off with the boarding party, no one else on the pirate vessel understood more than a few words of Spanish. With Jengo and several other intimidating men absent, the wily expatriate Spaniard knew this was his best chance of escaping.

Dan Abrams was quick to pick up on the shift in attitude as well. "Well then, we'll simply have to prevent them from leaving," he said with a confident half smile and a lifted eyebrow as he rounded on the man.

Juan Molina spat on the deck scornfully, and rubbed it out with his big toe before he looked up. "If you dare to fire on them, we will all die here. They have more guns and more crew. I know how my people think, Señor, and they are as fierce and cunning as they are suspicious. Make any sudden move toward them and they will blow you out of the water and be done with it. You have taken on a fool's challenge, and now you will lose."

James Reuben smacked his fist into the fat man's face, knocking a tooth loose and bloodying his lip. "You'll remain respectful, or it will be my pleasure to beat some humility into you," he warned. The Spaniard's eyes smoldered with hatred, but he rubbed his jaw and smiled without mirth.

"The truth…it only hurts those who speak it," he said.

Gully eyed Dan Abrams, who nodded. The desperation and disrespect apparent in Molina's voice signaled that he'd come to the end of his usefulness.

"Have a couple of lads escort our prisoner back to his quarters; tie him up, gag him, and lock him inside," the aggravated captain snapped. "And then bring me the best swimmer aboard, and let's see if he wants to make himself a bloody hero."

Juan Molina was hauled off struggling and protesting loudly, trying to break free of his captors.

A sailor swinging a marlinspike suddenly loomed up before Jez; he'd been sleeping on a coil of line, and she'd nearly tripped over him. With a grunt of effort, she sidestepped her attacker while bringing up her own weapon. A quick and brutal two handed swing of the axe stove in his head between the eyes and felled him like a tree. She had to jerk the blade free with her foot on his chest while he was still spasmodically kicking, and wiped blood and brains on his shirt.

That had been close. She needed to be more careful.

She ducked down low, as there came a quickly stifled outcry somewhere well ahead. That ended in a muffled bonging noise and a couple of splashes... and then silence, followed by the sound of bare feet pattering across the deck. Someone who had tried to ring the alarm on the ship's bell had been dealt with, so Jez assumed that whoever went over the side was a Spaniard, and the silent racer was one of their own freebooter lads heading toward the forecastle. She scuttled along after him.

Walter had warned them to spare all who immediately surrendered; but not to hesitate in killing anyone who might raise an alarm or put up a fight. Any soldiers aboard who didn't instantly lay down their weapons were dead men. They needed to proceed as quickly and quietly as possible. The galleon would not fire on their own treasure ship, but they had archers and crossbowmen aplenty to station on the fighting platforms once alongside, and at any moment could send over several boarding parties of their own. As well as having forfeited most of her guns, the nao didn't seem as well garrisoned aboard, so once they'd secured command, the simple threat of further mayhem to any non-compliance should be sufficient to coerce the crew to obedience.

The plan was to pile on sail while firing the remaining aft guns on the treasure ship's escort, hopefully taking out the galleon's fore mast while the sprit sails were still furled. Since there was no fourth Bonaventure mast on that ship, the more maneuverable *Devil's Handmaid* would attempt to blow out the mizzen and then circle evasively to avoid a broadside, coming around in between the two to cut them off. A ship that size could be sailed on the main mast alone, but losing two sets of canvas would severely slow things down. While the war galleon was still sorting itself out, the nao would pull away; awaiting the outcome of the fight with the pirate vessel.

Providing they took the Spanish warship as a prize without sinking her, they'd elect an acting captain and bring over some feisty lads to keep order, with a handpicked skeleton crew to sail it. Jez hoped Walter would earn that command. While the treasure was being transferred, any troublemakers would be severely dealt with. Those who refused to join the crew would be battened into the hold of the nao...once it was emptied of all valuable cargo...and set adrift. No doubt some men would beg to be taken aboard. Regardless of their nationality, the average merchant sailor never seemed to care who was in charge, as long as he was treated humanely. All unneeded crewmen would be put off at the next convenient spot.

There were no certainties with that sort of action; but then, there were never any assurances in pirating. As Andy Boone was fond of saying: You lived for the moment, or you died like a dog, but a common man never knew such freedom and profitable adventuring anywhere else but aboard a fast ship with a savvy captain and a spirited bunch of cutthroats at your side. Even considering the constant danger and the brutal nature of the fighting, it was exhilarating, and Jez never felt more alive than here; stalking the deck like a panther, her nerves always on edge, ready to pounce at a moment's notice. Any ship they took, every fight she'd been in, the lesson had been to live by your wits and kill or be killed. What was once a gangling slip of a love-struck fourteen-year-old girl was now a grimacing marauder of the high seas who dealt harshly with those who defied her for coveting any prize she could carry off.

This was the adventure she craved and the independence she had longed for...the liberty to choose her own life based on what she could accomplish. Jengo, Pakke, and even her mother had all fought bitterly for their own freedom; something the highborn of the world never needed to think twice about. Dan Abrams had left his British Navy post because of the atrocities he witnessed aboard, where hierarchy and protocol delivered by force dictated who bowed to whom, and promotion was based more on ancestry and wealth than merit. His years as a slave was something that fierce Jengo seldom spoke of, though he bore ridged lash marks on his back and scars from manacles and collar. Walter Armitage had gone to war to support his country, only to return and find the girl he loved had been ravished and spurned by an idle young nobleman. Even the wanton women of the brothel her own mother owned had no expectations, so they shared their bodies with many rough-handed men just to earn a place to sleep, food in their bellies, and a few trinkets. Jez flat refused to have her life defined by her gender, and so she had run off to create her own destiny. She'd hack her way through the entire Spanish fleet to preserve it.

She could hear multiple sounds of scuffling accompanied by blows and oaths; a signal that they'd been seen and open skirmishes had begun. Walter had said pistols were a last resort, as the crack of a gunshot would often carry well over open water, alerting the warship that some chicanery was afoot. When the hue and cry went up that there were raiders aboard, Jez pulled her cutlass and raced forward with the axe in her off hand, bellowing like a wild beast.

She fought like a tempest unleashed, with no hesitation to her actions now; a fury of untamed and uncontrollable destruction. Alternating striking and parrying with either hand as needed, she took a few minor cuts but did more damage than she gained. She just narrowly missed having her brains scrambled when someone swung at her the iron ball end of a long-handled loggerhead tool, which was normally heated and plunged into barrels of tar to stir and soften it. She weaved and dodged in time and it hit the mast behind her instead, bouncing off and dropping down to leave a tarry mark on her shoulder and a numbness that made the offhand use of the axe far harder. She thrust and slashed with the cutlass, until she could bring the axe around to chop off the wooden handle, and then swung the cutlass to take a slice out of the arm that had held it. Fortunately, it was a sailor and not a soldier, and while he had the longer reach and more upper body strength, he'd done no more than brawl in waterfront dives. She eventually got the best of him, and cut him down.

While she was dealing with the man trying to bash her head in, a rapier meant to pierce her heart got caught in her loose shirt and its owner ripped it free, leaving her left sleeve dangling. Someone else took that soldier out; she had no idea who because of the confusion of bodies around her in the semi-darkness. A burning sensation made her look down and she noticed a cut on her upper arm that oozed for a bit before crusting over. She ripped away the torn sleeve, which came off raggedly, and kept on fighting.

Every time she attacked someone, Jez steeled herself by focusing on the exploitation and abuses she'd seen and heard of, and how the treasure aboard would only compound them. What was stowed in the hold of that ship belonged to the strong and the bold of the lands it was raped from, for too many unfortunate souls had toiled and suffered to create such wealth. It would be grossly unjust if only the privileged few in faraway lands got to enjoy it. If it reached Europe, no matter who benefited from it, more soldiers and sailors would be impressed and shipped off to fight and die on foreign soil to further advance the schemes of those in power. More fettered lives would be bought and sold abroad, allowing the already wealthy to add additional coin to their coffers on the backs of slaves treated like animals. So much better to tear it from the plump and greedy hands of the oppressors now, and then dump it into some local port town, where businesses would thrive and hungry bellies be filled. This raid, she told herself, was justified, and that thought allayed any guilt for the duration of the bloodbath.

Shots rang out now and then. No need to hold back now. As she slashed and clawed her way through the melee, she eventually made it all the way up the weather deck, heading toward the bow. There were bodies everywhere, and blood pooled in spots. She found herself momentarily alone, grateful for a breather in the intense fighting, though it didn't last long.

The sounds of a struggle came from above her. There was fighting on the forecastle deck above, and the sounds of bodies being heaved overboard. It ended in a sudden shot along with a multitude of curses and oaths. A familiar voice yelling in anger was suddenly cut short with the sound of a heavy blow.

That turned her blood to ice. Still if she rushed in, she'd be dead before she got halfway there.

Jez shoved her bloody cutlass back in its hanger, and drawing a pistol, crept up past a hatch where the choking reek of the stink pots that had been tossed down where sailors and soldiers had been sleeping still wafted up. Scuttling rapidly across the open deck, she was headed for the port ladder to the forecastle when she heard a noise, and quickly crouched behind an unused knighthead. Someone was clambering up the port side companionway rather clumsily, still coughing and retching. She stayed back and waved the axe where it could be seen from below. As she had expected, a shot came rang out and knocked it from her grip as the musket ball careened off the metal, and her hand went numb. That was soldierly shooting, so better the axe head than her own! Walter had drummed into her the wisdom of caution and subterfuge.

Jez gave a low groan as if she'd been hit, waiting with pistol drawn until a head popped up, allowing her to return fire at almost point blank range. The man bucked and yelped as he went over backwards down the hatch. She shoved the empty pistol into her baldric and drew the other and waited, but there was silence, so she scuttled past, creeping up the port side ladder to the forecastle deck. Just getting her eyes above the deck level, she glanced around and stiffened.

There were several soldiers standing below the foremast. They were huddled over two prone bodies...by what she could see of them, both were pirates. Their own dead they had ignored after a cursory check. A Spanish crewman lay nearly headless, with his blood already congealing and sticking to their boots.

It took a few tense moments to figure out what had happened. Once the cry went up that there were pirates aboard, someone must have discovered the ship's bell was missing. Noises did not carry well in the fog, which had thickened because they were still fairly close to the small islands. Her mates had obviously taken out the Spanish sailor while he was trying to load a swivel deck gun to fire a warning shot, which even at the opposite end of the ship should have been loud enough to alert the galleon that the nao was under attack. The Spaniard's crumpled body lay up against the front rail, below the ruined bit where the gun had been. As the pirates had cut the man down and toppled the weapon overboard, some hastily awakened and armed Spanish soldiers had boiled out of the forecastle. One of them had gotten in a lucky shot. The three of them now stood with their weapons drawn, looking down at the fallen pirates and jabbering excitedly.

A squat and lumpy pirate she could not quite identify groaned and writhed in pain from where he lay on the deck, bleeding out from a gunshot wound. Another taller, and more familiar form sprawled silent and still just beyond; a huge bruise covering half his face, indicating that someone had recently brained him. He wasn't moving and she couldn't tell if he was alive or dead. Jez's heart sunk.

The closest soldier was rather short and dressed in finer clothing, his hair dark and curling, with a small pointed beard and great upturned mustaches. She could not see much of the other two because they were in the shadows, but no doubt this was their commander who stood nearby, calmly reloading his pistol, ramrodding a ball home as he gave quiet orders. One soldier was kicking the taller of the corpses in the ribs, trying to determine if he was dead. He bent and flicked back an eyelid, and then felt his throat pulse, before jabbering something to his companion, who sheathed his blade and tucked his pistol into his belt before they began tossing bodies over the rail. Together they hefted the limp body of the big man and Jez could see enough then to be certain it was Walter. They made to toss him over the side.

She screamed an oath and fired at the commander. Overwrought, her shot went wild; but Jez had already drawn her cutlass and was charging in blindly to save the one man she valued above all others.

Someone emerged unseen from the shadows beyond the mast and smashed her in the face with a belaying pin. There was a crack and she bit painfully into her tongue. She reeled dizzily and dropped the cutlass, gasping and choking as blood ran from her broken nose down her shirt, mixing with the tears she shed for the man she had loved and now lost, as his body tumbled out of sight.

The Spanish commander jabbered at her in a surly tone as he held his now loaded pistol leveled at her heart. He had never done more than duck before coming up with his own weapon. The man who hit her forced her down by the shoulders with the idea that the Comandante would take the pirate's head off with his own blade, but catching sight of something intriguing, he ripped her shirt open and grinned at the advancing soldados.

Jezebel Johnston sank to her knees in defeat. Her captor used the tip of his rapier under her chin to raise her head.

"Mira, hemos encontrado un tesoro! Esta es una mujer pirata," he said with a wicked laugh as he swept the sharp tip of his cup hilt rapier downward and scratched a bloody X on her now exposed left breast.

Not many men aboard a pirate ship can swim. It was Pakke who readily volunteered to do whatever the captain he so admired asked of him. He stood barefoot and shirtless on the predawn bow, listening intently. Gully stood nearby, a thoughtful look on his weathered face. James Reuben had gone off to the ready the guns for the coming attack.

"I hear you are a strong and swift swimmer," Dan Abrams said with a smile. In answer, he got a big smile and a nod.

"Pakke save Jez when Mouse go overboard," the Panamanian Indian boy boasted, and thumped his chest. "Sea that day was rough. This easy swim."

"You're a gutsy one," Dan Abrams said, patting his shoulder. "Still you'd best hear me out before you agree to this, because what we'd have you do is quite dangerous. That galleon out there," he pointed out toward the Spanish warship, whose stern lanterns shown as glowing disks in the fog, "is making ready to sail off once the wind is up, and while we would likely catch up to her and offer a broadside, she'll just come round and blow us to bits. That is, unless her rudder stops working. Then we'd have her just where we want her. Of course, that would have to happen soon, to be effective." He eyed the boy, to see if Pakke understood, but there was only a faint glimmer of comprehension in his eyes.

"Pakke no can steer big ship," the boy said uncertainly, and both men laughed.

"Indeed," said Abrams, "neither could I at your age! What we need is for someone to swim out there with some boards and jam the space between rudder and sternpost, so they can't navigate a turn," he explained carefully with motions of his hands, and saw the light dawning in the boy's eyes. Pakke was bright and had learned a lot since coming aboard. "Can you do that lad?"

"Pakke is brave and strong, but wood break easy. Need hard thing," the boy answered, "Like in Andee's story."

The captain's face bore a confused expression. He tipped his head like a dog and blinked a few times before turning toward Gully. "Oh blast it, what the devil he talking about?" Dan Abrams asked his quartermaster.

Gully pursed his lips. "I'd say it's one of Rat Stew's old tales, something about a conquistador who fell overboard, got his breastplate squeezed in the rudder, and crippled his own ship during a firefight. Most of the company could likely repeat it from heart."

"Is that... even *possible*?" Dan Abrams asked in a low voice.

"P'raps," Gully said, "but I've naught the one te say whether Rat Stew made it all up. You know how he gets after hoisting a few."

"Unfortunately yes, but they tell me he was daring and canny in his day. So... do you think metal would be better?" Dan Abrams asked quickly, for they were running out of time.

"Most likely, aye, twould be best," Gully answered. "Ye already have somethin' in mind I take it?"

"As much as I hate to part with it, yes I do have just the thing," Dan Abrams said with a snap of his fingers before he stomped off to his quarters. He came back bearing the cast metal mask with the goat horns that he'd taken out of the cabin on the Portuguese slaver carrack they'd raided earlier in the season. "If our lad here can somehow bear the weight of this while he swims out there, it should do nicely." His face had a self-satisfied look, for most of the crew feared the foul looking thing and a few had whispered that since it had come aboard, their luck had changed.

Pakke looked at it dubiously, because it was quite heavy. Yet he had swum a similar distance towing an exhausted Jez in far rougher seas, and she weighed more than that. He'd find a way to make it work and be a hero in the eyes of captain and crew.

"Pakke will do this," he said with surety he almost felt.

"Good lad. You've earned yourself a single pick of the take for your fearless attitude," Dan Abrams told him. *Providing he survives...*

A couple crewmembers tied the thing to his back, and Pakke went down a line over the side and slipped into the water, looking for all the world like a big sea turtle as he struck out in the near dawn darkness, trying to keep the lights of the warship ahead in sight.

"I do hope he makes it back, he's a game fellow," Dan Abrams said before he went back to the stern to have a quick conversation with the night helmsman.

Through a haze of pain and grief, Jez listened to the grating tones of the men who stood triumphantly around her. She knew very little Spanish, but the intent was clear enough. They had stripped her of all her weapons, and were going to make an example of her by allowing the crew to rape her repeatedly before putting her to death.

From where she stood being ogled and groped by armed men, she could see little of the rest of the ship. It was Puggy who still lay shallowly gasping on the forecastle deck, his broken axe discarded, holding his bleeding belly and moaning. Another soldier had drawn his blade, and grinning like a demon, he taunted the dying pirate with it. The sailor who had hit her in the face was sent below to fetch something…likely line to secure her hands and feet so she couldn't escape while they did as they wished with her. The sounds of battle were dying out, and she feared the worst.

They'd lost. She hung her head again, watching the blood trickle down her shirt from her shattered nose as they prodded her with blades to turn around and walk, not caring anymore what happened next.

They had not discovered the knife in her boot. She was saving that to take out the commander, figuring he'd get first go at her. Then she'd take her own life. There was nothing left to live for anyway…not with Walter dead.

Pakke was a strong swimmer, and the sea was relatively calm, but the piece of metal strapped to his back made it hard to stay afloat. He struck out mightily for the galleon, but with the fog thinning and the land breeze just beginning to pick up, it was now slowly moving away, and so it took him the better part of an hour to reach it. By then his arms and legs were burning and he was exhausted. He cut the ropes binding it to him, and barely managed to keep it from slipping away into the deep. Holding onto the lowest exposed gudgeon, he manhandled the mask around and carefully wedged it into the gap between rudder flap and sternpost. The curve of the thing made a nice tight fit, but it wouldn't go in far because of the angle of the open space as the warship was being steered, and it kept trying to pop free. He shoved harder, almost catching his fingers. To make it stay, he wedged his knife blade in with it as well. Kicking off, he turned wearily to swim the distance back toward *Devil's Handmaid* just as dawn was lightening the eastern horizon.

There was a grinding noise and a metallic screech that was only somewhat muffled by the slapping of the water around him. Someone had noticed right off that the steering was affected, and came running aft to see what might be wrong. A shout and excited jabbering behind him said Pakke was spotted. He dove down and swam for his life.

As the air warmed, the fog had begun to lift and spotters on the arms platforms began to fire both crossbows and muskets. There was the sound of objects hitting the water all around, and then a searing pain went through one calf. He'd caught a crossbow bolt. Pakke gulped air and then dove down under the surface again, fighting against the current to get out of range before he had to surface and breathe. He stopped and floated a moment and with gritted teeth, pulled the quarrel free. It had mainly caught the outer part of the calf muscle and no major blood vessels, but the leg felt weak. Leaving a trail of blood behind him as he swam off again, he looked around frantically.

He couldn't spot his own ship, because *Devil's Handmaid* was already on the move.

With the gradual lifting of the fog and the strengthening breeze of the predawn hours, the galleon had hoisted her sail flag and was putting on canvas as she prepared to move away. If the nao boarding party had been successful, they'd know it soon as she became visible. Dan Abrams gave the order to move out.

"All able hands a'deck Master Gulliver; top men to stations, gunners to batteries. Strike that arse wiper we're flying now and raise our true colors as soon as that wallowing tub ahead fires on their escort," he added, indicating his personal flag. "Add the red jack to it as well...perhaps knowing they'll be offered no quarter will give them something to think about besides fighting!" Dandy Dan was always at his best when there was prey ahead.

"Ah, Master Ping," he boomed as the Chinese sailor came stalking up the ladder to the quarterdeck, "You have an uncanny sense of when you're needed. Take the wheel then. Full and by, but change our heading to follow that blasted Spaniard. We shall beat to weather if we must to keep up, but let us remain evasive if she begins to come around at us."

The often-silent helmsman and expert pilot nodded slightly and touched his forehead with a forefinger before assuming his position.

"Do ya b'lieve Pakke actually made it out there Cap'n?" Gully asked as he started down the ladder toward the weather deck.

"We'll know soon enough I suppose," was Dan Abrams reply. After consulting the compass in the binnacle, he headed down himself, spyglass in hand, striding confidently toward the foredeck.

Just before he bounded up that ladder, there were shouts across the water from the Spanish warship, and bowmen on the fighting top shot down toward their aft. He watched with satisfaction as with their sails filling, the rudder refused to turn and the great ship heeled over in protest at the lack of harmony between canvas and wheel. Lines were quickly adjusted to right the ship, and men were going down over the stern to investigate what had stopped the tiller from working.

"We have her!" He cackled like a maniac and almost danced a jig on the foredeck.

"Full ahead Master Gulliver," he shouted aft. "Have them stand by on the guns; this needs to happen fast. Chain shot to the bow chaser…I want those mizzen sails down if possible. Ready the port battery first with canister shot, we're taking that ship as a prize if I've anything to say about it!"

He hailed a sailor running by, and gave him orders. "Have the lookouts spot for the native boy. If he lives, we'll toss a line and attempt to bring him back aboard. He's earned himself a permanent position in my crew today."

As two men propelled Jez toward the ladder down to the weather deck, a shadow clambered clumsily over the gunwale where the foremast shrouds were tied down to the chain plates. Another detached itself from a position near the coiled lines hanging from the rigging just below and crept toward the foredeck ladders, but crouched in a dark spot when Jez and her captors loomed overhead.

The third Spanish soldier had stayed behind to deal with the dying pirate and then gather the confiscated weapons, but he never got a chance to do anything. He lost his life when an unseen and unexpected assailant loomed up. Wrapping an arm around his neck with a hand clamped over

"We have them!"

the soldier's mouth and nose, it choked the life from him. The struggling victim sank his teeth into flesh, but battle nerves and desperation will make a man shrug off all pain. Like a wounded wolf of the sea, the creeping figure quickly liberated the man he'd killed of blade and pistol, running him through for good measure before turning to stagger off in the direction he had seen Jez being dragged.

Jez and her escort had just spotted the body of the burly sailor who had hit her with the belaying pin lying sprawled in death on the weather deck below, his throat slit and blood pooling around him. The Spaniard who held her captive muttered something incomprehensible through gritted teeth as the one behind him pulled a pistol and glanced around wildly.

"Estos merodeadores son como fantasmas!" he complained. Seconds later, a blade rammed into him from behind. With a gurgling cry of shock, he dropped at his comandante's heels, scrabbling weakly and vomiting blood, as his weapon went careening down to the deck below.

The commander turned at bay with his pistol in hand, more worried about his own safety than in securing a female prisoner. Anyone behind him wouldn't have a clear shot with the woman in the way, so he dragged her around before him.

Jez pretended to stumble and went down on one knee, providing whoever was out there a clear target. The Spaniard hauled her upright by her arm and a hank of hair, and she kicked out viciously, catching his leg and staggering him just before he fired on the big man looming up at them, who had mistakenly grabbed an empty pistol in his haste. The tall pirate dodged as the gun went off at close range, and the ball barely grazed his arm. Jez scrambled to her feet and lunged for the commander's sword, only to be met by the head snapping blow of a pistol butt that made her reel drunkenly as the world spun upside down

"Más tarde vas a sufrir por eso!" her assailant snapped at her. She went down again and fought to remain conscious as the half-seen pirate was frantically fumbling to free the blade that was still stuck in the body of the dead soldier. It had caught in the ribs, and would not easily pull out. The man had landed on his own sword, trapping it beneath his prone body, and there was no time to roll him over and fish for it.

"Ahora mueres pirata!" the Spaniard sneered as he drew his own sword with the ring of fine steel.

With a final desperate yank, the pirate came up with the sword just in time to parry a vicious cut, but his hands were shaking and blood ran down his arm to his sleeve from where the musket ball had taken a chunk of flesh with it. He would not have much stamina.

While they were squaring off, Jez managed to clear her head enough to stumble back upright and grab the Spanish commander by the off arm, yanking him sideways in an attempt to distract him. Rather than change direction with his blade and risk being skewered, he roughly flung her away, for he was less worried about an unarmed woman than the snarling pirate who was wielding the bloody blade. As dazed and battered as the man seemed, he had the stance and skills of an experienced combatant.

As both opponents pressed forward and their weapons began to clash and clang, she remembered she still had a one of her own. She reached into her boot and then scrabbled to her feet, leaping at her former captor with a scream of defiance and her own long knife in hand. The Spaniard was well occupied in lunging at and parrying blows from the man he was fighting, so she had an opening, but he was moving so fast she missed the neck and caught him in the face, opening his cheek to the bone and slicing off half his ear, which dangled and twisted on mere threads of skin. He screamed in pain as blood welled, and smacked her away with his hilt, leaving himself open a moment, and the pirate got in a slash to his ribs before he had to back away from a frenzied flurry of swipes and thrusts.

The Spanish commander was a capable swordsman, and he was able to keep them both at bay, but the vicious onslaught of the big pirate and the constant nuisance of the woman with the knife were wearing him down. He pressed in on the woman instead, hoping to kill her and then take out the other pirate, but she moved like a cat. Meanwhile the man kept at him, and now he was hard pressed to defend his position and not get backed up over the deck railing. The three of them fought in a chaotic melee of slashing, darting forms, but it was still a mismatched battle because the Spanish commander's blade came up faster than his half-dazed opponent could match. He eventually backed his primary assailant against the mast and moved in for the kill.

Before he could thrust it home though, Jez buried her knife in his left side and he went down gasping.

"Never turn your back on a live opponent...not even a woman!" she said viciously, as she ripped the blade backward and out. She liberated the quivering man of his weapons, and then ran him through. Nodding to Sol, who had just come racing up the starboard ladder, she stumbled over to throw her arms around Walter, and he held her close in shaking arms.

"I thought you were dead!" she said with a half sob.

"Close to it. They really scrambled my head. I woke up when I hit the hawse chain, and was able to pull myself up onto the anchor cat."

"If I had lost you..." the words gurgled through the blood in her throat from the broken nose. She turned and spat, and then wiped her face. "I'm a mess.

"I tried to tell you this was no easy life," he said in a voice thick with emotion and the daze of a major concussion along with a few broken ribs, and complicated by exhaustion.

"I don't care, as long as you're still alive," she insisted.

"For the most part," he said, his eyes glazed and head pounding.

"How touching this all is! You knew she was a woman all along, didn't you *Master* Armitage?" Sol interrupted in an accusing voice.

"Does it matter?" Walter snapped tiredly, looking up over Jez's shoulder.

"It likely will to the company," the thin man said with disgust.

"We'll worry about their reaction later. Keep your mind on our business for now, because we took this old tub too easily. I don't trust these bloody bastards; they have some reason for dangling this treasure before us like they have, and leaving it so poorly protected. Is the ship secure?" the arms master demanded with an edge to his voice that said Sol had best get back to work.

"As much as it can be, with whatever's left of our party," came the offhand answer. "Enough of them papist devils suffocated down below," he jabbed a thumb downward, indicating the lower decks, "that we'll have barely enough to sail this tub now. They've only barshot and a rack of balls aboard that someone forgot. The rest is grapeshot for the deck guns."

Walter was not up to long-winded discussions. "Fine, use what you have. Tell them to get men aloft to start unfurling sails, and some to ready those stern guns. We're taking her out of this fight as soon as possible, but we've got to cripple that escort first!"

Sol knuckled his forehead in a parody of respect for a superior before he stomped off to see how the rest of their party fared.

"I'm going to kill him some fine day," Walter declared in a low voice.

"If I don't get him first," Jez said with equal vehemence. They both knew he was going to cause them no end of trouble once they all got back aboard *Devil's Handmaid*.

A groan nearby broke the tense moment. They let go of each other and walked over to squat at the Puggy's side. It was not the first time he'd taken a ball, but it was going to be the last. He was white faced and limp with blood loss, and couldn't even lift his head.

"I can't believe he's still alive," Walter said. "You're a tough sort, Puggy."

"P-pain... bad... I-I'm c-c-cold... Mercy," he begged feebly, and Jez felt a prickle of shame that she'd forgotten him. She'd seen enough wounds now to realize there'd be no recovery from this one, which at almost point blank range had blasted well into his entrails. He'd bled out for a while, and she could smell the stink of perforated bowel in it. He might linger for a few days, but the fever and infection would kill him slowly. She looked up at Walter, and he nodded solemnly.

"A man has the right to choose his own time," he said tiredly. "Do it."

Jez handed Puggy her knife, which he accepted gratefully. His hands shook, and he dropped it, so she had to help him grip the handle by wrapping both hers around his bigger ones, holding it upright and steady against his chest where the heart was. He met her sad gaze and smiled weakly before he managed to thrust it home by himself, using what little remaining strength he had left. His eyes went wide, there was a last desperate gulp of air, and then his fingers fell away. His big ugly face, which had been twisted in agony, went slack as he finally slumped in death.

Jez never shed a tear as she pulled her blade out and wiped it on his shoulder. She would miss the homely man, who'd always been kind spoken to her, but this was better than lingering on, suffering for days as the sepsis slowly killed him. She closed his staring eyes with two fingers before standing up and stepping away.

"How many of us are left?" she asked Walter.

"Just over half, last I knew. Barely enough to control this tub, though there weren't as many aboard as we'd expect to... uh.. protect a treasure. Sol, Jengo, and I had been down inside the cabins but we couldn't get past the gun deck because of the fumes. We managed to kill most of the officers and a few soldiers while they were sleeping in their beds; the rest were retching their guts out from the reek of those stink pots Andy cooked up. Fortunately, after some examples had been made, the deck crew had their hands up. These fools... ah... they left only a small guard aboard. Most of the men are common sailors... n-not... fighters. They'll obey if... if they know w-what's good for them."

He held his aching, spinning head in shaking hands a moment and she looked at him with concern. "Walter, are you going to be alright?"

"I hope so..." he said before he collapsed in her arms.

CHAPTER ELEVEN

The lower decks seethed with activity. The powder room curtains had been wet down, and the area around it was crowded as filled canisters were being hauled out and up the companionway. On the gun deck, hammocks were stowed and the big guns below them were readied for the upcoming encounter, while racked loading tools were brought down and handed out. Buckets filled with water for swabbing barrels were set in place next to stacks of balls and prepared bags of grapeshot. Men scrambled to and fro, getting in each other's way and cursing.

Without Neville, Pakke, or Jez to assist him, Andy was extra busy in the galley. The old man stumped back and forth, muttering to himself as he put the oven's flame out and made sure whatever coals weren't needed for igniting slow matches to light the guns or cauterizing wounds, were hauled up to be dumped overboard. The threat of fire while under attack was serious, and there was too much powder around to take chances. Hardtack and jerky was passed out in lieu of a meal, and then the big preparation table was cleared and scrubbed with a chunk of holystone, and the floor covered in sand with a bucket someone hauled up from the hold. As no more food could be served until after the battle, the cook table's wide surface would be used by the crew member designated as surgeon… on this trip one of the carpenter's mates who was not averse to sawing off limbs…and the sand was there to catch the blood and provide more stable footing when it got slippery. Buckets and empty kegs were set by as receptacles for any necessary amputations. Andy's carefully hoarded hard spirits and medications were broken out, the chest unlocked and made ready nearby. The old man usually assisted whenever there were casualties, for he had at least a passing knowledge of the contents of vials and pots, and even with three missing fingers, he was passably good with a thread and needle.

Gully had been busy running fore and aft above, bellowing orders to get the ship underway. He kept having to dodge men tossing sand on the deck, which would provide safer footing once the blood began to run.

Visibility had returned, and they were gaining on the galleon, whose sails had been trimmed and adjusted for coming about, but the big ship was unable to negotiate the turn. Instead, she had heeled drunkenly, which almost set the decks awash before the crew righted her.

"The boy pulled it off!" Gully said with relief. "Hard to starboard then lads, we'll take her now, afore they figure it all out." A general cheer went up, for the wolf of the sea was unleashed at last, and the hunt was on!

"Duffy me pal," he called up to the mainmast lookout, who had the best eyes aloft, "see if ye can spot our Pakke out there. If we can manage te git close 'nuff afore we make our run, we'll toss him a line and haul him in."

Devil's Handmaid's sails were filled and she leapt forward on the waves. The forward spotter called down that men on the galleon were going down from lines tied to the stern rail to try to loosen the rudder. Others scrambled to reset sails, while bowmen on the towers were firing on something in the wake behind the Spanish vessel.

As the galleon began to pull forward to protect her lesser armed traveling companion, there was a puff of smoke, a flash, and a resounding 'BOOM' from the nao ahead. A hurtling bar shot, well aimed, ripped through a good bit of foremast rigging on the warship before it nicked the timber. As it dropped it chunked off part of the foremast platform, which smashed into the spar below. The timber cracked and buckled, and men tumbled like flies out of the rigging and into the water. A good part of the foremast canvas slumped raggedly down to drag over the side, further slowing the vessel.

The Spanish captain was fully prepared to fight, for he'd not been completely taken in by the false message. He was furious, though not totally surprised that the nao had fallen to pirates, for the accompanying vessel had been designated as bait. By dawn's light, the fog began to lift and he already had the broadside guns prepared and run out as he gave the order to fire the stern chasers.

The ship following them was still too far behind to do more than take a near miss from his galleon's powerful starboard stern gun. The larboard stern shot fell harmlessly into the water.

That was just a warning telling the pirates to back off. He secretly hoped they wouldn't, because he had an interesting response planned that he'd love to try.

Dan Abrams and Ping knew their business. With the angle they were coming in at the galleon, the speedier and far more maneuverable brigantine would be hard to hit squarely. The warship would seek to simply breech the hull and sink them.

"So they intend to play rough! High time to let them know exactly whom they are trifling with, Master Gulliver," Abrams ordered in a booming tone so everyone could hear. There were cheers all around the deck.

"Captain's orders lads…lower that blasted standard o' theirs an' run up our battle colors," Gully shouted. "Don't forget the bloody jack." Men scrambled to pull down the Spanish flag and raise Dandy Dan's personal ensign, a Jolly Roger featuring a bone chewing, red eyed skull with crossed cutlasses behind it. The smaller plain red flag below it signified that all aboard the ship they targeted would die if there were any further signs of resistance.

"Ah, Master Reubens, your timing is impeccable," Dan Abrams boomed as he spotted his chief gunner coming quickly with several other men loaded down with shot and powder to arm the bow chaser. "If at all possible, I should like the hull of that ship kept intact enough to be sea worthy under load; though we care naught for those aboard. Concentrate on taking out sails for now. Once we've crippled their aft mast, we'll want rakers of grapeshot. The faster we clear the decks, the better."

"Aye, I'd figured that Cap'n." He was so busy getting his lads to load and carefully aim the long bow gun, James Reuben barely looked up. This first shot would count more than any other they'd take, and the angle had to be just so. They'd not get another chance to wreck the sailing capacity of the galleon without exposing themselves to far more dangerous broadside fire from her big side guns. It had to be timed just right for them to be within the correct range for the diagonal volley he'd had the men below set up. That would take down many men on her decks. Then they had to be out of range before the galleon got off another dual round from her stern guns. The Gunnery Master had decided to handle this one himself.

"Fire in the hole!" he called out, and carefully touched the match to the priming. Men scrambled backwards and held their hands over their ears as the extra-long gun roared before them, belching flame and smoke as it careened backwards in the tackle, barking a whirl of hurtling chainshot. It flew fairly true, dropping a little more than James Reuben had planned, but still sliced through shrouds like a hot knife in butter, wrapping the galleon's mizzenmast and splintering it enough that it cracked and the top half fell to starboard of the stern, creating an impromptu sea anchor. Screaming men rained down, hitting decks and hull with sickening thuds and splatters, or into the water with hard splashes that sent them choking to watery graves.

"*Well done* James!" Dan Abrams chortled as he watched through his spyglass while the mast toppled, tipping rigging and sails in the water. Men on the decks were desperately trying to cut lines free and a few chopped at the splintered end of the broken mast with axes, while others threw bodies overboard and manned swivel guns against boarders. The mess was obstructing their starboard gun sighting and the men who had gone down to free the rudder were flailing helplessly as they were dragged under by the heavy mess of wet canvas. "We've got to strike now lads, so pile on all we have and let's come 'round with a postscript!"

As *Devil's Handmaid* closed in, all aboard were jubilant. This encounter had gone far easier than they expected, and Dandy Dan's reputation for being a canny captain was reaffirmed.

After firing the stern chasers at their former escort, getting the nao back underway was taking far longer than anyone would have anticipated. Not only was there a language barrier, but the remaining crew were injured, demoralized, or surly and uncooperative. Without Walter Armitage to interpret with what little Spanish he knew, Sol, Jengo, and what was left of the pirate boarding party had to use hand gestures, weapons, and fists to restore and keep order. They made a few sickening examples in hasty executions after tying up and torturing men who had fought against them. Still it wasn't until Jengo got angry and demonstrated his own version of what would happen to them if they resisted that the crew capitulated.

An unrepentant Spanish sailor of some size had leapt at the big dark skinned pirate, spitting curses and slashing with a knife. After snapping the man's wrist with a quick grab and twist, Jengo hoisted the howling Spaniard overhead and held him on high a few dreadful moments. When all eyes were on him, he smashed the screaming and struggling man down over the quarterdeck railing to break his back audibly, and then tossed him overboard like a child's rag doll. The giant of a man spit on both palms, slapped them together, and glared down at the rest of the deck crew.

"Who wants to die next?" he bellowed. While the sailors below him who had eyed the spectacle fearfully couldn't understand the words he said, their meaning was obvious. The huge Negro pirate with the fierce expression was going to break them one at a time until they either paid him respect or he killed them all.

The rebellion was over, and Walter Armitage had played no part in quelling it. He lay insensible in an officer's bunk…which had been hastily cleared of body and bloody bedding…pale and moaning. After screaming for help to carry him down the forecastle ladder, Jez longed to sit with him, but they were too short handed. She fastened the door securely against any of the Spaniards getting to him, and then went back on deck, where Jengo and Sol were overseeing their departure. She'd managed to find a shirt to replace the one that had been torn and left her partially exposed, but her secret was out, and any men she'd come aboard with gave her some curious and not-always-friendly sidelong looks. Sol was openly antagonistic.

"Get out of my sight *wench*," he said with venom and spat in her direction. Jengo was busy directing two men to haul their longboat aboard, so he didn't see that exchange.

"You still need my help up here," she said with narrowed eyes, a hand on the hilt of a sword she had purloined for her protection, since she'd no idea where her own cutlass had wound up. The new blade was a cup hilt Bilbo, a utilitarian piece, but it had a good balance and feel to it. At that moment, she was tempted to bury it to the hilt in his guts, but they needed every pirate aboard alive to keep the impressed crew under control, and Sol was managing that rather well.

"You're nobody special on *my* ship. Go sit with your lover and leave the real men to take this tub asea. We'll not be needin' yer feeble assistance any longer. Yer both off at the first dry spot we find."

Those were words said with an edge, and she caught the underlying meaning immediately…even before he pulled the pistol and leveled it at her.

"You can't take this treasure for yourself Sol! The entire company battled for this prize. I did my share aboard; I've stood side by side with you, way up in the rigging, or on the deck facing storms. I've fought and killed my share of men!" Jez swept an arm back wildly, indicating the combat noise that was going on in the sea behind them. "Look for yourself! Cap'n Dan and the others are back there taking their chances against that galleon so that we'll all have a rich winter. You can't just sail off without them! I vote we stick to the plan. Who's with me?" she called out, hoping to hear at least one voice of dissent.

There was total silence. Sol laughed.

"Let's get one thing straight right now *Jez*; you're no man, so yer X mark on Dandy Dan's articles means nothing to us. A woman don't belong on any ship, and they don't get no vote. Yer place is in some whorehouse; flat on your back with yer legs in the air, servicing those who do." He sneered, trying to goad her. Neville, who had drawn close to watch the exchange, laughed, and she heard Rusty's hardy guffaw from somewhere down the deck.

The hot blood of several generations of proud seafaring men and recalcitrant slaves rose in her, and Jez took a few deliberate steps forward, her hand on her sword hilt, showing him she was not afraid to challenge him. "I'll honor duel you for saying that. I have the right," she insisted.

"Keep interfering with my command, ye little tart, and you'll give me enough reason to kill you," Sol said as he coolly stepped back, the hammer of his pistol cocked. "Get off my deck *now*,"

Jez stopped. If she died here, he'd kill Walter too. As if reading her mind, Sol continued with a swagger, "Maybe I'll just tie your sweetheart to the mast, and then bend you over a barrel and show you both what happens to haughty bitches as don't know their rightful place in the world. Then the lads can have a go at ye too, just so ye don't ever ferget too soon."

Neville snickered and asked, "Can I be first to teach her some manners after you're done Cap'n Sol? I so want to hear her squeal like a piggie. She's got a nice round arse you know! Like I told you, I seen it when she was pissing in the bilge…"

"Shut up Mouse!" Sol shouted angrily.

"Why you little betraying bastard!" Jez interrupted furiously as she and Neville lunged at each other. Sol grabbed the thin boy and flung him aside, and he landed flat on his back behind his mentor, out of breath and gasping for air. Jez never heard the other man come up behind her, but she was grappled with an arm like iron bars before the blow was delivered. She crumpled to her feet without ever knowing what had hit her.

"She'll sleep a while," a deep and resonant voice said as the owner shoved the uncocked pistol, whose grip had just knocked Jezebel Johnston out cold, back into his baldric.

"Yer too soft hearted, ye know that Jengo?" Sol said with a snide smirk.

"I didn't agree to kill her Sol, just to get her out of the way. Now what we doing with them two?"

The thin man thought for a moment. Bringing Jengo into the mutiny made things far easier, but the former slave had a fierce sense of honor to those he counted as comrades in arms. He'd never agree to killing former crew mates unless they challenged him openly. There was no way to engineer that now…not with them both out cold. It would seem like murder, and that would lose him Jengo's respect and cooperation. Sol needed that fierce and glowering presence to keep his hastily impressed crew in line.

"If it was up to me, I'd slit their throats and throw them to the fish, but a captain's word is his bond," Sol answered with a cold smile. "Shove her and Armitage into one of those small jolly boats this floating wreck has aboard. Give them a little water and some provisions, and set them adrift. We need to get this hulk out of here before we get fired on as well. Looks like old Dan's losing his end of the battle."

"These are not friendly islands. They could easily die out there," Jengo complained as he began to motion to a couple of suddenly docile and obedient crew members to quickly ready one of a pair of skiffs that was aboard and load the two unconscious pirates into it along with food, water, a blade apiece, and some rum. A piece of canvas protected them from the weather, included at Jengo's insistence. No treasure or coin was shared though, for by breaking their oath of the articles, these two lovers were no longer considered part of any company. Down the side, their boat was lowered, and then it was cut free.

Sol spat down after them. "All yer mollycoddling will come back and bite you in the arse. Armitage may not survive because they stove his head in good, but that little cunt of his will, and she'll come looking for us."

"She's just a girl Sol. I owed her that much for the times she had my back," Jengo answered.

"That's *Captain* Sol to you, *Master Jengo*," the smaller man said with a self-satisfied smirk as he watched the skiff drift away behind them. With some luck the little boat would get caught in the crossfire between *Devil's Handmaid* and the galleon, and Dandy Dan's favorite boot-lickers would die anyway. In the meantime, there was a treasure to secure…one that would buy an entire fleet of ships.

Sol raced up to the stern and glanced out at the combat going on behind them. Even though they seemed to be winning their end of the battle, the crew of the galleon would have their work cut out for them getting their ship back to where it could sail swiftly enough to even catch a rowboat. By then, Sol would have his own ship back in Charles Town, New Providence, and no lone Spanish warship would dare enter that port.

Life was good when a bold man knew just when to make his move.

The company of Dandy Dan Abrams were mostly a seasoned bunch of buccaneers, and they knew what the odds were. They weren't prepared however for the nerve of the Spanish captain or his ingenuity in saving his best weapon for last. He had kept the most precious treasure of all aboard his own ship, so whatever happened to the nao they had used as a decoy to draw out the English pirates that were always plaguing them was now of little concern. Those fools would find out soon enough how much treasure was truly aboard that wallowing wreck.

He hadn't expected these sea scum to send out a successful boarding party that could take over the other ship and then fire its only remaining big guns on her own escort. The loss of *El Halcón*'s mizzen mast and rigging as well as the additional crew was grievous and regrettable, though not insurmountable. They still had plenty of soldados aboard just burning to be in a battle, and for this very special mission, had stocked well on shot and powder. Masts would have to be replaced and sails repaired, but every pirate he killed was one less to interfere with Spain's manifest destiny.

A gambling man by nature, he played his bluff. They had cut away the broken mizzen mast, but a lot of the lines and some sail still dragged. As the pirate ship came within range he had instructed his gunners to shoot right through their own tangled rigging and sails, scoring a low hit with an exploding shell that set the bow of the pirate ship alight. That was followed by a timed and staggered volley at point blank range, aimed not at sinking the ship, but setting it blazing. As the small vessel quickly caught fire, he reasoned that should keep these pirates busy until the galleon's other broken mast was cut loose, and her rudder freed. Then they'd come about and sink her.

In her continual battles with the English and French, Spain needed a trump card…something that no treasure could buy. Following rumors, the long-lost formula for what was once known as '*Ignis Graecus*' had been found in the lands of the far east, where some ancient adventurer had smuggled a manuscript that included coded directions for creating a batch. It had the peculiar quality of being able to burn ships while they were still afloat, and would even stay alight on water…nor could it be put out by any liquid. It was the perfect weapon, and Spain needed to be the only one to possess it.

The manuscript had been stolen by spies acting as trade emissaries, and then came across the Pacific well guarded. Quietly it was carried by a Jesuit priest known to be loyal to España, though all he was told was that he must protect a state secret, which he kept hidden in a Bible. The Padre rode a mule to Vera Cruz with only a couple of loyal native guards to protect him against attack, so his presence was not remarked upon. The captain's galleon had picked the Bible up there as part of his manifest, and he was instructed to get the enclosed document translated and await further instructions.

The leaky old merchant vessel became part of the ruse. It had been a slow journey though, for the ancient ship was in rough condition, though her position low in the water and carefully shadowed by the accompanying galleon created plenty of speculation about the contents of the nao's hold.

They had picked up the pirate ship following them on the west side of Cuba. Fortunately, Havana was the next stop. There, the captain of *El Halcón* had been informed, was the one man who could possibly translate the script into Latin. The nao, he was told, must appear as though it was loaded down with treasure that was ripe for the taking. So they had sold her antique cannons at the next port to make her more seaworthy and added additional barrels and bundles to the hold, in case there were pirate spies afoot in the great port.

Once delivered, they had tucked that parchment and its source in between the pages of a family prayer book, which the translator gave to his unsuspecting niece to present to the Capitán of her ship the night she met him. With a few days layover in Havana they'd have been able to put together a couple small casks of this material to use as an experiment, firing the useless nao before they reached the Flota. "*Yet, what better way to test it than on pirates?*" the galleon's captain had surmised.

And now it was proving its worth many times over.

The pirate ship known as *Devil's Handmaid* managed to get off one well-aimed but ineffective volley before their entire ship went up in flames. The ship's upper deck, masts, and rigging burned rather quickly, with screaming men falling or jumping into the ocean to escape the inferno. As the figurehead of the red devil woman caught fire and fell into the water, the Spanish captain smiled as he sipped wine and gave the order to sail on, for there was no point in staying to watch it become a sinking hulk. The damage had been done, the test had been successful, and they'd not need to waste any more time here.

Mother Spain could now easily rule both land and sea, once that very important formula was delivered. A pity they had to kill Senorita Campo's uncle, because the man was quite the scholar. Yet this secret must be kept quiet at all costs. The captain himself would have to decide which men of his crew needed to die before they docked at Seville, and the loyal soldados aboard would certainly carry out that odious task.

They would likely make him an Almirante for his service!

EPILOGUE

A small brown body clung to what looked like a section of floating log, and clambered up atop it. Because he lay there exhausted, no one saw him. The boy's eyes were open, and he watched sadly as *Devil's Handmaid* went up in flames. He knew then his best chance of being rescued had evaporated.

When their village was raided by Spanish slavers, his father had told him that a man did not cry; he accepted his destiny and lived with dignity. His father had died a slave, but Pakke had fought for his own freedom, and he was not giving that up to the Spanish again. So he bobbed along unnoticed on the long chunk of wooden mast, letting fate decide for him whether he'd live or die.

Jez came to and sat up groggily next to Walter, pushing the canvas covering them aside just in time to see the treasure laden nao pulling away. Behind them, the battle between *Devil's Handmaid* and *El Halcón* raged on with exchanges of gunfire. She was shocked when the pirate ship suddenly burst into flame, and watched in horror as each successive bombardment started another blaze. It was a fire that would not go out…it even burned on the surface of the ocean!

What exactly was that galleon armed with?

Devil's Handmaid quickly became a charred wreck, and her heart ached for her brethren aboard. Poor Andy, dear Gully, Master Reuben, and Pakke. Dandy Dan Abrams as a captain had been of a volatile and fickle temperament, but he had been good to her, and she was sad that he had come so close to his big prize of the year and had now lost everything; including his life.

Well, as Walter was fond of saying, life was for the living. At least she still had him. She tried shaking him awake, satisfied to at least hear him groaning and see his eyelids fluttering. Looking under the seats, someone had taken pity on them, not likely Sol, Rusty, or that bilge rat Neville. It had to be Jengo. She would remember that, and give him an honorable chance at death the next time they crossed paths. The rest would die like dogs for their treachery.

The best thing to do was to get out of range of any ship that might fire on them, and then find some place to land and take stock of their situation. They had enough food and water for a couple days, and the canvas would protect against exposure. There was no way to rig a sail on the tiny boat, but she could row. Jez was used to hard work in unpleasant conditions. So she set the oars in the rowlocks and began to move the small boat out of the main current, back toward those small cays they had hidden in while waiting for the great treasure ship from Spain to show itself.

The hot Caribbean sun was merciless. Hunger cramped her belly, and thirst dried her mouth, but she ignored them. The provisions had to last. A lesser woman would have given up in defeat and surrendered to her fate, but anger drove Jez past despair into a black and foul humor. The idea of vengeance gave her the strength and courage she needed to keep going long after she was exhausted and her injuries had taken their toll. One way or another, she'd live however long enough it took to find those back-stabbing turncoats and make them pay for what they had done.

First, she had to get herself and Walter Armitage to safety.

She rowed the rest of the day while Walter lay pale and breathing harshly, his sleep troubled by demons that made him cry out softly and twitch. While the sun reddened her skin to a terracotta shade, she kept him covered by the canvas, and stopped now and then to dribble water between his cracked lips. She gave herself only enough time to nibble a bit of a hardtack, not even bothering to knock the weevils and maggots free, and sip a similarly small amount of water. She had no idea how long it would be before they saw land. By evening, her arm muscles cramped, her legs were sore from sitting, and there was nothing on the horizon except for endless ocean.

Despairing, she looked west into the rapidly sinking sunset, and caught sight of a set of sails cresting the horizon. They were still a long way out, but they might see her if she made enough noise. She shipped the oars and yanked off the sailcloth; the sun was too low to harm Walter now. Gingerly she stood up in the small, flat-bottomed boat. Straddling Walter, she yelled, waving the sail like a banner, which caught the last rays of the setting sun.

The ship drew closer, and she could see by the flag it was French…that at least was a relief! No language barrier. Someone on the foremast lookout spotted her signal, and they changed course slightly to investigate.

As the sloop *Dame de Nantes*, a French privateer, drew closer, they hailed Jez and she answered back in such a way that they immediately threw down a line, which she made fast so they could tow her in.

Jezebel Johnston would live to seek her revenge after all.

THE END

ABOUT OUR CREATORS

Author

NANCY HANSEN - An avid reader and prolific writer of fantasy and adventure fiction for over 25 years, Nancy A. Hansen is the author of the novels FORTUNE'S PAWN and PROPHECY'S GAMBIT, the anthologies TALES OF THE VAGABOND BARDS and THE HUNTRESS OF GREENWOOD, and the novella COMPANION DRAGON'S TALES: *A FAMILIAR NAME*. Her short stories have been featured in multiple issues of Pro Se Presents, and she has a tale in THE NEW ADVENTURES OF SENORITA SCORPION, while the E-story TO RULE THE SKY is offered as a Pro Se SINGLE SHOT. Nancy has also contributed stories to both Airship 27's SINBAD: THE NEW VOYAGES Volume 1 and Mechanoid Press' debut book, MONSTER EARTH, and the charity anthology THE LOST CHILDREN. Nancy currently resides on an old farm in beautiful, rural eastern Connecticut with an eclectic cast of family members, and one very spoiled dog. (

Artist

ROB DAVIS began his professional art career doing illustrations for role-playing games. Working with a number of independent publishers he began lettering and inking, then penciling comics—most notably for Malibu Comics on *Scimidar* with writer R.A. Jones. Rob began working on likeness-intensive comics like TV adaptations of *Quantum Leap* and Star Trek's many incarnations: primarily on the *Deep Space Nine* comics for Malibu but also on DC's Star Trek comics. Under his own publishing banner Rob has produced the graphic novels *Robyn of Sherwood* with writer Paul Storrie and *Daughter of Dracula* with writer Ron Fortier. Rob is Art Director, Designer and Illustrator for Airship 27 Productions. partnered with writer/editor Ron Fortier. Rob is the recipient of the Pulp Factory Award for "Best Interior Illustrations" in 2010 for his work on *Sherlock Holmes: Consulting Detective*. He works and lives in central Missouri with his wife and two children.

Cover Painter

TERRY PAVLET. It all started in the days of B&W reruns and you could buy a comic under a buck, whose artistic skills showed up in kindergarten (so he was told), introduced to comics by his mother in a brown grocery bag of yellowed paged coverless issues, when the bug hit. From there on, he has been with comics ever since. He provided interior illustrations for several roleplaying game books from West End Games. Also worked for Comics- DC (logo), Image (interiors), Dark Horse (covers), Disney (cover - unpublished Kim Possible) RPG/CCG- Fantasy Flight Games, Wizards of the Coast, White Wolf, etc.
Book Publishers- Ballantine Books, Flax, Whitman Publishing Co., etc.
Indy Comic Publishers- Masterpiece Comics, Blind Bat Press, What the Flux Comics, etc.

Graduated from the Milwaukee Institute of Art and Design with a BFA-Illustration, Graphic Design, and Advertising and Associate Degree-Painting

His motto: *How do you need it and when?*

SET SAIL FOR ADVENTURE

The greatest seafaring adventurer of all time returns to the high seas, *Sinbad the Sailor!*

Born of countless legends and myths, this fearless rogue sets sail across the seven seas aboard his ship, the Blue Nymph, accompanied by an international crew of colorful, larger-than-life characters. Chief among these are the irascible Omar, a veteran seamen and trusted first mate, the blond Viking giant, Ralf Gunarson, the sophisticated archer from Gaul, Henri Delacrois and the mysterious, lovely and deadly female samurai, Tishimi Osara. All of them banded together to follow their famous captain on perilous new voyages across the world's oceans.

So pack up your you traveling bags, bid ado to your loved ones and get ready to sail with the tide as Sinbad El Ari takes the tiller and the Blue Nymph sets sails once more; its destination worlds of wonder, mystery and high adventure.